Reflecting Gold

Endorsements

In *Reflecting Gold*, author Cynthia L. Simmons hones her literary voice. Weaving American history, intrigue, betrayal, hope, and faith with her skills as historian, teacher, and observer of hearts, Simmons spotlights the value of gold and integrity in times of war and peace.

—**PeggySue Wells** is the bestselling author of 29 books including *Chasing Sunrise, Homeless for the Holidays*, and *The Ten Best Decisions A Single Mom Can Make*

Cynthia L. Simmons's wonderful series continues with *Reflecting Gold*. I was enthralled, entertained and educated by the other books in the series and this new addition continues the "gold" standard. From this series, I learn about history and culture in an era gone by. Ms. Simmons is a master storyteller of historical fiction. May she be blessed and continue! We need to hear her insights about our history.

—**Kathy Collard Miller**, international conference speaker and author of 58 books including *God's Intriguing Questions: 60 New Testament Devotions Revealing Jesus's Nature.*

Reflecting Gold will keep you turning pages. Mary Beth Roper and her husband must solve a mystery while navigating a war-torn world. What a fun way to learn history!

—**Lee Ann Mancini**, author of *Sea Kids*, Host of Raising Kids Podcast, Adjunct Professor at Southern Florida Bible College and Theological Seminary.

In Cynthia's sequel to *Pursuing Gold*, *Reflecting Gold* delivers to the reader everything a well-written novel should: plot twists that flirt with intrigue, romance, and mystery, all while giving a nod to the Civil War era. If you're looking for something that will instantly transport you to a simpler time, this book is it.

—Michelle S. Lazurek, multi-genre award winning author and literary agent.

Reflecting Gold highlights the historical and novel-crafting talents of Cynthia L. Simmons. Her tale of intrigue and drama comes threaded with elements of faith and well-researched details. Enjoy her inspiring story while deepening your understanding of the past and the timelessness of faith.

—Tina Yeager, LMHC, author, speaker, life coach, and host of the Flourish-Meant Podcast

Reflecting Gold

Cynthia L. Simmons

ELK LAKE PUBLISHING INC

PUBLISHING THE POSITIVE
Plymouth, Massachusetts

Cover and Interior Design: Derinda Babcock

Editor(s): Marcie Bridges, Deb Haggerty

Author Represented By: WordWise Media Services

PUBLISHED BY: Elk Lake Publishing, Inc., 35 Dogwood Drive, Plymouth, MA 02360, 2021

Library Cataloging Data

Names: Simmons, Cynthia L. (Cynthia L. Simmons)

Reflecting Gold / Cynthia L. Simmons

364 p. 23cm × 15cm (9in × 6 in.)

ISBN-13: 978-1-64949-310-1 (paperback) | 978-1-64949-311-8 (trade paperback) | 978-1-64949-312-5 (e-book)

Key Words: Civil War; Chattanooga; gold standard; banking; Confederacy vs. Union; Romance; Holistic medicine

Dedication

To my sweet husband, Ray. I cannot thank you enough for your enduring love and wisdom.

Acknowledgments

Special thanks to my writing coach, Sandra Byrd, and to my editors, Marcie Bridges and Deb Haggerty.

Chapter One

Mary Beth Chandler squinted against the morning sun as she and her husband trotted along the wooden sidewalk to C&R Bank. Her brow grew damp as she tried to match Peter's pace. She brushed her hand across her forehead and peered down the street. The sun prevented clear focus, but— was the front door ajar? A thief? Not another attack on the bank. They had survived a couple in the past two years.

Surely not! Chattanooga had almost no crime, but she must believe what she saw. After her father's recent death, she had inherited half the bank and felt the heavy responsibility. "Peter, look at the door—"

"No!" Peter released her arm and broke into a run, stirring up dust as he hurried across the street.

As he bolted away, Mary Beth almost lost her balance, but she lifted her skirt and followed, trying to ignore the dirt coating her dress. Breathless, she reached the bank just after her husband. Scratch marks covered the door, and the burglar had hacked off the doorknob.

Her husband's face was tight and hard. "I hear someone inside. Stay here and don't allow anyone in, not even employees."

"Be careful." Her stomach tightened as he headed into the bank to face unknown danger. If she'd had a weapon, she would have followed, but Peter carried a pistol inside his jacket. He'd told her he wanted to be prepared when the Union Army came marching in, as rumors of their movements increased. However, she had no desire to lose a loved one again. Her father's recent death had sunk her into depression and left her without family nearby except for Peter's kin. However, she adored Peter.

Wearing a floppy hat complete with flowers, Mrs. Phipps arrived, swishing her voluminous skirt. Peter had hired her as an assistant bookkeeper after her husband died, but she made numerous mistakes. While other employees struggled to train her, he considered changing her to bank receptionist. In spite of having grown thinner, Mrs. Phipps looked as if she were ready to visit President Davis rather than work in a bank. She fingered the cameo at her throat. "Is something amiss?"

Mary Beth held back a groan of disgust and nodded toward the bank where the damaged door stood ajar. If someone had emptied the safe, Mary Beth and Peter might end up on the street. However, Mrs. Phipps, too, would suffer since they paid her salary. Patience.

"I fear a burglary."

Bang! Boom!

Mary Beth jumped and shrieked. That had to have been a gun, and the shots came from the basement—where the bank kept money. She started forward into the bank. God help us!

"Peter? Peter!"

"You can't go in there," Mrs. Phipps screamed, grabbing Mary Beth's shoulders and shoving her backward onto the wooden sidewalk just beyond the door.

As Mary Beth landed, her gaze fell on a planter full of purple cornflowers decorating the bank entry. How ridiculous their beauty seemed at such a moment. Her husband might be dead.

NEARBY
MOMENTS EARLIER

Anna Chandler's blood sizzled as she ambled alongside Mathew Grant, the bank manager. Comfortably plump, he wore a gray pinstriped suit. His gray hat concealed his receding hairline and fair hair. How nice to have a little romance in her life again.

"Isn't it a lovely morning, Mr. Grant?"

"Indeed, Madam. The companionship is quite agreeable." A slow smile spread across his intelligent face. "Except it's very hot already."

Anna hoped he felt warm because he was in her presence but smiled back at him. "Actually, I prefer heat. Anytime."

At the intersection of Broad and Arbor Lane, Grant took her elbow and guided her across the street.

"How very kind." Anna tucked her chin and grinned.

"My pleasure." Mr. Grant tipped his hat.

Anna's mind ran over the delightful events leading to this morning's walk. Matthew had indicated his interest in her several days earlier, and they had arranged an accidental meeting, so they could walk to the bank together. However, as a widow with children, she would do nothing to alienate her offspring. She considered this a pleasant flirtation.

"And what of Mr. Weston?" Grant spoke up, his voice just above a whisper. "Does he call on you?"

"Horace?" She chuckled. "He merely manages my trust fund. Andrew didn't want me to be totally dependent on the bank. Weston's interests lie in expanding his personal empire."

"I see no problems then." Grant nodded with seeming relief.

Just then, they rounded the corner onto Market Street.

"But what is this? Mary Beth is on the sidewalk?" Anna noticed broken daisies in the large planter beside the bank door, but that mattered little compared to the distress on Mary Beth's face.

"Something has gone awry." Grant said, as they both rushed toward the bank.

Anna darted around him and reached Mary Beth first. Should Mary Beth be carrying a child, such an accident might cause her to lose the baby. A year had now passed since the wedding, and Anna longed for that first grandchild. "My dear! This will never do."

Mary Beth pulled herself to her feet and pushed Anna aside. "I don't need assistance."

Anna leaned close to her ear. "Did you feel lightheaded? It's quite common in the early months. You must take great care."

"No, indeed." Mary Beth brushed herself off. "It's Peter. I heard gunfire from inside."

"Gunfire!" Anna gasped and then noticed the damaged door. She'd been focused on her daughter-in-law and hadn't seen the destruction. "Peter!" Her heart leapt as she pushed the women aside and hurried in.

"Mrs. Chandler! You cannot—" Mrs. Phipps spoke up, but Anna ignored her. No one would keep her from her son.

Mary Beth charged after her mother-in-law, grabbing at her arm. "Peter does not want anyone in there, Mrs. Chandler."

Anna shook her off.

Mary Beth groaned as her mother-in-law hurried down the steps leading to the safe room. She hated being ignored. Besides, Peter would be upset.

"Excuse me." Mr. Grant stepped around Mary Beth also.

"Sir. It's not safe. I heard shooting." Why didn't they listen to her?

Grant kept walking as if he didn't hear.

Mary Beth turned to Mrs. Phipps. "Stay there. I'll return in a moment." Then she hurried downstairs after them, hoping no one was injured.

Anna's prayers flew heavenward even faster than her feet. Her heart slammed against her chest. A mother should not have to bury her child.

She hurried past the teller windows and the offices toward the steps leading to the basement. The odor of smoke choked her. "Peter?"

"Mama?" Peter appeared at the foot of the steps. His wavy brown hair was disheveled and his forehead sweaty. "I asked Mary Beth—"

"Peter." Her lips tight, Mary Beth hurried around Anna. "I tried to keep them out, but everyone will be down soon, even Mr. Grant."

Peter brushed his rumpled hair off his forehead. "Mama, you should have listened. The thieves fired at me."

Anna ran for him and cradled his face in her hands. She pictured him as a boy. "They shot at you? Are you injured?"

"Mama!" Peter moved away from her grasp. "I am fine. Grant, go for the sheriff."

Mrs. Phipps now hurried down the steps. "Make sure the cash drawer is there. I saw it beside the safe last night."

Peter raised his voice. "What? Was it full of money?"

"Of course." Mrs. Phipps removed her hat with a flourish. "If you recall, I'm not allowed to touch gold or any coin. Everyone fears I shall give incorrect change."

Peter raised an eyebrow. "You can communicate."

Grant, who had turned to leave, stopped. "Mrs. Phipps! How many times—"

Peter grabbed Grant's arm and put a finger to his lips.

"Scolding me again?" Mrs. Phipps, who stood on the steps above him, lifted her chin. "I'm blamed for everything."

"Dreadful." Anna couldn't believe what she heard. Peter should never have hired that lady. "Matthew, I'd best accompany you to the office. I might injure Angela Phipps if I remain behind."

"Mother, I'd like you here." Peter's voice had an edge. "Mary Beth, do you mind doing an inventory of the gold and deposits with Mama?"

"I'll be glad to." Mary Beth nodded.

Peter motioned them toward the door of the safe room. "I'm going to examine blueprints of the bank right away."

"Blueprints?" Anna rolled her eyes. What an odd choice for such a time. His late father would have examined the safe—and counted the money—himself. She hoped her son wouldn't sink her husband's bank.

An Hour Later
C&R Bank Office

After studying bank blueprints, Peter rubbed his eyes and sat back in his office chair allowing his gaze to roam over familiar objects—the bookcase across from him, the engraved desk his father purchased, the wing chairs for bank guests. His late father had furnished the room, and sometimes Peter longed to chat with him whenever he faced a new crisis. Instead, he prayed. Wise choices mattered now.

Peter's clients trusted him, and he would never violate that, even if he must work to restore lost income. He begged God for wisdom several times, hoping he didn't disobey Scripture. Reverend McCallie had once preached against 'meaningless repetition," but Peter couldn't help himself.

His secretary, Mr. Riddle, knocked and entered. He carried several papers and wore the usual pencil behind his ear. "Sir, I have several letters for you."

"Would you ask my wife if she can take a break to talk? Also, I need a bricklayer to come and close that window in the basement today. See if Mr. Archibald Crips can do it. We can help each other, I need his work, and he needs the money."

"Right away." Mr. Riddle's brow wrinkled as he left the room making notes.

Peter returned to the blueprints spread on his desk until Mary Beth walked in. Her mouth formed a straight line as she sank into the chair across from him. "What do you need?"

Such beauty. Peter admired her face and figure, but he hated to see the muscles in her face so tight. Dr. Smith believed anxiety might play a role in her infertility. He stepped behind her and massaged the muscles in her shoulders. "We need to address security."

She rubbed her hands down her face, loosening a blonde curl beside her cheek. "I agree, but I don't know what more we can do. This is terrible."

"Yes, but we survived several difficulties already." He walked toward the desk and tapped the papers there.

"I've been pouring over the blueprints. My dad and yours constructed the basement well."

"So?" She crossed her arms. "It didn't prevent the burglary."

"The thieves left through the basement window."

"But—" She sprang to her feet. "But they came in the front door."

"Yes."

"Let's prevent—"

"I agree. A reinforced door for the front, and—"

"We didn't have one?" Mary Beth shrugged. "I can't believe Papa didn't think of that."

"They manufacture stronger ones now." Peter rubbed the back of his neck as he thought of the cost. He explained his plan for taking out the window. "As times change, we must also change. Unscrupulous people would like the money we hold in trust, and I have to keep up with new ways to protect our customers."

Mary Beth paced across the room. "We have three doors. Will we do something to all three?"

"Correct. I started that process already. The second door, just past Grant's office, will be upgraded. We seldom use that one anyhow."

"What about the safe room?"

"Banks are moving toward securing the entire room. Adding the heavy door to the safe room will complete the vault."

"I wish we'd done it sooner." She walked into his arms, resting her head on his shoulder for a moment. "It's very interesting the one day the cash drawer is left out of the safe, the thieves decide to break in."

He filled his lungs. His wife had a way of noting facts that escaped his notice. He pulled away from her embrace, so he could look into her green eyes. "Do you suspect someone from the bank gave out information?"

"I do." She nodded. "The most obvious person is Mrs. Phipps. What do you think about her comment that everyone blames her?"

"Unfortunately, her mistakes create chaos." He shrugged. "Her talents don't lie in banking, but I can't see her inviting thieves. That would impact her livelihood."

"Hmmm." Mary Beth sat on the edge of the desk. "I'm going to keep an eye on her. Maybe she's trying to steal money. If she's innocent, let's help her find another job."

"Are you sure you want to deal with Mrs. Phipps?" He moved close enough to run a finger down her cheek. "I would save you from the distress."

"No. I'm the best person." She tweaked his nose. "Since I'm a woman, perhaps I can figure her out."

Peter hoped so. Having the bank robbed was his worst nightmare, but every banker must prepare for that possibility. If only he could find a door that would keep everyone out, insiders and intruders, which apparently might be one and the same.

SAME DAY
11:30 A.M.

Massaging the bruise on her shoulder, Mary Beth reentered the safe room where her mother-in-law counted gold at a battered wood table to her left. Mrs. Chandler worked on the contents of the main safe, which sat across the room with the door ajar. The air smelled heavy and stagnant; an underground chamber locked away from the outside world. Mary Beth's claustrophobia and anxiety kicked in as she entered the room most important to the bank's success.

She noticed a pencil sitting on the second unopened safe in the exact same position as she had left it the previous day. A good omen? This bank robbery could ruin them. What a shame that would be after all they had overcome in the past. She took several deep breaths trying to calm her pounding heart. She must believe God could guide them through this crisis.

"Are you all right, dear?" Mrs. Chandler touched her on the shoulder.

"Uh, yes, of course." Her shoulder hurt from the fall, but her mother-in-law would worry if she mentioned the bruise. She hurried to open the safe. What a relief to see undisturbed stacks of gold coins. She hauled them to the table, spreading them in stacks of ten. Her mind reeled from counting and recounting, but she didn't dare make a mistake. Peter's sensitive conscience would trouble him if they lost any money, and of course the bank supplied most of their income.

She handed the tally to Mrs. Chandler. "This is the last batch."

"Thank you. I tallied several checks from the bank in Cleveland, which the bank president has verified. That money should come in this week." Mrs. Chandler took the paper, adding it to the stack she held.

Mary Beth groaned and rolled her neck about to release the cramped muscles. "I thought we'd never finish that job."

"Be thankful for the money you still have," Mrs. Chandler said.

That statement sent a shiver through Mary Beth, but she held her tongue.

Peter entered the room and slumped wearily into a chair. "How's the process coming?"

Mary Beth looked toward his mother. "She's adding now."

Mrs. Chandler waved the stack of papers she held. "I've checked and rechecked. All the burglars took was the cash drawer."

Mary Beth consulted a paper from upstairs. "But according to Mr. Evans, the cash drawer held a hundred twenty-five dollars."

"Horrible!" Peter jerked his head backward. "That's too much gold to keep upstairs."

"Your father and I kept much less at the teller windows." She gave Mary Beth a pinched look.

Mary Beth looked away, flushing. The unwanted loss upset her too since the numbers represented more than a month's salary for a military officer. She rubbed a knot in her neck wondering how serious this might be. Surely Peter would tell her.

"We must take precautions," Peter snapped.

"Indeed, you must." Mrs. Chandler crossed her arms and raised her chin.

Mary Beth turned away. She didn't enjoy the implied accusation from her mother-in-law, but she determined to be kind. "Thanks for your help, Mrs. Chandler."

"Yes, Mama," Peter said.

"I'll do anything for my son," Mrs. Chandler crooned as she embraced Peter.

As always, Mary Beth felt like an outsider.

Chapter Two

Robins trilled a melody as Mary Beth gazed across the valley below, where Chattanooga lay in the crook of the Tennessee River. Spectacular. Down the side of the mountain, the greenery intermingled with huge stones. Land and water stretched out as far as she could see. The desk clerk at the hotel said a person could see seven states from this vantage point. Getting away should help her relax. If only the knots in her muscles would dissipate.

Attempting to distract herself, she looked into the valley and tried to pick out the downtown streets so she could locate the bank, but she couldn't. After yesterday, she felt a need to guard the remaining gold night and day. She must remember they had outwitted a conman and a counterfeiter. A hand touched her back, and she turned. Peter stood beside her.

"It's stunning." He slid his arm around her waist. "I could stand here all day."

"Could you?" Relieved he stood on the opposite side of her sore shoulder, she let him pull her close. His engaging smile revealed the dimple in his cheek. How well she knew his face, his dark wavy hair, and his deep blue eyes. She'd been his playmate when his fair cheeks were still chubby, and now she could describe how he donned his tie. Lately she'd seen more lines around his eyes. "I can't stop wishing I were in the office today to make sure everything is safe."

He pulled her closer. "We are increasing security. Besides, Grant and Evans will be extra vigilant after the break-in. Relax."

Her husband often told her she worried too much, and she attempted to remember good things, blessings from God. "We are fortunate to have found Mr. Evans. He's such a quiet, unassuming man, but his work is superb. I am glad Mrs. Phipps does not work today."

Peter chuckled. "I wonder if she tries to annoy you."

"Speaking of being annoyed, did you notice your mother and Mr. Grant yesterday?" She shook her head. "I was shocked at how intimate they seemed in conversation."

This time Peter grimaced. "I'm not sure I'm ready for a stepfather, but she's been a widow for a couple years now."

"Ah, Mr. and Mrs. Chandler." At the sound of a voice, Mary Beth turned to see Mr. Weston approaching them. He wore a dark suit, and his brown hair was combed back, revealing a streak of gray on the left. Weston maintained a home outside the city and one on Lookout Mountain as well. Several times a year, he offered events for Chattanooga citizens. And this one took place at the Whiteside Hotel, a multi-story white building with bay windows, dormers, turrets, and decorative trim. He waved toward the back of the hotel. "I was worried you couldn't come. We are now serving lunch, and I feel sure you'll find something to your liking. Your mother just spoke to me about the unfortunate event of yesterday. I do hope you have recovered."

Recover? Weston didn't own a bank. He'd never understand the responsibility wouldn't be easily forgotten.

One must stay diligent and wise. Mary Beth offered Peter a weak smile.

"You timed this party perfectly, sir." Peter offered his hand. "I'm much more rested after the beautiful ride up here. The scenery seems to improve every time I come."

"Yes, I've always said the four-hour trip is just long enough. Any longer and you'd feel weary from sitting." Weston accepted Peter's hand and then extended his arm to Mary Beth. "May I have the privilege of escorting your pretty wife?"

Peter nodded, and Mary Beth accepted Weston's arm.

"Anna speaks of you working in the bank, which is most unusual for a woman of your station. But you aren't there every day, are you? I suppose you knit or play the piano?"

Mary Beth's face grew warm. Why was he calling her mother-in-law by her Christian name? "Several soldiers came to Mrs. McCallie's home after the battle of Stones River when the hospital was so full. I often help her nurse them."

"Remarkable." Mr. Weston said. "You could be doing much more frivolous things. Do you still make your herbal medications?" His eyes twinkled as he smiled at her. He didn't appear to be flirting. His attentions were gentle, fatherly.

"I do. For Mrs. McCallie and the local hospital."

"Have you ever considered selling them? I could help, you know. Several times I've launched fledgling businesses."

Was Weston serious? Mary Beth glanced at Peter's bland smile as her throat clogged. Her mother-in-law talked about her activities? How embarrassing. At one time, she'd volunteered to nurse the wounded at the military hospital. Bringing medicines was such a small contribution. Besides, making money from herbal preparations had never occurred to her. "You are too kind."

"Not at all. I would love to invest in such a venture. However, the weather is far too lovely for such talk." They arrived at the serving table where fancy plates displayed generous helpings of fried chicken, roasted vegetables, and fresh fruit.

Mary Beth's stomach growled as she inhaled the aromas. She hadn't seen such a feast since the war started.

"Enjoy the meal." Weston released her arm at the serving table and turned to Peter. "The same invitation goes to you too. Should money become tight, and I've heard it might, I'd be delighted to buy stock in the bank."

SEVERAL HOURS LATER

Peter's gaze roamed the park seeking his wife. He hoped she had stayed close to the picnic area. She'd mentioned wanting to walk, but she wasn't sure-footed on uneven ground. Huge trees had added shade in the bright sunshine, but since the sun was going down, she might stumble over exposed roots or boulders in the landscape. Earlier, when he'd seen her walking along the edge of the precipice, he'd caught up with her to ensure her safety. Besides, he enjoyed her company.

"Peter." His mother walked up holding Mr. Grant's arm. Mary Beth trailed along a little behind her. "I've been looking for you. Horace is loading carriages to take us back down the mountain."

Horace? Didn't she mean to call him Mr. Weston? When did they get on a first name basis?

"Good evening, sir. I shall leave both Mrs. Chandlers with you." Grant bowed. "Since we closed the bank early, I brought my elder sister. I must escort her home now."

"My dear." Peter offered his arm to his wife and took a deep breath. Seeing his mother with another man turned his stomach. He couldn't blame her, but he must grow accustomed to someone taking his father's place. "Are you and Mr. Grant courting?"

"No." She lifted her chin. "I am fond of his company and he enjoys mine."

"You also seem quite close to Mr. Weston." Peter glanced at his wife for affirmation and received encouragement from Mary Beth's nod. "How many men are you flirting with?"

"Yes." Mary Beth spoke up. "I'd like to know too."

"What?" His mother frowned. "Horace has no designs on me. Besides, your question isn't appropriate."

THAT EVENING

Mary Beth glanced about the bedroom that had once belonged to her father. How she loved this room. Her father's affection seemed to linger here. She had replaced the heavy brocade curtains with light blue and switched the large bed for a smaller one. A highboy rested against one wall and the shelves beside the bed held soft blankets. A crib would complete the room, if only her husband would acquiesce.

"There you are." Peter's eyes widened as he entered and then glanced about the room. "You've been working hard. Is someone going to stay here?"

"Yes." Mary Beth did not want to bring up the topic, but he seemed to be asking. She took a deep breath to fortify herself before she broached the topic of children. "This will be the nursery. All we'll need is a crib."

"Mary Beth." His face hardened. "We have discussed this over and over."

She sighed, not wanting to have this conversation again. The last few nights she dreamed she held her baby, and when she woke, the longings engulfed her even more. If only she had avoided mentioning a crib. "Why not ask Reverend McCallie to pray for us?"

"We can do that, but that is still a separate issue. Think about other things. Maybe my mother can teach you embroidery or something."

"I am already doing herbal medications for Dr. Smith, and helping Ellen McCallie nurse soldiers, and working at the bank." Mary Beth was getting overheated. Peter used to be more sympathetic before they married, but now he fussed at her if she told him her worries. "I do not need more to do."

"Dr. Smith said he saw no signs of pregnancy. With inflation, money is tight, so we need to wait on the Lord."

"I made the curtains myself and I reused the brocade ones elsewhere." She closed her eyes as she ran her hand over her slender waistline. Everyone at church assumed she would have a child by now, and they were asking her each Sunday. One lady even knitted baby socks two weeks ago. Her whole body ached with longing. The doctor told her a change in diet and extra stress tended to make conception more difficult, and the war caused both those conditions. But she kept praying and hoping. "I haven't wasted anything."

"Dr. Smith believes you will bear a child in time. You have become impatient." He put his hands on his hips. "Use your talents to sew or do something to keep your mind busy."

Mary Beth's lips trembled, and warm tears filled her eyes. "But Reverend McCallie said we must have faith, and that's what I'm trying to do."

Peter pulled her toward him. "I don't think the Reverend meant you to set up your nursery quite so early."

Mary Beth pushed Peter away. Perhaps she misunderstood faith, so she must think and pray on this topic. She hated these discussions, but she was honest with Peter. Very well. She'd attempt to broach another topic. "Is that a newspaper under your arm?"

"Yes. It's the Rebel. They say the Union commander named General Rosecrans is moving toward the city. Of course, we can't be entirely sure how close he is. But he's close." He opened the paper and glanced at the front. "See?"

Great! More talk of war. Selling herbal medications might be a great way to get her mind off the death and destruction that could be headed toward them.

❦

SUNDAY MORNING
JUNE 21

Mary Beth was already steaming with summer heat as she and Peter strode to church. Their conversation from the night before seeped into her dreams, leaving her sad and uncomfortable. Everything seemed to remind her she was not pregnant. Oddly enough, even the dusty road beneath her feet brought pregnancy to mind, devising ways to protect her baby from the dirt.

"You are so quiet." Peter looked down at her. "What are you thinking about?"

Mary Beth wanted to lie and say the approaching armies because that did worry her some. She weighed the cost of telling the truth. If she could be honest and yet kind, she might learn what motivated Peter. "I-I feel like you are less compassionate with me now that we are married."

Peter stopped walking to gaze into her eyes. "What made you conclude that?"

Mary Beth appreciated his gentle tone. At least she had not made him angry. "I feel scolded when I bring up wanting a child. That makes the ache go deeper. You used to let me talk and hold me rather than give me a lesson. Your words arouse more painful emotions."

"Isn't it more compassionate to resolve the problem?" He ran his finger along her cheek.

"You mean you are trying to solve the problem?"

"Yes. But you must understand I am sad too. Based on the doctor's advice, I want you calmer so it's more likely you can conceive. I love you too much to see you gloomy."

"Will you let me talk about this a little bit?" Mary Beth touched his face. "I am less anxious if I share how I feel."

Peter gazed off in the distance. "We must see compassion in different ways. I shall think on this. Oh, I wanted to talk about a new approach to bank security."

Talking didn't solve the problem, but at least she and Peter seemed to understand each other better. And she cared about the bank. "Of course."

"I've been considering limiting access to the vault, and having our employees sign in and out. It's ridiculous that we can't discover who left the cash drawer out of the safe."

Dismayed at the change in subject, she had a hard time focusing. She wanted to talk more about having a baby, but she shouldn't be so selfish. She shook her head, "How would we enforce that?"

"The key will stay in my office, and employees would have to sign to use it."

A flock of birds weaved about the sky overhead, at first close together, and then further apart. Mary Beth could imagine Peter as the leader of the flock, always besieged with requests. "I daresay you will get nothing accomplished if our employees make requests all day."

"I've considered opening the safe at intervals during the day."

Mary Beth rubbed her eyes. She really must sleep better tonight. How terrible they must go to such lengths. "But wouldn't that ensure the teller always had a lot of cash? Someone could pull a gun and demand money."

"We'd start with a smaller amount and pull coins from the drawer more frequently. I've also considered an evacuation plan. We might need to leave if the Union invades."

"Oh, dear." Mary Beth jumped at a sudden noise.

Bushes by the road shook and Peter's sister, Ruth, hopped out with her friend John behind her. Leaves clung to Ruth's thick brown hair, which she yanked loose. The shape of her face and eyes resembled Peter's. John's dark hair glowed in the sunshine like freshly polished shoes. How much they'd grown. Ruth was now thirteen, and her special playmate was ten. Despite John's limited communication skills, he had demonstrated a useful cleverness in the past, and Mary Beth adored him for it. She laughed. "Oh, I thought I was about to be attacked."

Ruth spoke up. "Do you mind if we walk to church with you?"

"I'd be honored." Mary Beth decided against alarming the children. She stooped to speak to Ruth's friend, who held a paper. "Hi, John. What's that?"

John handed her a drawing of the church. It was a perfect representation of First Presbyterian of Chattanooga where the Chandlers attended.

Ruth looked after John and understood him when most of Chattanooga failed. He was a sweet child who seldom spoke. Mary Beth had learned to love his gentle ways. "Did you do that, John?"

He nodded but made no eye contact.

"Excellent!" Mary Beth tousled John's hair. He was different than most children, but he also had talent. He'd drawn a new hairdo for Mary Beth for her wedding.

Peter nodded. "Great work, John."

"John draws a lot these days. He's got some really good ones." Ruth wrinkled her nose. "Horace Weston came by in his carriage for Mama. I told him I'd rather walk with John."

Mary Beth turned to Peter. "What is going on with your mother? Is she courting Mr. Grant and Mr. Weston?"

"You heard my inquiry last night." He shrugged. "I can't step in and demand to know her business."

"Mr. Weston kisses her hand, a lot." Ruth scuffed her heel in the dirt, as if taking out her frustration on the road. "I don't like him. The past two days, Mr. Grant visited our house instead. At least he doesn't kiss her."

John ran ahead to a patch of clover just off the road. Mary Beth smiled as he picked a few flowers. How nice to be so pleased by life. "Peter, will your mother's behavior reflect on the bank?"

"I hope not," Peter said.

They'd passed the spot where John was picking flowers. Mary Beth glanced behind her to see John running to catch up.

"Mama seems busy. I want to stay with you a while, Mary Beth. Maybe for a long time." Ruth slowed down and walked alongside her.

Mary Beth turned to Peter. Having a child in her home would keep her mind off pregnancy. Maybe. "What do you think of that idea?"

"I don't mind, of course. But I wonder what Mama will think."

John circled around the other three and handed Mary Beth a wreath of clover flowers.

"Is this for me?" Mary Beth asked.

He nodded, his dark eyes intense.

"Thank you. I shall hang it around my neck." She gave John a hug and wished he were her son. Images of having a baby in her arms flooded her mind.

Maybe God was giving Mary Beth youngsters to love.

Chapter Three

Monday Morning

A knock caught Peter's attention, and he looked up to see Evans at his door, holding ledgers. He wore his usual dull white shirt and brown jacket the same color as his eyes. His sandy brown hair blended with the color of his fair skin. Peter would have described him as quiet, almost invisible. Today, he wrinkled his thin nose as if he'd eaten something distasteful. Peter hoped his newest employee didn't have more dreadful news. After all, they'd just lived through a bank robbery, which took a huge chunk from their profits. "Mr. Evans. You appear to have a problem."

"Indeed, I do." Evans handed two books to Peter. "Mrs. Phipps has mutilated the accounts receivable ledger as well as accounts payable. She appears to have no capacity for handling numbers."

Peter wanted facts, not opinions. "Please define mutilated."

"I don't know any other word to use for this, sir." Evans frown created a perfect upside-down u. "Her math is horrible, and she confused the two ledgers. General ledger information was recorded in the accounts payable. She marked through mistakes and wrote above her marks. Illegible. We need to recreate the entire book."

"Let me see." Peter flipped through the account books. He did a few calculations in his head as he looked over the last pages. This happened the day of the robbery, which meant his wife did not monitor Mrs. Phipps. "Thank you for bringing this to my attention."

"Mistakes must be fixed. Bank security, you know." Evans leaned closer and lowered his voice. "Mrs. Phipps may have done it on purpose. When employees embezzle, they often create small math errors to cover their work."

Peter hated employees to talk about fellow workers, but he didn't reprimand Evans. He'd rather employees talk to him than about him. With the troublesome books in hand, Peter stood. "Thank you. You may return to work."

Slumping, Evans slithered from the room.

Peter studied the ledgers and did a few more calculations. Mistakes Mrs. Phipps made altered bank assets by three hundred fifty dollars—a significant sum. When he added that amount to what the thief stole, the total created a loss they couldn't afford. He hurried out to his secretary's office. "Mr. Riddle, send for Mary Beth. You'll find her at home."

He must make plans to deal with Mrs. Phipps.

LATER MONDAY MORNING

When Mary Beth arrived at the bank, the foyer was quiet. To her right, Mrs. Phipps's desk sat empty, and no customers hovered about the teller windows. What an opportunity! She'd have a chance to interview Grant without Peter. Maybe she could learn more about the burglary. Her tendency to ask probing questions irritated Peter at times, and she preferred peace between them. After a quick glance around, she headed into Grant's office.

Grant was flipping through files as she walked in.

"Good morning." She kept her eye on the door, hoping Peter wouldn't come downstairs. "Do you mind if I ask a few questions?

"Sure." Grant closed the cabinet and slid on his navy jacket. "What do you need?"

"What happened at closing the night prior to our burglary?"

Grant raised an eyebrow and crossed his arms. "Customers left by five, but I didn't lock the door until five-thirty. I carried receipts back to my office, and I counted the money in the cash drawer. Mrs. Phipps came to ask me to let her in the storage room because she needed more ink ..."

"Mr. Grant?" Evans shuffled into the office. "Several customers just came in."

Mary Beth motioned for Grant to go. "Let's do this later."

A line of customers stood at both teller windows, which would keep Grant and Evans busy. She headed for the steps leading upstairs.

Mrs. Teague hurried in from the street toward Mary Beth. Her energetic smile made her green eyes glow. "Oh, Mrs. Chandler, how nice to see you."

"It's delightful to see you too, Mrs. Teague," Mary Beth answered as she walked toward the empty desk where Mrs. Phipps usually sat. She was quite fond of this lady who did so much for wounded soldiers. "Do you have something I can help you with?"

"I have checks to deposit." Mrs. Teague brushed red curls off her forehead. "It's for the Newsome Hospital fund, you see. I'm so glad the bank keeps our contributors confidential. More people will give if it's anonymous, and we certainly need funds."

Peter set up the account for Mrs. Teague and gave her special privileges since the money went to help injured soldiers. Mary Beth offered her a most gracious smile. "Since there's a line at both windows, I'll do that for you."

Mrs. Teague handed her the deposit information, and Mary Beth noted the cash and the amounts that would be drawn from other accounts. She drew up a deposit notice, and handed it to Mrs. Teague. "That should take care of you."

"Thanks ever so much." Mrs. Teague bustled toward the door.

Mary Beth hurried to the teller with the information after she put away the checks. She handed the papers to Evans. "Here's some transfers from our customers into the hospital account."

He nodded as he accepted her receipt. "Morning, ma'am. Have you spoken with Mr. Chandler?"

"I'm heading there now." Mary Beth paused at the door.

"You'd best do something immediately." Evans cleared his throat. "The error is serious."

Mary Beth surmised he referred to the mess Peter called her here to fix. Her chest tightened as she nodded. Evans seemed inclined to perfectionism. He did his job so well, and Peter seldom overreacted—she hoped his opinion wasn't as bleak.

MONDAY
NOON

Mrs. Chandler ignored her lightheadedness and floated into the bank. She had dressed to capture Matthew Grant—a soft peach dress that set off her blue eyes and graying brown hair. The tiered skirt had been fashionable when the war started, and a hat completed the look. If their friendship continued to grow, she might not be a widow much longer. That made the hot day more pleasant.

As usual, Mrs. Phipps sat at the desk in front of the door, except this time, she held her hands over her face, sniffling. Anna stopped, "My dear, what is the trouble?"

"Errands kept me busy all morning. Bank business, mind you." She sighed and unfolded her damp handkerchief. "As if that wasn't enough, Mr. Evans said my bookkeeping would destroy the bank."

"I daresay he's exaggerating." Anna leaned close. "Never believe a man who slumps. They don't see the world clearly."

Laughing at her own joke and the confusion on Mrs. Phipps's face, Anna strolled over to Mr. Grant at the teller window. "I want to withdraw three thousand dollars, please."

Grant offered a wink. "I cannot do that, Madam."

"Then I shall expect you to take me to lunch." Anna twisted a curl.

"What if I can't get away?" Grant leaned toward her.

"Then an expensive dinner would do." She giggled.

"Mr. Chandler would like to see you, if you have time."

"I have all the time I need, Matthew." She fluttered her lashes. "Do you?"

"Yes. Come back when you're ready, and I'll have Mr. Evans stand in for me."

After tossing a coy look toward Mr. Grant, Anna headed upstairs to the bank office, but she found Peter's desk empty. She peered into the adjoining office where Mary Beth sat glued to account books, surrounded by papers and files, very unlike a mother. "My dear, where would I find Peter?"

"He's in the basement beside the vault." Mary Beth dropped her pencil. "That is, it will be the vault when we install the heavy metal door we ordered. The bricklayers are closing up the window downstairs. He was hoping you'd stay the afternoon and monitor the workmen."

Anna would need to move her lunch to dinner with Grant, and that might work better. He would not feel the need to rush back to work. Grant would understand. Besides, she'd do anything for Peter. "Of course."

"I know he'll appreciate that." Mary Beth looked down and turned a page in the ledger before her.

"Do you work here every day?" Anna moved further into the office that once belonged to Mr. Roper, Mary Beth's father. "I want a grandbaby. Maybe you should worry less about banking?"

Mary Beth looked up, gasping. "What?"

Anna closed her eyes and let memories wash over her. "Cuddling your baby, rocking him to sleep … it's precious."

Mary Beth's face blanched.

"I shall find Peter." Anna headed out of the office and down the stairs, but she had to grab the railing to steady herself. These dizzy spells made her worry about her advancing age. If she didn't have a grandbaby soon she might never know that joy. And some mornings, she had no energy. Mary Beth had made Peter very happy. Such a sweet girl. Anna would apologize later. She had been too harsh not only with her daughter-in-law but with Mrs. Phipps also. What had happened to her tact?

In the basement, she found Peter observing the bricklayers. "Mama, did Mary Beth explain what I need you to do?"

"Yes." Watching these men didn't excite her, but Peter was taking security measures. She could imagine herself at a romantic dinner with Matthew while she helped her son.

Maybe she would soon be a bride. If she grew much older, she'd be too ugly.

LATE MONDAY AFTERNOON

Peter stepped into Mary Beth's office to discuss the plans he'd drawn up. Light was fading in the room, and an oil lamp illuminated the ledgers she worked on. She rubbed her temples and groaned while poring over her work. Her gloomy expression bothered him, and he chose to put aside his main agenda for a moment. "You appear distraught."

She looked up. "I am not thinking warm thoughts of Mrs. Phipps. These books remind me of scrambled eggs. I need to see the transactions from yesterday and put them in again."

"I apologize for foisting that job off on you. Once this remodeling ends, I will find a position for her elsewhere. She carried out a list of errands for me this morning, so she can be useful." He put a hand on her arm. "Put that away for now. Let's come in a little earlier tomorrow, and I will redo the ledger myself."

"Oh, that does make me feel better." She slammed the book shut and leaned back in her chair. Tension faded from her face. "Thank you."

"See. Sometimes fixing the problem is the right choice." Peter pulled a paper from his inner coat pocket. "I've drawn up an evacuation plan."

"Evacuation plan?" Mary Beth frowned and placed a hand at the base of her throat. "How close is the Union army?"

"Everyone is guessing right now." He didn't need to reiterate the fact the Union wanted Chattanooga because of the railroad. Peter pulled up a chair beside hers. "I think we should be prepared."

"It's hard to think of leaving. I grew up here." Mary Beth whispered.

"I understand. This is my home too, but my plan is to protect ourselves and our clients. Being prepared will help in a crisis." Peter pointed at the paper he handed her. "I have you and Evans grabbing the ledgers while Mr. Grant and I pack up the gold. We should also plan to leave separately, except you and me, if possible. We'll meet up again in Big Shanty, which lies south of here. It's a small town north of Atlanta. I remember the town because the spies stole the train there."

"I prefer to stay with you." She grabbed his hand.

"I agree." He kept his voice soft. "But if we cannot, we must plan a place to meet. Always keep enough money for a train ticket and remember Big Shanty."

Mary Beth crossed her arms, hugging herself. "How far is that?"

He rubbed her back, hoping compassion would ease her anxiety. The situation would have to be desperate before he chose this plan, but it might happen fast. "I think I read it was eighty or ninety miles. That's far enough to be out of harm's way until we can regroup.

"What if one of us isn't here?"

Peter rubbed his jaw. Having a plan would give her security, even if it wasn't perfect. "We'd do our best, and we will discuss this with the others."

Mary Beth pushed away from the desk. "If we knew who we could trust, that would help. Which one loaded the cash drawer and gave the okay for a burglary? Mrs. Phipps?

"Lately she appears afraid to do anything."

"Maybe her skills lie in teaching. On the other hand, I don't know how I feel about Mr. Grant taking the gold. Did he or your mother start this flirtation? I thought I could trust him, but the way the two act bothers me."

"Mother annoys me more than Mr. Grant. Even though she denies Weston is flirting, I believe he is." Peter thought for a moment. "I can trust Grant."

"I feel better about Evans, but I will trust you. You judge people a bit better than I do." She pulled paper out of the drawer, ready to jot down notes. "I wish we'd interviewed our employees the day of the break-in. We may have to figure out who did this ourselves."

With an army coming toward them, his wife didn't need that pressure. Besides, he couldn't be sure one of their employees had betrayed them. "Let me talk to the sheriff to see what he's learned."

"I still think we should find out what our employees know. The sheriff has too much work already. Ida commented he was thinking of moving, so we'd best protect ourselves."

Peter gritted his teeth. He would approach the sheriff tomorrow and demand action. Otherwise, his wife would put herself in danger solving a crime.

Chapter Four

C&R Bank
Tuesday Noon

Stretching, Mary Beth rose and walked across Peter's office to the window overlooking the street. The sun blazed in a cloudless sky and birds outside twittered their delight. Their newest banking concern seemed less ominous in such beauty. Besides, her clever husband could manage the situation.

She had completed her bookkeeping and would hurry home to mix herbal medications until Peter returned from his meeting.

Thump, thump!

What a curious sound, unusual in a bank. She ambled to the door that led downstairs where angry voices floated up from below. Was that Mr. Grant? In all the years she'd known him, he'd never raised his voice. Perhaps she could soothe an upset customer. She headed down to the bank lobby, and her calm mood evaporated.

"Those rules are ridiculous," a man shouted.

"Sir, you mustn't speak to me that way," said Mr. Grant.

"If anyone has a right to question your practices, it's me."

"You don't own the bank!" Grant shouted.

Who threatened Grant? Her heart pounded as she stepped into the lobby. The place looked like a battlefield. A bulky Confederate officer dashed behind the counter and punched Grant. Several men she didn't know shouted encouragement while waving fists. The grocer, Mr. Nelson, peered into the teller window.

"No!" Her voice was lost in the scuffle. She had to stop this. Her whole body twitched.

Mrs. Cox from the bakery inched toward the door, and a tiny lady with a small flowery hat left the bank, sobbing. A gray-headed man with stained overalls rushed behind the counter just as Evans came out of his office and shoved the soldier to the floor. Grant and the overall-clad man dragged the soldier back to the lobby. Kicking and squirming, the Confederate broke free and punched the old man. The two went to the floor brawling.

Mrs. Phipps screamed.

"Stop fighting!" Mary Beth yelled, but she could barely even hear herself. "People should be able to do business. This is a bank."

She ran forward and tried to pull the officer off the elderly man, but Mr. Grant jerked her away, shaking his head. He mouthed words, but nothing she could understand. Her whole world was falling apart. Was this all due to the war?

The grocer shouted too, but Mary Beth couldn't make out words.

"Gentlemen!" Peter bellowed as he stalked into the bank waving a pistol. "Stop now, or I shall shoot."

A glance around the room told Peter he'd best control this situation. His heart raced like a horse pulling toward the finish line, but he ignored it. Women to his left hovered about the door, weeping. Men, who appeared to be acting as spectators, moved toward the walls. Grant was drenched in sweat and so was Mr. Fuller who worked at the dockyard.

A bedraggled Confederate officer stood in the center of the room. Perspiration rolled down his cheeks. His receding brown-gray hair was mussed, and several buttons hung by a thread from his soiled uniform. He glared at Peter as he reached for his sword.

The man's eyes challenged him. Fire raced through Peter. This man would not destroy his bank or hurt his wife. Peter pointed the pistol at the colonel. "Drop your gun and sword."

For a moment, the officer stood in defiance, his face hardened with the threatened of attack. Peter moved closer, steadily aiming his gun. If he must, he would fire and probably kill the man—something he never wanted to do. Sweat beaded up under his collar.

The intruder eased his sword and gun onto the floor, and Peter released a tiny sigh.

Soft chattering filled the room.

"Quiet!" Peter yelled. "Who was fighting?"

"He was." Grant motioned to the soldier.

"I were protectin' your teller, sir." Fuller spread out open palms. "That there soldier were rushin' behind the counter and beatin' up your employee."

Peter lowered his gun but kept glaring at the soldier. "Is that true?"

The colonel stepped backward. "I had good reason—"

"That's not what I asked," Peter said. "I shall give you a chance to talk, without the weapons. Mr. Grant, please take those to the back room."

"I am a colonel in the Confederate Army. My weapons are government issue. You can't take them."

Peter wanted to lynch the man, but he held his temper. "You disobeyed the law by attacking my employee. Your position does not give you that authority."

"In this case, it should," the colonel said.

Peter glanced about the room. Mrs. Phipps was white and shaking. She wasn't in any shape to follow instructions. "Mr. Riddle?"

Riddle stepped forward, whipping out his pencil and pad. "What do you need?"

"Send for the sheriff." Peter took the soldier's arm. "We're going to unravel the problem in the back, but we might need extra guns."

C&R BANK
MR. GRANT'S OFFICE

With Mary Beth beside him, Peter kept the gun aimed at the unwelcome visitor. Grant, his round face damp, occupied a chair in front of them. Beside him, the colonel's large-boned frame spilled over the straight chair. He was breathing hard.

"Colonel Bennet, please explain why you attacked my bank manager."

"Your employee disrespected me," Bennet said.

"What?" Grant's mouth fell open. "Not true."

"Yes, it is," the soldier said. "You wouldn't let me say anything, and I am a colonel in the military."

"Let me start over." Peter had never handled a customer this difficult. "Why are you here?"

"I want to know who established the loan guidelines. They are ridiculous." Bennet scooted forward.

Mary Beth sucked in air.

"I'm asking the questions. Not you." Peter snapped. His wife was uneasy and that made him angrier at the man who caused the problem. "Why are you here?"

The colonel sighed. "I'm new in town and want to buy a house, a short-term loan I can pay off in two to three years. I have papers from my bank in Louisiana which states I have good credit and detailing my account there. I've even found the house. All I need is a loan."

"You are applying for a loan?" Mary Beth shook her head. "Attacking the banker seems a poor way to do that."

Peter lowered his gun and frowned. "How did that provoke you to hurt Mr. Grant?"

"Your Mr. Grant informed me I must repay in gold or commodities. I should be able to use Confederate treasury notes." Colonel Bennet banged on the arms of the chair.

"And that is disrespectful?" Mary Beth said.

"When I asked why the stringent rules, he screamed at me," Bennet said.

Knowing Grant, Peter was fairly certain which person yelled first. "You object to the bank's rules and then expect us to give you a loan?"

Colonel Bennet stood and waved his arms. "Repaying the loan is impossible with inflation and a shortage of gold. Whoever sets your guidelines has no confidence in the Confederacy. He's a traitor. I'd like to find that man and report him as such."

A knock sounded on the door. Mr. Riddle stepped in, "Sir, I brought the sheriff."

"Excuse me." Thankful for the interruption, Peter stepped from the room, taking a deep breath. He faced a quandary. The colonel had discerned Peter didn't trust the Confederate's paper money. It was not legal tender or backed by gold. If he admitted his concerns, he could be accused of being a traitor or worse. No one had ever demanded he accept Confederate money—until today. This situation presented another potential threat.

In light of the colonel's behavior, Peter would press charges. He doubted his old revolver would restrain a seasoned soldier much longer. Sheriff Campbell's massive form filled the hallway, a welcome sight after the chaos the bank just suffered.

Campbell crossed his muscular arms and raised a bushy eyebrow. "Mr. Chandler, I understand you had some trouble."

"I did. A Confederate colonel decided to attack Mr. Grant, almost starting a riot. Please, arrest the man."

"Hmph. The military occupies our city, so I'll have to get them to cooperate. Where is he? In there?"

"Yes." Peter opened the door to Grant's office.

Campbell entered looking from Peter to the soldier. "What's his name?"

The soldier stood. "I'm Colonel Bennet."

"Very well." The sheriff tied his hands together. "Colonel Bennet, you are under arrest for assault and battery."

"I protest," Bennet said. "I came here hoping to buy a home, but the policies of this bank won't allow that. I shouldn't be arrested."

Campbell frowned. "You can protest to the judge."

Peter sighed as the sheriff escorted the soldier out the door. His trouble wouldn't end. The soldier's accusation would be the talk of the town. Peter hated this worthless paper his fellow citizens used for money and didn't want the whole town talking about his political views. He hoped his clients didn't choose to pull out their money when they heard the story.

LATE WEDNESDAY AFTERNOON

Ignoring the fatigue in her back and shoulders, Mary Beth strode up the steps to the bank office holding a withdrawal request. Peter wouldn't be happy about a family closing their account, and she wasn't thrilled either. However, the war brought changes and they must adapt. Banks must keep a certain amount of their assets on hand, and the gold in the vault was too low already. Insomnia bothered both of them since the incident with Bennet, and her eyes teared up at the smallest provocation, like yesterday when she saw a mother with an infant. Peter had raised his voice talking to Mr. Riddle on a couple of occasions, something he never did. Even the weather boded ill. Rather than the usual summer sunshine, heavy clouds hung over the city and distant claps of thunder warned of impending storms that never came.

Last year, when her father died, she had learned to pursue the Lord. She knew she must continue, but she battled fearful thoughts. She was attempting to seek the Lord for guidance as they faced new challenges. If only this tension would end soon.

When she entered the office, Peter was slumped over the newspaper with his eyes closed. His teacup lay on its side. The dark liquid filled his saucer so full that she'd have a hard time not spilling it when she cleaned. Perhaps the Union army was about to swoop down on them all. "Peter, are you okay?"

"Yes." He sat up. "I fell asleep and made a mess. What can I do for you?"

"I need the key to the safe." She grabbed a handkerchief from her pocket and dabbed up spilled tea.

"Sure." He pulled out a ring of keys and handed it to her. "Is someone withdrawing money?"

"Yes." She glanced at the paper she held. "Mr. and Mrs. Finn are leaving the city this week to move to Nebraska territory to avoid the war. They want to close their account."

Peter groaned. "I hate to see them leave, but I understand. After the robbery, our gold reserves are almost depleted."

"That's getting really dangerous."

"Yes. I wonder if their choice to leave had anything to do with this." He tossed a copy of the *Chattanooga Rebel* toward her.

> **Early this week, Colonel Bennet, recently assigned here by the Confederate Army, approached Mr. Grant at C&R Bank about a loan to buy property in town. Bennet reports Grant refused him a loan because the bank wouldn't accept Confederate paper money to repay the debt. The colonel also reported Grant became overwrought. The event ended in a brawl at the bank between the two men. Mr. Chandler, bank owner, sent for Sheriff Campbell who arrested Colonel Bennet on an assault charge. The colonel's superior officer requested Bennet be released to the military in light of upcoming hostilities. Bennet reported bank policy fails to demonstrate loyalty to the Confederacy. Both Mr. Grant and Mr. Chandler have refused to comment. Further investigation may be warranted.**

"Horrible. The news will reach all the farmers in the area too." Mary Beth plopped into the easy chair before his desk. "I didn't realize anyone from the paper called for an interview."

"No one did. I questioned Mr. Riddle and he said no one approached Grant either." Peter sprang from his chair and paced. "The injustice makes me furious. We have always tried to be fair."

"Fair. I guess it doesn't seem fair to Bennet." Mary Beth sighed.

"No, but I am fair to my clients. Not many banks pay interest if the client keeps a certain balance, and we allow them to write checks rather than carry cash. This article makes us look so evil. I thought I had to worry about a Union attack; however, our own soldiers will ruin us."

Mary Beth ran a hand over her face and tried to formulate a plan. "Let's see if we can get our own interview. We'll tell our story and give citizens a chance to see who we are."

"I told my story to the reporter the day of the incident." He slammed one fist into the other. "They have not printed it."

Mary Beth went behind his chair to rub his shoulders. "We would never hurt anyone."

Peter gave a wry chuckle. "Bennet might think so."

"Surely, the people of the city know us."

"Do they? I've never announced my opinions on slavery. This could go on and on. I chose the bank policy, not Grant. The colonel is angry with me, and no one is listening to my side of the story."

"You've always been honest and held to your values." Mary Beth loved him even if they had their misunderstandings about when to buy a crib. No one in the city could complain about Peter's behavior. "Your clients know your honesty."

"I'm staying on the gold standard, so I won't lose my client's money. That paper money Congress issues has no value."

Mary Beth agreed with Peter. She had heard the same sermon from her father. However, if the military turned against Peter, they would be in trouble.

Chapter Five

A basket filled with medicines in hand, Mary Beth knocked on the McCallie's door. Reverend McCallie pastored her church, and she'd become friends with his wife, Ellen. The morning was warm but still pleasant. Mary Beth turned to observe butterflies hovering around morning glories adorning the porch railing. Their graceful movements uplifted her. Perhaps their presence indicated the Almighty approved of her plan. She hoped to seek advice and comfort from Ellen this morning and had prayed God would make it possible.

The front door opened with a squeal. Mary Beth gazed at two-year-old Grace McCallie who stood at there, her dark eyes widened. "Hewwo."

"Hello, Grace." Mary Beth knelt to get at eye level with the little girl who had her mother's tiny frame. It was a wonder she could reach the doorknob. Mary Beth's heart contracted with a tinge of worry. The toddler had never answered the door before. Ellen McCallie took in soldiers Newsome Hospital could not hold. Besides, some of her patients were Union soldiers. "Is your mommy here?"

Grace nodded, her gaze roaming up and down, examining her guest.

How Mary Beth wanted to embrace the precious little girl who looked so small and lonely. "May I speak with her?"

Grace's brown eyes widened. "Mommy! Mommy."

Moisture dampened Mary Beth's eyes. If only she could have a child. She eased into the foyer, closed the door, and deposited her basket. She picked up the toddler and rocked her a moment. How awesome it must be to have a child who wanted you so. "Let's go find her. Will that be okay?"

Grace nodded and snuggled into Mary Beth's shoulder.

"I promise to help." Mary Beth carried the girl into the living room, which had two vacant bedrolls on the floor. Across the hall, the pastor's study was empty. She walked toward the back of the house where she found the huge kitchen also unoccupied. Next, she ascended the staircase which creaked with each step. A couple of soldiers lay on blankets in the hall. From the left bedroom came the sound of coughing. "Private, I think we should send for the doctor. Right away." Ellen's voice carried into the hallway.

Grace extended a hand toward the room. "Mommy!"

The soldier mumbled a reply as Mary Beth, still holding Grace, crept to the door. "Ellen?"

Ellen McCallie came to the bedroom door. She wore a simple beige dress over her thin frame with her brown hair secured into a bun. "Hello, Mary Beth. I see you found Grace. Last night several of my patients worsened. I've been busy since dawn."

"I brought you some medicines and bandages." Mary Beth put down the toddler who ran to her mother. "I can stay the morning to help. Peter won't expect me until noon."

"What a relief!" Ellen smiled as she picked up Grace. "Two men rejoined their regiment today, and a couple more will go home soon. Several men, however, cannot go to Newsome Hospital because they fought with the Union. But they live nearby."

"This war rips apart friends and family. How terribly sad." Mary Beth touched Ellen's arm. She and Peter weren't the only ones who suffered.

"It is indeed, and we shall soon have even more fighting with the Union army moving this way."

Mary Beth shivered and chose to avoid that topic. "Ellen, you look so tired. How can I help? What do you need?"

"Grace would probably like her breakfast." Ellen, her arms full of the toddler, rubbed Grace's back.

"Let me watch your patients so you can feed Grace," Mary Beth said. "I'll offer the soldiers water and change bandages."

"What a blessing you are!" Ellen headed downstairs with the toddler.

Mary Beth's heart ached as she saw how mother and baby clung to each other. If only she could have her own, but she must not let those thoughts dwell in her mind.

She stepped inside the bedroom Ellen had vacated. One man struggled to breathe, and the other appeared very pale and lethargic. Today Ellen would not have time to talk. Besides, how frivolous her own fears seemed in light of death. The butterflies were not the message she expected. What was God saying to her?

SUNDAY MORNING
JUNE 28
FIRST PRESBYTERIAN CHURCH

Mary Beth kept her gaze on Reverend McCallie as he completed his sermon at the wooden pulpit. His long face, high forehead, and deep-set eyes had frightened her when she was younger. However, after she lost her father, she had learned McCallie's gentle heart. Today he had focused on James chapter one and told them to rejoice during suffering. Considering their new banking problems, Mary Beth longed to discuss that thought with Peter at lunch. The war and its privations brought frustration, not rejoicing. Even the church building suffered. The staff couldn't afford flowers for the foyer or pulpit. Plus, the hardwood floors and pews showed wear and lacked their usual polish.

Organ music filled the air when the service ended. This Sunday more soldiers filled the church than did citizens. Mary Beth was accustomed to chatting with friends around her rather than rushing out the door but military men surging toward the exit made it impossible to see her chums. Mary Beth eased her way along the bench with Peter and Ruth hoping to merge into the mass of gray uniforms. If only the war would end before the Union arrived in Chattanooga.

When she finally joined the soldiers in the aisle, she looked back to make sure she could still see her family. Ruth was right behind her, and Peter back further still, surrounded by soldiers. Up ahead, Fannie, an old friend, had just stepped into the hot June sunshine. Mary Beth longed to catch up. The throng thinned as she exited the church. She reached out and tapped her friend's shoulder. "Fannie? Fannie, how are you?"

Fannie turned, making eye contact for a long minute. But instead of speaking, she then turned and hurried down the church steps.

What? Mary Beth refused to believe Fannie ignored her. Her stomach hurt.

Soldiers mingled with citizens pushed Peter away from his wife, even though he could still see her and his sister. "Excuse me, please. My wife is up ahead."

Those around him let him move forward, and he nodded his thanks, continuing to inch forward toward the door. As he reached the foyer, he moved faster.

"Surely the bank officials should relax their standards for one who is fighting to protect us. The man is a colonel. He should be trusted."

Peter glanced around for the source of the words. A group of officers stood on the porch to his left. How uncomfortable to be the object of conversation and unable to defend your choices.

"There's very little gold available these days." A soldier nodded and donned his hat.

"Indeed, and prices keep rising," a soldier with a goatee said.

Peter moved toward them, intending to introduce himself and enter their debate; however, the men walked away and headed down the church stairs. A cluster of girls passed between them.

Mr. Haskell, the town lawyer, came alongside Peter. He spoke loud enough for everyone outside to hear. "Mr. Chandler, what a pleasure to see you. How is banking these days?"

Peter breathed a sigh of relief. At least he could no longer hear the others. He offered his hand. "Good, Mr. Haskell. Thank you for asking. I do hope your family is well." Peter noted the crowd of men scattered.

"They are indeed," Haskell said. "Jane has been asking after your wife. We shall have to plan another outing soon."

"I would enjoy that, sir."

The café owner took Peter's arm. "You are doing fine work, sir. Don't be swayed by those who do not understand your job. It's difficult for everyone these days."

Humbled by his comments, Peter nodded and shook his hand.

"Good afternoon!" The café owner hurried down the steps.

"Excellent advice," Haskell said. "And should you ever need legal counsel or someone to confer with, I would be honored."

"I appreciate that sir."

Haskell disappeared down the steps and Peter turned to search for Mary Beth. She and Ruth stood at his right at the top of the steps. Why was his wife frowning?

"Fannie?" Mary Beth couldn't believe her friend walked off. She was almost certain Fannie had seen her.

"She ignored you," Ruth said, taking Mary Beth's hand.

"Are you sure?" Mary Beth still couldn't believe what happened. She gazed toward Fannie's retreating back. "Why?"

Ruth pushed a lock of thick hair over her shoulder. "She saw you, yet she decided not to stop and talk. That was rude."

Mary Beth hoped no one had seen. How embarrassing to be ignored. More than ever she wanted to talk to Ellen McCallie. Unfortunately, Ellen's patient load never seemed to decrease. If one ailing soldier left, three more took his place. She turned to find Peter who shook hands with the town's lawyer.

Peter took her arm and guided her toward home. "It appears there's gossip going around town about the bank."

Mary Beth sighed. "Gossip? Is it about the incident with the colonel?"

"Yes."

Did Fannie's slight have to do with bank policies too? How terrible. She would keep praying for guidance.

An Hour Later

Peter gazed down at his sleeping wife who lay atop their blue velvet bedspread. With her blonde curls spread out around her head, and her peaceful face at rest, she radiated beauty. He could gaze for hours at the perfect curve of her cheeks and the gentle slope of her jaw. Her rosy lips tempted him to kiss her, but she needed repose. If only he could relieve the burdens and meet her needs, but his human limitations prevented that. He'd read poems to her after lunch until she fell asleep on the sitting room couch, and he had moved her to the bedroom to ensure she rested. How God had blessed him.

His father managed to provide for the family and inspire confidence in his wife. Peter needed that gift.

He slipped away from the bed and tiptoed across the woolen rug to the door. After pausing to pray for his dear spouse, he eased the door shut. Time to pray and plan. Bank protocol might need to change. He tiptoed down the stairs and turned right at the bottom of the stairs toward the library. Haskell's report had alarmed him. Rising prices and shortages already plagued them, and his present banking practices might land him in jail as a traitor.

LATER SUNDAY EVENING

Mary Beth settled on the sofa in her sitting room across from her old friend, Ida Campbell. Clothed in a navy skirt and white blouse trimmed in lace, Ida eased down beside her. She wore her brown hair parted in the middle and braided into a bun. Mary Beth had seen a similar style in New York before the war, and she wondered if the styles had changed. What a frivolous thought. Maud entered the room with a tray of hot tea.

"I appreciate you dropping by." Refreshed after a good nap, Mary Beth could give her friend a genuine smile. "Any news?"

"That's why I came," Ida said. She giggled and covered her mouth. "I'm getting married."

"Wonderful." Once Ida married, Mary Beth could plan outings with them as a couple. "Is he someone I know?"

"You probably don't. He's stationed here. We met the day he arrived. I was out taking a walk, and he caught me when I stumbled. His name is Sergeant Stanford."

Mary Beth scooted forward on the couch. "What are your plans?"

"I'd like you to help me with the dress. It'll be a remake of the one my mother wore."

Mary Beth clasped her hands and laughed. What a pleasant diversion from nursing and banking. "Of course, I'd love to. When is the wedding?"

"My parents are planning to move west, and I want to marry before they leave," Ida said.

"Yes. I've heard the rumor, and I had hoped that's all it was." Mary Beth dreaded the family leaving, but maybe Ida would stay in the city. "No one can replace your father."

"Costs are going up, and the city council doesn't want to hire anyone else. Have you seen the price of coffee? Four dollars a pound. Dreadful."

Mary Beth had never like coffee. "Tea prices are rising too, but I can grow herbs to make tea."

"What is this I hear about the bank?" Ida frowned and put down her teacup. "There's a rule saying you must pay back loans with gold? There's not enough of that these days."

"Oh, there's a reason for that—"

"I cannot imagine. Unless you have so much money that you do not care about the rest of us, and lots of folks about town are coming to that conclusion."

Ida stomped out of the house, leaving Mary Beth stunned and confused.

FIRST PRESBYTERIAN CHURCH
LATE SUNDAY EVENING

Anna sank on her daughter's bed while fingering the delicate pink embroidery on the bedspread that took months to finish, matching pillows and all. She was devoted to her offspring, and now she was trying to understand Ruth's request. "Ruthie, dear, would you please repeat what you just said?"

Looking down, Ruth stood across the room with both arms around her chest, twisting a lock of thick brown hair. "I want to move in with Mary Beth and Peter. Please?"

Another request. Anna thought about the room cross the hall, which now sat empty. Before Andrew died, Ruth had begged for new furnishings in shades of lavender, and Anna had stitched matching draperies and bedcovers. Ruth seemed pleased, at least at first, but one evening she moved into the guest room down the hall. She never said why, which Anna found frustrating. How do you please a daughter who will not communicate? "I don't know."

"Tonight?" Ruth pleaded.

Anna had always longed for a daughter and imagined the two of them shopping for clothes and bonnets. Peter was dear, but he could never understand a woman's love of color and fabric. He was kind and tolerated her chatter on the topic. The past few weeks, Ruth had drifted even further away, which distressed Anna. "You want to stay with Mary Beth?"

"Not stay." Ruth gnawed at her fingernail. "Move in."

"Why?" The word didn't come close to describing the ache in her heart.

"I like her."

Anna never realized a simple three-word sentence could pierce one's soul. Like? Was there any place for love in the heart of her thirteen-year-old daughter? She always wanted the best for Ruth, but this hurt. Must she give up her baby at such an early age? "I'm quite fond of Mary Beth, but should you leave, I would miss you terribly."

Ruth looked down and rubbed her toe on the floor. "It's not far."

"I don't understand why you don't want to stay here." Anna let her gaze wander about the rose and pink accoutrements. "You have a lovely room here, and you are close to John. Mary Beth's house is much further for him to walk."

"I just like Mary Beth."

Anna took a deep breath. She had to know the truth, even though it burned a hole in her heart. "Are you saying you don't like me?"

"No." Ruth sat down on the bed.

"Then what?" Anna kept her voice soft. She'd do anything for her baby. Anything. But this ache ran deep.

"Mr. Grant comes to see you."

Anna covered her mouth and hid the shudder that wanted to run through her body. "You don't want to see me with another man. Is that true?"

Ruth wilted onto the bed, and Anna pulled her daughter close but sensing her resistance. "I love you, and nothing will ever change that."

Ruth whispered into Anna's shoulder. "I love you."

Dampness gathered in Anna's eyes. She held her daughter close until Ruth dozed. After she eased her sleeping daughter under the covers, Anna went downstairs to the sitting room. "Peter?"

"I'm here, Mama." He stood and dropped a kiss on her cheek. "Mary Beth and I agreed to let Ruth come. Of course, we wanted your permission."

"Ruth doesn't like Mr. Grant. She worries about another man replacing her father." Anna tried to imagine marrying again, but despite her flirtations, she still clung to her husband's memory. "If she wants to go live with you and Mary Beth, she may do so. I hate having her leave home, but I know you will keep her safe."

Peter smiled and hugged her. "I doubt she will stay long. You know Ruth."

He didn't understand. He couldn't. Anna was losing her baby girl.

Chapter Six

The sun shone from a dark blue sky edged with a few fluffy clouds as Mary Beth, Ruth, and John trudged up Cameron Hill to Newsome Hospital. City officials had converted a warehouse into a place to care for the wounded, and military men had constructed rustic wooden buildings on the perimeter for military staff.

John, who'd grown several inches in the past few months, carried the heaviest basket of food and provisions. Ruth had a selection of bandages, and Mary Beth carried her latest herbal remedy for skin irritations. Mary Beth had volunteered at the hospital before she married. The hospital held a special place in her affections, and she liked most of the staff.

As she neared the facility, a group of soldiers barred the way. "John and Ruth, stop and wait here for me," she said.

Rather than stop, John circled around making noises that sounded like battle.

An unsmiling soldier approached her. "This is a military facility. What is your business here?"

She swallowed at the sight of the rifle in his hand. "I brought provisions for the wounded. I know the head nurse, Mrs. Decker."

"Your name?" The man frowned, annoyed.

Mary Beth had visited many times before and no one ever stopped her. Surely an unarmed woman with two children didn't pose a threat. Was General Rosecrans hovering outside the city. "Mrs. Chandler."

"One moment." The soldier retreated.

John continued his trek about her as if he had no fear. He didn't trust many people, but Mary Beth was pleased she'd earned his confidence and felt protective of him.

Another soldier waved her forward and she motioned for the children to follow. The man led them to a desk just inside the hospital foyer. "Wait here."

Mary Beth looked about. The familiar odors of medicine and food reminded her of the days she worked here a year ago. Mrs. Decker's vacant desk still sat in its usual place with a stack of notes, pen, and inkwell. A wounded man on crutches inched his way through the foyer.

A few moments later, a large-boned man came to the doorway from the outside. He had a receding hairline and dark brown eyes. Her heart lurched. "Colonel Bennet! What are you doing here?"

"Indeed? Madam." He clipped his words. "What business do you have here?"

Mary Beth met his gaze as she recalled his behavior in the bank. "You were arrested—"

"My superior officer negotiated my release." He narrowed his eyes. "Such petty disagreements become inconsequential in the face of invasion."

"Mrs. Chandler!" Mrs. Decker entered behind the colonel, her dress and white apron spotless. She rushed forward and embraced Mary Beth. "The soldier got your name wrong, and I couldn't imagine who was here. Colonel, Mrs. Chandler brings provisions from town, and we are quite fond of her."

"The café owner across the street from the bank sent the food." Mary Beth motioned to John's basket which Mrs. Decker now held. Surely the colonel would now see her in a better light. "You'll find bread, soup, and jars of fresh milk."

"Thank you." Mrs. Decker offered a smile that rivaled the sunshine as Ruth put her basket on the desk. "I'll have someone put it all away. The men will be so grateful."

"Indeed?" The colonel raised an eyebrow. "I'd like to know if you pay Mrs. Chandler with gold or Confederate bills."

Mrs. Decker's smile faded and her gazed flitted from Mary Beth to the officer. "No. She charges nothing."

"Then I don't have to arrest her for being a traitor?" He moved closer wearing a don't-you-dare-scowl.

Mrs. Decker gasped. "Traitor?"

Mary Beth lifted her chin. She'd like to slap the man for suggesting such a thing. "I wouldn't dream of asking for money—gold, paper, or otherwise."

The colonel narrowed his eyes. "Which side are you working for?"

Mary Beth took a step backwards. "I bring supplies to wounded soldiers, and you question me like a criminal?"

The colonel pounded the desk. "Anyone who will not use money produced by the Confederacy makes us suspicious. I understand you also nurse Union soldiers at Mrs. McCallie's."

"Mrs. McCallie has taken in one Union soldier who grew up here." Mary Beth paused, knowing she had to be accurate. "She might have two. I don't ask. I appreciate her compassion, so I help her."

The colonel inhaled, and his frame enlarged. "Reverend McCallie works closely with us while you husband appears to defy us."

Mrs. Decker turned white and covered her mouth.

Mary Beth's chest tightened. "I assure you my husband and I take no positions on the war beyond protecting our assets—and those of our depositors. Those Union soldiers are too mangled to fight again."

"Now you admit there are more." Bennet raised an eyebrow. "And they could be spies."

She pulled John and Ruth to her side. If they weren't frightened, she was, but she mustn't let them see. If the colonel was trying to frame her, he might succeed in the current situation. "You have our gifts to the wounded. May we leave now?"

Arms crossed and legs spread, Colonel Bennet stared at her for a long moment. "You may leave; however, if I were you, I'd make a change in bank policy. I'll give you a week. After that, I'll have to arrest you on suspicion of spying. We usually have a quick trial and then hang the prisoners."

Moments Later

After meeting with a client downtown, Peter strode down the wooden sidewalk to the bank. The morning sun overheated him, and he longed for the comfort of this office. According to his pocket watch, it was past time to pull cash from the tellers and deposit the money into the vault. He sped up.

A hand clapped him on the shoulder from behind. "Chandler! My favorite banker."

Peter stiffened as the lieutenant came alongside. He knew the slim, red-headed soldier from a year earlier when McDonald tried to sell bogus bonds to him. Later, when McDonald was drunk, he lost his temper and fired at Peter.

As usual, the lieutenant's appearance was impeccable. All the brass on his uniform gleamed. Peter thought McDonald must care more about his clothing than his behavior. "I'm surprised to see you out of jail, Lieutenant."

"The judge found me not guilty, so I'm a free man." A light wind ruffled the soldier's red hair. "It's always good to see justice done."

Peter knotted his fist and wondered how McDonald had been freed. The man had no scruples. Maybe he'd paid someone to overlook the evidence.

"A little while ago, I tried to open an account at your bank. No one seemed willing to accept my Confederate bills." McDonald frowned. "I did not believe the newspaper, so I decided to see if it was true. Are you hoping the Union wins this war?"

If they lost the war, Confederate notes would be worthless paper. "I protect my clients by remaining on the gold standard."

"Foolish." McDonald turned away.

If the Confederates stopped trusting Peter, they might seize the bank.

Same Morning

Accompanied by John and Ruth, Mary Beth climbed the steps to her house. She devised snappy insults for Colonel Bennet and imagined his reaction. Thoughts of scolding the man lifted her spirits even though her insides still trembled at his threats. She'd discuss his actions with Peter.

Maud entered the foyer and ushered everyone into the sitting room. "Yous be a wantin' some iced tea, so I'm a goin'a fetch ya some."

John bounced down the hall after Maud into the kitchen. Mary Beth smiled at his antics. He enjoyed watching Cook, which would keep him busy for a while. She turned to Ruth. "Are you coming with me? Or John?"

Ruth laughed. "I don't like watching the cook."

Mary Beth sank onto the couch and blotted her dampened brow with her handkerchief. "I'm always thankful for the comfort of my sitting room after a jaunt about town."

"You didn't mention we'd be standing up to a grumpy soldier." Ruth shuddered as she plopped into an overstuffed chair across the room. "His frown is formidable. I wasn't sure whether he would use his sword or his pistol."

Mary Beth scrutinized Ruth. Now she'd love to kick the colonel for making Ruth fearful, too. "I assure you I wouldn't have allowed him to hurt you."

"Yoo-hoo? Mary Beth?" Ida's voice called from the porch.

Mary Beth sprang to her feet. She'd forgotten Ida Campbell planned to bring a dress to alter. "Ida, please do come in. We just returned from taking provisions to Newsome Hospital, but I am anxious to see what you need me to do."

Ida nodded, handing the parcel to Mary Beth.

Mary Beth and Ida both removed strips of paper revealing a full skirt gathered into a lace covered bodice. Tiny seed pearls lined the scoop neck.

"Ooooh, that's so pretty." Ruth touched the lovely white fabric.

"Indeed, it is stunning." Mary Beth would enjoy working with the luxurious fabric. "You need to try it on so I can see what needs to be done."

Mary Beth led the way to her bedroom where she

retrieved her sewing supplies from her boudoir. How luxurious the fabric felt in her hands as she helped Ida slip it on.

Ruth stepped back. "Beautiful!"

"I agree. It's lovely and there's not much to do." Mary Beth inserted some pins in the bodice. "I need to take it in here, and the skirt could be longer in the front."

"Mama had extra lace. Could you use that?"

"Yes. That's the best fix." Mary Beth clapped. "I was trying to think how I might get more fabric in the midst of war."

Ida groaned. "That reminds me, my parents will have a hard time paying for the wedding unless they can sell their house. Why won't Peter allow the loan?"

"I assure you it has nothing to do with your family." Mary Beth offered her most gracious smile. "My father and Peter's father founded the bank on the gold standard. The paper money colonel wants to use is worth nothing, so—"

"Worth nothing?" Ida broke in.

"It's not backed by gold."

"But it's all we have." Ida frowned. "You don't trust the government?"

Mary Beth had no desire to discuss such a delicate topic. She'd rather accidently pin the dress to Ida's skin, not that she would. "I'd best start sewing right away."

"You didn't answer me." Ida's face turned red. "That means you don't like the Confederacy."

Mary Beth stepped away. "Do you want me to fix this dress or not?"

LATER THAT EVENING
PETER AND MARY BETH'S HOME

Mary Beth intended to tell Peter about the threat the moment he returned, but he'd brought home a client and his wife for dinner. Fortunately, Cook had purchased a pork roast that day, providing plenty of food. She forced herself to entertain her guests rather than worry Bennet's men would arrest her without warning. Once the couple left, she breathed more freely and took tea to Peter, who had retreated to the library. He'd placed his open portfolio on the huge, engraved desk her father once owned and pulled out bank documents. "It's late to be working."

"Yes, but I need to get this ledger fixed." He tightened his lips.

She peeked over his shoulder after placing the tea tray on the desk. "Still working on the one Mrs. Phipps butchered?"

He laughed. "Mr. Evans used the same wording, and I now agree. Butchered describes what she did perfectly."

"Evans is succinct." She poured him tea.

He accepted the china cup she handed him and took a sip. "Perfect. Once I finish, we will know where the bank stands."

"I'm glad Cook purchased meat today or else we might not have entertained quite so well."

He nodded. "I warned Bessie and asked Maud to tell you."

Mary Beth closed her eyes and tried to recall if Maud had passed on the message. "Perhaps she did, but I don't recall. You see, Colonel Bennet threatened me today. I've had a hard time thinking clearly tonight."

"What!" Peter slammed the ledger shut. "It takes a real coward to threaten a woman. He's going to hear from me."

"Wait." Mary Beth held up her hand. She imagined another brawl like she saw in the bank, and the idea made her feel sick as she gave him the details. "He did not hurt me. Are you sure it's wise to confront him?"

Peter stood. "But he did threaten you, right?"

"Yes." His reaction surprised her.

Peter frowned and shifted his weight as if less certain of what to do. "What exactly did he say?"

Saying the words tasted like death but she explained his agitation over banking policies. "He also knows I help nurse Union soldiers with Mrs. McCallie."

"He's not threatening her. Instead, he frightens you when I'm not around." Peter's face reddened, and he marched toward the library door. "I'm going to find him."

Mary Beth put her hand on his arm. "I think we should give Colonel Bennet a loan. It may be the only way we stay alive."

"I prefer not to change bank policies." Peter paused at the door. "We put them in place for a reason."

"What about staying alive?" She pictured a noose. Mary Beth's father had been a banker her entire life, and she understood the gold standard. Paper was worth nothing and could be easily copied. Bankers protect depositors by insisting on gold or taking commodities they could sell. When they extended a loan, bank staff gave the customer checks rather than handing them gold. The customer wrote checks, gradually reducing the gold leaving the bank. She didn't want to change policies, but she also feared Colonel Bennet.

Peter stopped. "How much money will they need?"

"It's the Campbell home. A recent appraisal set the value at three hundred dollars."

Peter bit his lip. "Maybe we could manage it if Campbell would accept part commodities? Grant usually has some to sell."

"Mr. Grant told me Bennet brought a letter from his bank verifying his credit and his property. What if we changed the loan requirements based on those elements?"

Peter ran his hand along the back of his neck. "I shall speak to Campbell to see if he's willing. If so, I'll draw it up tomorrow. We'll insist on the person being a military officer with a credit letter from a bank outside the city and property in another state. That makes the requirements fit Bennet but not broad enough for anyone in the city. That might keep us out of prison and calm public opinion." He left the room.

Mary Beth's throat clogged. Would they have enough in storage to bargain with? If only this new policy would solve the problem.

THIRTY MINUTES LATER
MILITARY BUILDING OUTSIDE NEWSOME HOSPITAL

The room where Peter waited had a straight chair and a rustic table. A single candle burned to dispel the blackness. Time inched by as he paced the length of the room. Colonel Bennet might think him crazy for coming out so late, but Peter must assuage Bennet's boiling temper.

At last, the door rattled, and the hulky frame of the colonel walked in. "So. It's you again. When my assistant told me you were here, I didn't believe him. What on earth is so urgent?"

Peter was quite aware he was the smaller man, but that would not hold him back. He stood tall, arms crossed. "I understand you threatened my wife today."

Colonel Bennet laughed as he dropped into the rustic chair. "She must have told you I thought she was a spy."

"Indeed." Peter was unsure how the soldier would respond, but he had a fist ready. "She came with two children bearing provisions for wounded soldiers. I imagine even a private could see she was harmless."

"Well, you certainly seem overheated." Colonel Bennet said. He waved a hand as if dismissing the charges. "I made reference to the bank and to its policies, not to what she brought."

His frivolous attitude fueled Peter's fury. "But you threatened her with jail and insinuated she was a spy. We all know what happens to spies."

"Ah, she understood that, did she?" Bennet slapped the table as if rejoicing.

Peter walked closer and leaned toward him. "With respect sir, your behavior was inappropriate. Never threaten my wife again. If you have a message, be man enough to say it to me."

The colonel's eyebrow rose. "Are you changing bank policy?"

"I didn't come here to chat about the bank." Peter longed to thrash the man. "I'm discussing how you treated my wife."

"She understood my message." The colonel leaned back with a satisfied smile.

"And I'm saying, you should be talking to me." Peter hoped he looked as angry as he felt. "Should you want to discuss banking or take out a loan, don't talk to the bank manager. Come to me."

The colonel's smile widened. "I think I will. Soon."

Bennett was impossible. He could make you want to murder him.

LATER THAT EVENING

Peter was never sure whether to knock when he entered his mother's house or just walk in. After all, he'd grown up there, and in many ways, it still felt like home even though he lived in his wife's childhood home. He walked up the steps to the ornate wooden door and rapped several times prior to entering the foyer. Once he passed the huge coat stand to his left, he hurried to the sitting room. When he stepped in, the odor of furniture polish surrounded him, and he felt like a young boy again. His mother sat in her usual chair to the right of the fireplace, her hands busy with a crochet needle. A painting of Peter's late father hung over the mantel and his confident expression dominating the room. Peter sighed at the memory of the man he'd planned to work alongside. "Mama?"

"Peter!" His mother pulled off her reading glasses and dropped her needlework. "What a delight to see you here. Would you care for tea? Or have you eaten dinner?"

"No, mama. I need nothing." He thought about the tea he left in his library as he sat down in the chair across from her. "Mary Beth and I came to a conclusion about Confederate money. The entire town is up in arms over the faux pas with Colonel Bennet. Folk at church have shunned us, while others wonder if we are spies for the Union."

"That seems terribly unlikely." Peter's mother hurried to Peter and dropped a kiss on his cheek. "People here have known you forever."

"Mary Beth cares for Union soldiers in Mrs. McCallie's home." Peter returned his mother's kiss. "That, plus the bank policies on money we will accept, add up to spying."

"How ridiculous. They shall say I am a spy next."

"However, I am here to notify you we are altering the loan requirements to fit Colonel Bennet's qualifications."

His mother plopped into her chair. "I suppose you are making me feel good prior to pronouncing a death sentence."

"No." Peter explained the plan.

Mrs. Chandler's eyebrows rose. "Will you accept any of this paper in payment?"

Peter had given a great deal of thought to his answer. "The Confederate Constitution states we can only use silver and gold as legal tender. However, Tennessee passed a law stating people should consider Confederate treasury bills to be worth putting in the bank. Considering the dilemma we face, I will negotiate the terms of repayment. Obviously, I will attempt to accept very little Confederate money."

"Peter!" His mother sprang to her feet. "How could you? This will be the ruin of your father's bank."

"Mama, it's something we had to do. Bennet is threatening us, or Mary Beth to be more specific."

"No, you did not have to do this." His mother stamped her foot. "And I will take out my money. If you sign that loan, I'll start taking out my own money."

"That action will ruin the bank," Peter said. "Remember Dr. Smith said Mary Beth's anxiety is keeping her from conceiving. You will add to that considerably if you continue this course."

Chapter Seven

TUESDAY, JULY 7
9:30 A.M.
C&R BANK

Unconcerned about the July heat, Anna Chandler had a spring in her step as she entered the bank. The ringing bell over the door reminded her of wedding bells, and she hoped Matthew Grant was thinking the same way. She'd promised her son she'd stay with the workmen today while they installed the vault door. Since she also planned some innocent flirting with Grant, she'd dressed in her loveliest day-gown for the occasion. She glanced to her left to see if she could catch Matthew's eye at the teller window, but he was focused on the customer before him.

With a saucy flick of her skirt, she headed upstairs to Peter's office to find out when the contractors planned to arrive. Perhaps she'd have time for a short chat with her soon-to-be fiancé before they arrived. As usual, her son sat at the ornate desk her late husband had purchased years earlier. Today, Peter studied a paper with a slight frown on his face. She danced in the room and snatched it from his fingers. "What's this?"

In order to accommodate the needs of military officers who reside in Chattanooga, C&R Bank will

now accept documentation from other Confederate banks as to these officers' financial standing and credit history. In addition, they may repay the loan with a mixture of commodities, specie, and Confederate treasury notes. However, treasury notes tendered must not exceed 1% of the original loan.

"Mama!" Peter compressed his lips into a tight line as he retrieved the document from his mother. "I'm still working on that."

Anna's good mood evaporated like a drop of water under the blazing sun. Now she was searing with heat. "Have you lost your senses? Your father would be livid if he knew you chose to abandon the gold standard. I will not stand for this. I thought I'd made that clear yesterday."

"You don't understand—"

"Indeed. I do." Anna snatched the paper back and crumpled it. She placed her hands on her hips. "You are putting my money in danger. It's a good thing your father stipulated Mr. Weston manage my other holdings."

"I'm also putting my money at risk because our lives could be in danger. The problem is Colonel Bennet—"

"That soldier is not my concern." She slapped the newly wadded document on the desk. If only she had some control over bank policy. She and Andrew ran the bank together, and her late husband was thankful for her input. "I shall withdraw everything I have in the bank if you do this."

Peter sank into his chair, dropping his head in his hands. "The loss of my deposits would close the bank."

Peter whispered a prayer as his mother swished her full skirt and left the room. The scolding he'd just received reminded him of the time he'd brought a muddy frog into the sitting room, except this time he wasn't guilty of poor judgment. He intended to word the document so he still had the ability to refuse a loan on some small technicality. He had been considering that exact wording when his mother walked in. She didn't consider he was a grown man with a wife to protect. Bankers must always balance risk. That's one reason his father had allowed customers to use checks. They preferred to keep the gold in the bank rather than hand it over the moment they extended the loan.

Now the page was too wrinkled to use. He opened it to copy the wording.

"Peter?" Mary Beth entered his office. "I need to talk."

The lovely blue eyes seeking his softened his mood. She was truly a gem, and he was glad she was his wife. He pushed aside his mother's anger and smiled. "Sure. Take a seat."

"Ida wanted me to alter her mother's wedding dress, but she attacked me yesterday for bank policies." Mary Beth sat on the edge of the desk, right beside his chair. "I don't know what to do. I did promise to help her, but I felt hurt when she left yesterday."

"You can refuse." No one would hurt his wife. Now he was getting heated again. Just last night, he'd risked his life going to see Colonel Bennett to protect Mary Beth. "You are too nice sometimes. Be willing to stand up to her."

"But she's been a friend for so long."

"That doesn't matter."

"Peter?" Mary Beth looked around and sighed with relief. "I thought Ruth was with me. She doesn't need to hear you speaking so sharply."

"I spoke harshly? I didn't realize it. Sorry." He grabbed the paper he needed to copy. "I haven't yet convinced mother to go along with the changes in bank policy. She said she'd withdraw all her money."

His wife gasped. "No."

"I doubt we even have enough in the safe to give her."

EARLY WEDNESDAY EVENING
BEFORE THE PRAYER SERVICE

Mary Beth walked into the almost empty sanctuary and noted the scent of wood polish hanging in the air. The evening sun poured through the stained glass windows bathing the room in red, blue, and yellow. She had come to seek advice from Reverend McCallie and she hurried to the office behind the platform. McCallie occupied a swivel chair while reading over hymns. "Pastor?"

McCallie stood and fastened the button on his jacket. He offered a smile, and his deep-set eyes were warm. "What can I do for you, Mrs. Chandler?"

"Advice." She shrugged then explained the bank's predicament and the way the church people seemed to avoid them. "We still come to church, but we feel like outsiders."

He sighed. "I was unaware you felt that, and I am saddened. I had hoped our members would speak to you rather than judge without knowing the whole story. This sort of politics should not be part of members of Christ's body. However, I know we all fail. The news impacts me deeply, and I want you to know I care for both of you."

Mary Beth's eye welled with tears at his sympathetic tone. "You have never made me feel unimportant."

"I appreciate knowing the problem so I can pray. Satan loves to divide the church, so recognize this as the enemy at work in people who are forgiven, but not perfect yet. Doubtless these folks listened to gossip and don't know the entire story."

"What can we do?"

"My advice will not be easy, because I have had to do this too. Continue being kind and loving those around you. The Bible speaks of heaping coals of fire on the heads of those who treat you poorly. The fire is kindness."

"The hurt makes me want to get even, but I know that's wrong."

"Mary Beth, I admire and love you both as a couple. God loves you also. I recall you saying you wanted to pursue God with all your heart when your father was dying. Don't give up. Rather than seeking to get revenge, reflect God's love while clinging to his grace and kindness. I have been embroiled in such situations too, and I felt the way you do. Sometimes life hurts, but our reaction to the pain helps us grow. I genuinely believe this will pass."

Reflect God's love. She must think on ways to do that.

A deacon hurried in. "Reverend, do you have the hymns ready for the service?"

"Excuse me, Mrs. Chandler." The pastor turned his attention to the music minister.

Mary Beth intended to ask about her inability to conceive, but it would have to wait. She slipped out to the sanctuary.

July 9
City Café Across From C&R Bank
Noon

Peter handed his menu to the waiter and leaned back in the comfortable café chair. His best friend from college, Rob Hatcher, sat across the table from him. Rob had large brown eyes and a thatch of thick dark hair which today was rumpled, making him look younger than his twenty-seven years. While in school, Peter and Rob had whiled away many hours attempting to fish but had failed to catch anything. Rob's sense of humor had made the rigors of college survivable. His surprise visit to the city energized Peter. For the first time in days, he felt lighthearted enough to play one of his college pranks. "Do you remember when we used to feed the ducks at the school pond?"

Rob threw back his head and laughed. "Yes. Once we got them gathered around for bread, they didn't expect bits of wadded paper."

"That big one would actually devour the paper before it sank."

"That's right. I'd forgotten that." The waiter brought tea, and Rob took a sip. "Sometimes I worried he would turn up dead, and the college staff would come after us."

"What are you doing these days?" Peter asked. "And how did you find me?"

"I have a business nearby, in Cleveland. We paint signs for businesses. I was asking residents about the best bank should I need a loan. Everyone told me C&R Bank was the best in the area."

Peter smiled. "You must have asked before our colonel came to town. He's created some ill will because he doesn't like our loan policies."

"You know what they taught us about listening to your customer." Rob chuckled. "But I've had difficult patrons too."

Peter explained the situation with Bennet.

Rob whistled. "He really is after you. How did you deal with him?"

"I've changed my loan requirements for him because I respect the military's efforts to protect us. Basically, he now qualifies for a loan. Given that Tennessee violated the Constitution when they pronounced their own treasury bills to be legal tender, I have a good court case for not accepting. I expect him to cooperate."

"We spent so much time together, I can guess what you are thinking." Rob raised a long, boney finger. "Knowing you, I think you'd give up your life rather than lose someone's cash. That's why your bank is so good."

Peter's face grew warm. He'd never liked praise, but today it was nice to hear such a compliment from a friend who knew him.

"On the other hand, if we didn't have that paper money the government is printing, we'd be in trouble. Inflation is so high that we can't raise our prices fast enough." Rob shoved a hand through his hair. "If I were you, I'd consider accepting the Confederate money like everyone else."

"I'm already in trouble for changing a little." The waiter brought Peter's food, but his appetite was gone. "My mother threatened me if I didn't reverse my decision. I cannot reason with her."

Rob leaned over to take a huge bite of his steak. "Sounds serious, Peter."

"Any thoughts on getting through to my mother?"

Rob laughed. "I wish I could. I can pray for you. That's all I can do."

Peter's pleasant mood darkened. He didn't want to be reminded of the danger.

FRIDAY MORNING
JULY 10
C&R BANK OFFICE

Mary Beth glanced about the faces gathered around the desk in Peter's office. Mr. Gray, the bank lawyer, held a sheaf of papers in his hand. Alongside him, Colonel Bennet sat straight and tall on the edge of a chair. Sheriff

Campbell, his muscular arms crossed, stood by his chair. They came to sign loan papers which the colonel would use to purchase the sheriff's house. Part of her couldn't believe this was happening. What a monumental moment—the day the bank deserted the gold standard.

Peter stood. "We are ready to begin—"

"No." Colonel Bennet shook his head while fingering the papers in front of him. "I won't sign anything until I read it."

"Indeed. We wouldn't expect that." Peter nodded to the lawyer. "Mr. Gray, will you pass out the contract?"

The slender man stood and handed a document to each person. Colonel Bennet donned a pair of wire-rimmed glasses then bent his hulky form over the document.

"This is incorrect." Bennet stood and slammed the paper onto the desk. "This said I must repay the loan with five percent Confederate bills. I cannot agree."

Mary Beth groaned aloud and then clapped her hand over her mouth. Peter would be angry. He detested men who attempted to get what they wanted by deceit.

"We can alter that to say you will pay in commodities," Peter said. "But that is what we discussed, and you had no problems at the time."

"I can assure you, Peter Chandler isn't a man to lie," Campbell said. He folded the pages in his hand and pointed them toward Bennet as he finished speaking.

Mary Beth applauded Campbell in her heart. Evidence seemed to indicate Bennet was manipulating for better terms.

"I want to renegotiate the loan, "Bennet said. "I don't like these terms."

Peter glanced at Mary Beth, and she shook her head. "Our answer is no. If you want different conditions, then you have no loan. You might try the bank in Cleveland."

Peter stood and Mary Beth followed, her heart beating faster. She hoped the loan fell through so they wouldn't have to further deplete the gold left in the vault.

"Wait." Colonel Bennet shouted. "I want the loan. My wife will love the house. She's been looking for a home in a small town a hundred or so miles from her parents."

Peter put his hands on the desk and leaned toward the soldier. "Your accusation was that the bank wouldn't take Confederate cash. I am accepting a small percent for this loan. Those are the terms.

"Very well. I will sign." The soldier picked up a pen, "but your demands create a hardship. I may have to offer commodities."

"Let's add a note to the contract." Peter dipped his pen in ink and wrote a small addendum at the bottom."

Bennet signed the contract and addendum, then pushed it toward the lawyer.

Gray's long fingers curled around the document. "I shall draw up the deed and bring it to the bank."

Bennet then shoved a packet of money toward Peter. "My down payment. You may count the gold if you wish."

Peter handed cash to Campbell for the house. "You requested commodities as well as gold, so Mr. Grant will escort you to the warehouse for your share."

"Thank you, sir." Campbell pocketed the gold and left the room.

Done! The room swirled around her, and Mary Beth sat back down. Money came in all the time, especially loan repayments and interest. But how much gold remained in the vault now?

Chapter Eight

JULY 15
8:30 A.M.
C&R BANK

Anna hovered at the door of Matthew's office wondering how long it would take for him to notice her presence. She had donned a gown accenting her fair coloring, and the tilt of her floral hat demonstrated her sense of style. How she craved for romance. Matthew finally looked up as she walked toward the door. "Good morning, sir."

Grant returned her greeting with a genuine smile. "Good morning, Anna."

"In all the years I've known you, I've never entered your office." She inched inside.

"I hope it meets with your expectations." Grant kissed her hand. "I am, of course, open to suggestion."

Anna fluttered her lashes. "You require some input from a lady?"

Grant raised a brow. "Indeed. Do you have a suggestion?"

"I would be delighted to help, that is, if you'd like."

"Indeed." Grant tucked his chin. "I'd enjoy having your assistance."

"How delightful for us both." She went past him, gazing at the desk and filing cabinets. "I shall give it some thought, but perhaps you might add a bit of color."

"You infuse a rainbow of colors the moment you walk in." Grant moved a bit closer to Anna. "Would you like to have dinner with me tonight?"

"Thanks." Anna offered her best smile. "I would like that."

"Anna, you can rely on me to take care of you. Remember that."

"Grant?"

Anna looked up to find Peter standing in the doorway. "Mrs. Bailey is waiting for you at the teller window."

Grant reddened as he brushed past Anna. "I'm terribly sorry, sir. I wasn't thinking of the time."

A HALF HOUR LATER
McCALLIE HOME

Mary Beth looked for a place in the crowded kitchen to put down her medications. The preparations for biscuits and gravy still covered the counter and a small canister of coffee sat beside the flour and lard. She pulled up an empty chair and deposited her basket there. No doubt Mrs. McCallie needed assistance with cleaning as well as with nursing. Perhaps today Mary Beth could also share her concerns about having a baby and ask Ellen to pray. "Where can I help?"

Ellen turned from stirring soup on the stove. "Sergeant Alcott is terribly uncomfortable, and Grace has been fussy all morning. I've been so busy with my patients lately, but I felt she needed me more than they did today. Oh, and

Private Butler needs his bandage changed. It's been oozing a purulent fluid that has an unpleasant odor."

"I have a preparation to make him more comfortable. I'll prepare some right away." Mary Beth measured a dose of medication into a glass of water.

"Wonderful. I've been worried about him." Ellen clasped her hands together and smiled.

Holding the glass, Mary Beth turned to her left and ascended the stairs. At the top she turned right into the room Butler occupied. Mary Beth headed to the window to open the shades before she turned to the bed at the opposite wall. A nurse must have light to observe the condition of her patient. The bearded soldier before her lay with one arm over his eyes. Despite the excessive hair on his face, his ruddy complexion was pale. His skin was cool and dry, which meant he had no fever. He'd suffered gunshots to his right thigh and to his left arm in a recent skirmish. "Sergeant, I have medication to make you more comfortable."

"Thank you, ma'am." The soldier lifted himself on his elbow and reached for the cup. He grimaced as he swallowed. "The cramps are intense this morning."

"This should help."

"This business of dying is hard work." The man lay back on the pillow and groaned.

"Oh, sir. I don't think there's any question of death. That is, you appear to be recovering."

"Augh! Would the doctor even tell me if I were dying, since I fought for the Union?" He ground his teeth.

"Oh, yes." Mary Beth smiled. "Dr. Smith has no loyalty to either side when it comes to caring for his patients."

"Mrs. Chandler?" Ellen came to the doorway and waved for Mary Beth to come into the hallway. "Dr. Smith is here, and he wishes to speak to you."

When Mary Beth stepped into the hallway, Dr. Smith motioned for her. "I fear the Private Butler will lose his leg unless we can apply that preparation you concocted. Did you bring any with you?"

"I'm sorry, no. I prepared the ingredients. The Echinacea is ready to mix with alcohol." Mary Beth noted the lines of concern around the doctor's eyes. "Shall I go home and complete the salve?"

The doctor stroked his salt and pepper beard. "Yes. Immediately. I'd rather this young man not lose his leg, but we'll have to start the liniment right away to have any hope."

"Cook is off today, so the kitchen will be empty." Mary Beth scurried down the steps to find Ellen in the kitchen. "Dr. Smith wants Butler on that preparation right away. I shall leave now."

Ellen beamed. "I'm terribly thankful you're so willing to serve. These Union soldiers might not get the care they need from a different kind of nurse."

Mary Beth made it home in record time. Ruth was in the kitchen hanging up herbs to dry. She gathered her ingredients from the pantry and laid them on the table.

"Excuse me, ma'am." Maud, Mary Beth's housekeeper came alongside. "I hope this be a good time, as I be havin' somethin' to say. And you ain't be liking the topic. I would like to be a workin' with me husband at Anna Chandler's house. He be fillin' the role of butler and housekeeper. You know we's been married for quite a while now, and I always meant to be workin' with 'im."

"Oh, dear." Mary Beth inhaled sharply. "How shall I do without you, Maud?"

"Miss Mary Beth, you be in good shape with that there husband of yours. He be a findin' someone better than me. I always said I do my best, but others can be organizin' better than me. Yous been so good to put up with what I could offer."

Finding someone to replace Maud wouldn't be easy. "I've never had a complaint with your work." Mary Beth took her hand. "And I'd rather not find a substitute."

"Yous be fine, Ma'am."

Mary Beth wasn't so sure. Maud could please her and run the house without a hitch. With the upheaval at the bank, Mary Beth wondered if Anna engineered Maud's resignation because Peter changed the bank's loan policies.

TWO HOURS LATER
C&R BANK

Peter looked with pride at the once-cluttered desk. Rather than work all morning, as usual, he'd chosen to organize his projects. His desk looked far better than it had at any time since he'd taken charge of the bank about two years ago. Now he intended to go home and spend some time with his wife and sister. Hopefully they could put aside their distress today.

He hurried down the steps to the bank foyer. He turned right to go behind the counter and then left to the offices.

Mr. Evans popped into the hallway. "Mr. Chandler, may I speak with you? The changes you instituted with the vault are creating some problems for us. Our job is much more difficult since we no longer have regular access to the safe…"

Peter pulled his mind away from thoughts of leaving the bank and listened. "Excellent. Write me a memo and tell me what you would like to see happen and why. I'll talk it over with my wife."

An odd sound in the foyer caught Peter's attention as Evans walked away. Was someone banging on the wall?

"Excuse me." Peter walked down the hall and turned right, going into the lobby. Evans followed behind. As Peter stepped into the room, he saw Lieutenant McDonald standing in front of Mr. Grant who carried a handful of receipts.

"Here's what you get for your insults." McDonald threw an uppercut punch into Mr. Grant's abdomen.

Grant grabbed his stomach, doubled over, and stumbled backward. Papers went everywhere.

Peter almost groaned at the confidential information spreading across the floor. He scolded himself and turned his attention to Grant. Based on the past, McDonald would probably not bear the guilt for this incident, since he often brought trouble. Peter ran between the two hoping to prevent McDonald from landing another blow. "Stop!"

McDonald, his coat open and flapping, hurried out of the bank, slamming the door behind him. The bell over the door jangled as a gold button rolled across the floor.

Peter turned to Grant who leaned against the counter, pale and breathless. "Are you injured?"

"I'm fine." The bank manager grimaced as he straightened.

Peter wasn't so sure, but he would give the man a few moments.

Evans chased a shiny button and came toward Grant. "Does this belong to you?"

Grant shook his head.

Peter took it. "I think it came from McDonald's coat. We'll put it aside for him."

Evans patted Grant on the back. "You look injured. I can manage things if you need to go home."

"No." Grant pulled himself to an upright position. His face, however, was drawn, as if he were in pain. "Give me a moment to catch my breath."

Peter wondered, as he pulled out his pocket watch, if he should open a boxing ring. "We usually close for lunch at noon on Saturday. That's only forty-five minutes from now, so we are closing early. I'm going to help you shut down the teller windows."

Mr. Evans spoke up. "No need. I can do it, Mr. Chandler."

"Thanks, Evans. But I particularly want to stay with Mr. Grant until he recovers." Being shy, Grant would be more open if the two of them were alone. Something went wrong, and Peter had to get the facts. "I shall see you Monday."

Evans shrugged and pressed his lips together. "Very well. I'll gather my things."

Peter picked up the receipts and locked the front door behind Evans. He busied himself emptying the cash drawers at both teller windows. After a trip to the vault to deposit the money, Peter found Grant in his office. His color and demeanor were much improved. "You look better."

Grant nodded. "I am. Thanks."

Peter sat down offering Grant time to consider. After a moment or two, he said, "Shall I send for Dr. Smith."

"No." Grant massaged his abdomen. "I shall go home and rest."

"What caused that altercation?"

"That was odd. I was headed to your office with those papers." Grant shifted in his chair. "McDonald came in asking if we now accepted Confederate money. I explained our new policy. The next thing I knew he shoved me. Maybe I shoved back, I don't recall. The entire event lasted thirty seconds or less."

Peter nodded. If only Mary Beth were here, she would know if Grant should take precautions after such an incident. "You can have him arrested and press charges."

Grant shook his head. "That might create even more turmoil for the bank."

Peter believed turmoil lay in the future anyway.

Chapter Nine

Mary Beth sat on the couch, surrounded by Ida's dress and the extra lace her mother had left over from the time of her own wedding. She sewed as fast as she could, racing against time to finish while keeping her stitches neat. Her thread became too short, and she snipped the remainder. After reaching for the spool on the occasional table beside her, she prepared a fresh needle and started again.

Peter entered the room and leaned over to plant a kiss on her head. "How's the work coming?"

She looked at the clock and groaned. "Not fast enough. Ida's wedding is tomorrow."

"I thought you were sewing all day?" Peter took a wing chair across the room. "I could have used your help today."

"Fixing this dress is taking longer than I expected. Besides, ever since I made a mistake while fixing Mrs. Phipps's errors, I have avoided the bank. I feel incompetent."

"That does not sound like you. It's irrational." Peter frowned.

She recalled the frustration on his face when she took him the ledger in question. "I apparently upset you."

"Nonsense. You were tired, and I promised to finish the work myself." Peter crossed the room and touched her shoulder. "Do you want me to be compassionate or help you?"

"I need compassion. I would have had these alterations finished, but Ida came early this afternoon for a fitting. She's lost more weight, and I had to take in the bodice." Mary Beth dropped the fabric and reached for a few more pins.

"You could have refused."

He was giving advice again, making her wish she had never accepted this task. "Ida is a good friend. I felt I should."

"I am sorry you found this task so difficult, but I admire your loyalty." Peter massaged her shoulders.

She let go of her needle and sighed with pleasure. "Oh, thank you."

"So, you would rather I make you feel better than problem solve?"

"Yes. I cannot change the choice I made."

"I was thinking of saying no in the future." He moved his hands to her neck, where he kneaded the muscles. "What time is the wedding?"

"Tomorrow afternoon at one. She wanted to follow the European custom for a Tuesday wedding, but she ignored the tradition of a morning wedding." Mary Beth rang the bell for Maud to fetch her more thread. "That reminds me, Maud announced she was leaving to work for your mother. I shan't know what to do without her."

"Do you have anyone in mind?" Peter asked.

"I don't, and that worries me. I shall tackle the issue once I finish sewing. But enough of my problems. How's the bank after the closing? Did you convince your mother not to pull out her money?"

"We now own Colonel Bennet's mortgage, and I gave him a higher interest rate to offset the risk I'm taking. We will earn money on the deal."

"And what about your mother?"

"My mother isn't willing to concede. She's given me a deadline of one week to reverse our policy and sell the mortgage to another bank. After that, she'll start removing her money."

"Dreadful. What can we do?"

"I intend to keep trying to talk to Mother, and I think I'll try to sell the mortgage to the bank in Cleveland, even though they might not give us gold. I don't like the stress my mother's putting on you. I shall also seek other investments to keep us afloat, but that will take time."

His mother could be incredibly determined.

TUESDAY
JULY 21
AFTER THE WEDDING

The aroma of beef and green beans filled the air in the church basement. Huge pitchers of iced tea sat on each of the long tables where wedding guests enjoyed the sumptuous meal. Mary Beth sat beside Ruth, who had loaded her plate with food.

"This beef is so tender," Ruth said, piercing a bite with her fork.

"Yes. And it's tasty. I ate as much as I could." Mary Beth turned her gaze to the round table holding the cake where the bride and groom stood, ready to serve the guests.

"The bride looks gorgeous." Ruth paused with her fork midway to her mouth.

"Mrs. Campbell's dress was exquisite. I'm going to speak with them before they leave." She hurried over to offer congratulations and to meet the groom. Hopefully, she and Peter could enjoy outings with the couple when they returned from their brief trip. She wished Peter had been able to attend, but she could introduce the two men later. "Best wishes, Ida."

Ida embraced Mary Beth. "Thank you for the needlework. I'm so grateful."

Mary Beth extended her hand to the groom, who had brown wavy hair combed straight back from a heart shaped face. He glared at her without responding. "Sergeant Stanford, Ida spoke of you so often. I offer my congratulations. I hope we see more of each other."

Stanford gave a stiff nod, puffing out his chest.

How rude. Mary Beth wondered if Stanford acted this way to everyone.

Mrs. Campbell walked up, dampness about her eyes. "Oh, Mary Beth, I'm so grateful for the alterations you made for Ida. To see my girl walking down the aisle in my gown took my breath."

"I was pleased to help, Mrs. Campbell. You've done a wonderful job with the reception. I haven't seen this much food since the war."

"We purchased food from nearby friends. They slaughtered one of their cows and provided most of the vegetables." She leaned close to Mary Beth and lowered her voice. "Money from the sale of our house paid for this. We'll have to start over once we settle down in our new home."

A pang of sympathy ran through Mary Beth. That explained why Campbell needed to sell his house. What a sacrifice. They must be so fond of their daughter to go to such lengths. "We will miss you. If a serious crime occurs, what will we do without the sheriff?"

Mrs. Campbell touched her handkerchief to the corner of her eye. "The city council will hire another. I suspect you'll have other things to concern you. Union things."

Mary Beth's stomach knotted. She preferred not to think of invading soldiers especially during a wedding. A movement to her left caught her eye, and she glanced up. Ida and her new husband headed out the door. Mary Beth hurried to say goodbye. "Ida?"

Stanford's brown eyes met hers for a moment, but he swept Ida from the room and out of Mary Beth's reach.

What an odd reaction. He acted as if he didn't want her speaking to his new wife.

A Few Minutes Later

The afternoon heat was so sweltering, Mary Beth had to pull out her fan as she hurried down the wooden sidewalk on Main Street. The streets were almost empty of her fellow citizens, as many, including Ruth, remained to enjoy the reception and feast. Mary Beth promised Peter she'd lift money from the tellers this afternoon while he met a client from out of town. Once she ran a few errands, she must return to the bank.

"Mrs. Chandler?"

She turned to see Mr. Evans behind her.

He lifted his hat. "I haven't seen you at the bank since the sheriff's closing."

"Good afternoon."

Evans grimaced. "I'm sure your husband shared the unfortunate incident with McDonald and Grant?"

"Indeed." Now that she wasn't walking, she was hotter than ever. Her feet ached to keep moving so she could complete her chores. "I should be on my way."

Evans looked left and right, as if making sure no one would hear. "I thought I'd mention a troubling matter."

She couldn't imagine what might bother him or why he didn't approach Peter. "Yes?"

"On several occasions, I've seen Grant become quite forceful, especially after he began his ... flirtations." He cleared his throat.

"Forceful?" Mary Beth's throat clogged. "Do you mean he was forceful while he flirted?"

"Oh, no." Evans pulled at his collar. "I mean he became more aggressive with me and with customers after he and the elder Mrs. Chandler began ... courting. Perhaps he thinks he will raise his influence at the bank if he makes an alliance with her. These two incidents at the bank don't surprise me."

Mary Beth sighed. She disliked having bank employees complain to her. She wouldn't make any changes without her husband's input anyway. "I'll approach my husband on the topic. Can you give us an example?"

"You've had two scuffles at the bank." Evans frowned and wiped his brow with his handkerchief. "What better examples do you require? Grant makes sure I don't have a chance to talk to you and your husband at the bank itself. Besides, I'm not sure your husband would listen, given that Grant is dating his mother."

Now who was getting aggressive? She cleared her throat and tried to construct the proper phrase, one that a bank owner would say. "I'll discuss this with Peter."

Was Grant different because of his relationship with Peter's mother? It might be true. She'd overheard Grant reprove Evans, but she assumed Grant was doing his job as bank manager. Mary Beth's world was changing fast, and she wondered who she could trust.

SEVERAL HOURS LATER
PETER'S OFFICE C&R BANK

Beautiful! Peter sat back in his chair, taking in the sight of Mary Beth before indulging in a huge gulp of tea. He enjoyed the view of his lovely wife, who occupied the chair across the desk. The warm weather had made tiny blonde tendrils curl about her face and suffused her cheeks with color. She'd hadn't worked alongside him for several days and having her back refreshed him. Bank problems receded. How pleasant.

His secretary, Mr. Riddle, entered with a tray of food. Ruth was close behind with more tea. "The café owner across the street sent you a meal, and it smells wonderful."

"How kind." Mary Beth took a whiff of the feast. "I think he wants to support us after the entire town complained about our bank policies. In the midst of all this, I can thank God for this gift."

Peter nodded. "Right now, I find it easy to praise God."

"I won't need anything, because I ate too much at the wedding." Ruth rubbed her stomach. "But the food smells good."

Mary Beth moved files and ledgers from the desk. "Isn't that wonderful? After I completed all my chores, I stopped in for some refreshment. The owner met me at the door and offered to bring us dinner."

Ruth grabbed tea. "I'll be in the storeroom reading that book on herbal preparations. I'd like to learn all I can from you."

The luscious smells made Peter's stomach rumble. He'd skipped lunch because a client meeting went longer than he expected, and he kept working afterwards.

His wife placed a plate before him with meatloaf, mashed potatoes, and fried okra. "The new owner is Mr.

Kauffman."

Peter didn't know if he could eat the entire feast, but he would certainly try. He rubbed his hands together. "I'm not going to complain, but I must thank this Mr. Kauffman in person. Let's become loyal patrons and encourage others to do so also."

"Indeed." Mary Beth sliced a bit of meatloaf. "Evans approached me today with a concern over Matthew Grant."

Peter savored a bite of crunchy okra, and he appreciated the skill of the chef. "I haven't given much thought to Matthew Grant. What was on his mind?"

"Evans believes Grant is more aggressive than he used to be. I asked for an example, and he mentioned both incidents in the bank lobby. He suggested that courting your mother gives Grant a particular status allowing him to be less genteel."

"I've caught him ignoring customers while flirting with my mother, but that was unusual. Peter put down his fork. "I could see him getting defensive if someone threatened Mother."

"Well, isn't threatening the bank a way of attacking your mother? She's quite protective of your father's work here. I've heard her say that. Isn't that why she wants to pull out her money? She fears you are ruining the bank her husband founded."

Peter clenched his teeth. He didn't like the thought of his mother's remarriage. But Grant appeared to be positioning himself to be a rival to protect his mother's interests. His good mood vanished.

THE CHANDLER HOME
JULY 29
5 A.M.

Head pounding, Mary Beth opened her eyes to darkness and pulled the sheet about her neck. She adjusted her pillow, longing for slumber again while knowing it wouldn't come. Her husband's slow even breathing led her to believe he was still sleeping, so she must be silent. She placed a hand on her stomach. She longed for food, but a gagging sensation accompanied the roiling. She slid her feet over the side of the bed and rose to a sitting position. Her body, however, protested and the room spun about her. Striving to be inaudible, she eased to the floor and pulled out the necessary basin under the bed.

Sh-sh! Her body wretched with violence and ejected a small quantity of liquid. She sank to the floor, exhausted. Maybe this meant she was with child.

"Mary Beth?" Peter's voice said. "Are you ill?"

"I tried not to wake you. I'm sorry." She shuddered at the acrid taste in her mouth, and a tear trickled down her cheek. She had work awaiting her at the bank. Right now they must know how much gold remained in the vault. "I don't have time to be ill."

"Nonsense. You need assistance." Peter lit a candle and knelt beside her wearing his robe. "I'll find Maud."

"She's not here. Remember I told you?" Mary Beth was so tired even talking took effort.

A knock sounded on the door, and Ruth's voice emerged from the other side, "Mary Beth? Is everything okay?"

Peter went to the door. "She's sick."

"I'll fetch Mother."

The door closed, but voices echoed in the hall. Mary Beth's body relaxed until warm hands—Peter's—scooped her up. His body was comforting. He placed her back in bed where the cool covers made her shiver.

A hand touched her face, and she jerked her eyes open. Anna Chandler's face hovered close to hers. "She's pasty white, Peter. Call Dr. Smith right away."

Mary Beth tried to sit up.

"Is it possible you could be with child?" Mrs. Chandler had a deep crease in her forehead.

If only that were true. Mary Beth preferred not to think about the topic because it upset her. "I think not. I've been spotting. What time is it?"

Anna Chandler shook her head. "Stop worrying about the time. Peter has the bank well in hand."

"It's six in the morning," Ruth said, taking her hand.

"I've got to be up." Mary Beth's body didn't do her bidding. "This is such a crucial time for the bank."

"Just relax." Ruth rubbed Mary Beth's arm. "Dr. Smith will be here soon."

Angry voices drifted in from the hall. Anna spoke, "Peter, if you hadn't been so foolish with the bank's money, I would not have been so harsh."

"Mama, you must not upset her. Dr. Smith thinks she caught something while nursing those Union soldiers. Perhaps …"

If only a family argument would break out some other time instead of when she was ill. Mary Beth prayed to have a baby and prayed for the bank. God must be her refuge right now.

Chapter Ten

Tired! Mary Beth glanced around at the clean but rumpled covers, the flowers from Peter on the dresser, and the tray by the bed with water and medicines. Thankfulness rose in her chest for those who loved her. Jane Haskell had come to help, and Ruth ran errands. Dr. Smith said she had contracted an illness from the soldiers she nursed, and he ordered complete rest. After two days, however, the inactivity almost drove her crazy. She should be at work with Peter or at least preparing medicines for the upcoming invasion. A twinge of nausea still lingered with the fatigue, but her mind begged for a challenge.

Jane popped her head in the door, her long brown hair fastened up. They hadn't spent as much time together since they married, and Mary Beth missed Jane. She'd told Mary Beth about her desire to go into nursing, but her father wouldn't relent. Mary Beth's illness gave her a chance to learn by doing. "Do you feel well enough to see a visitor?"

Mary Beth tried to straighten her thick blonde hair. She must look a mess. "Is it a woman or a man?"

Jane raised an eyebrow. "Ida … what's her new name? She seems upset, and you are supposed to stay relaxed."

"Ida?" Mary Beth adjusted her pillows so she could sit up. "She's home? Bring her in, of course. I can't wait to see her."

Breathless, Ida rushed in. Her wispy brown hair protruded from her bonnet as if she'd been running. A huge bruise marred her fair skin on the side of her face. "Mary Beth, I'm terribly sorry to bother you when you're ill, but this is an emergency."

"That contusion looks horrid." Mary Beth's heart raced. She threw off the covers and pulled herself to a sitting position on the side of the bed. "Someone attacked you?"

"No." Ida blushed and looked away. "This is nothing. I fell in the dark and hit the steps. Besides, I don't want my father to see my face right now. He'll be furious."

"What?" The discoloration resembled the shape of someone's hand. Not a blunt injury you'd receive from falling in the stairwell. "Then you'd best explain."

"My father agreed to sell his house only if Colonel Bennet allowed Ed and me to use the downstairs apartment where our servants used to sleep. We've just returned from our trip." Her voice faltered. "As I neared the house, I found …"

Mary Beth leaned forward, her curiosity aroused. "Yes? Go on …"

"Colonel Bennet was on the ground." She put her hands on her face. "You've been a nurse and might know what to do. I think he's dead."

Mary Beth got up, ignoring the lurch of her stomach. "You're right, this is urgent."

"What are you going to do?" Ida's hazel eyes widened.

Mary Beth staggered to the dressing table where she ran a brush through her hair. "You came for advice. Right?"

Ida nodded, staring.

"Then help me dress. Hurry!"

OUTSIDE COLONEL BENNET'S HOUSE
FIFTEEN MINUTES LATER

Holding the sides of her head, Mary Beth sank onto the stairs to the large front porch a few feet to the left of the corpse. The humidity, smell of blood, and the insects all over the man's body made her stomach churn. To calm the nausea, Mary Beth took deep breaths and gazed at beautiful oak trees, well-trimmed bushes, and flowers bordering the gravel walkway. However, the impulse to gag sent her to the bushes where she deposited her last meal.

"What a dreadful mess. I shouldn't have called you, Mary Beth. Ida stood in the shade of the two-story frame house wringing her hands. "He's dead, isn't he?"

Mary Beth didn't need to look again. She could picture the scene. Arms splayed, Bennet lay face down a few feet from the porch which ran the length of the house. A huge wound covered the back of his gray jacket. Spattered blood lay on the grass around and on the trunk of the beech nearby. "Yes. Shot in the back. I think he's been dead several hours. The blood looks sticky and dry."

"What shall we do?" Ida's nose wrinkled, and she moved further from the body. "Oh no. Here comes my husband."

Mary Beth glanced up to note Sergeant Stanford approach with a scowl. How sad. She thought of Ida as one of her most down-to-earth friends. Her helplessness today wasn't typical. Perhaps the change in her marital status had overwhelmed her. Mary Beth had already asked

Jane to contact Dr. Smith, who should arrive soon. "Get in touch with your father. Isn't he at the hotel?"

"Yes. He's at the Crutchfield house."

"Ida, what is that woman doing here?" Sergeant Stanford motioned toward Mary Beth as he sauntered up.

Mary Beth shrugged, wishing she'd stayed home. Dizziness and the bitter taste in her mouth made her long for the comfort of her bedroom. "I came here at her request."

"I request you leave. Now!" He came close enough for her to smell alcohol on his breath. His features knotted into a scowl.

"Indeed. Mrs. Chandler, I want you at home resting." Black bag in hand, Dr. Smith strode up and gave Mary Beth a piercing gaze. "Sergeant, your wife has nothing to fear from her. I understand we have someone injured?"

"Dead." Mary Beth pointed to the body. "His name is Colonel Bennett."

"Yes. He's the one who caused all the trouble for your bank." The doctor looked at her oddly before stroking his salt and pepper beard. He walked over and knelt by the body. "Oh, yes. He's been dead several hours."

Peter took in the blood-soaked corpse which lay face down in the yard. Buzzing flies and odor marred the ambiance of the lovely frame house, which the bank now owned. He hurried toward his pale wife sitting on the whitewashed steps of the porch. Whatever happened, he wanted Mary Beth out of harm's way. A surly sergeant shoved Ida to one side and walked right up to Peter. "What are you doing here?"

Peter pointed at Mary Beth. "She's my wife."

"Then get her out of here." Sergeant Stanford spit on the grass, as if he disdained all of them.

Peter went toward his wife and held out his hand. "I want to know why you are here."

Mary Beth stiffened and leaned away. "Ida asked me for help. Given her appearance, I thought she'd been attacked, so I came as fast as I could."

Peter turned to see Ida's face, hoping for an explanation of his wife's irrational behavior.

"What are you lookin' at?" The red-faced soldier thrust him away, but not before Peter saw the huge welt on Ida's face.

"What's going on here?" Sheriff Campbell strode up, frowning.

Stanford pulled Ida away.

"Ida?" Campbell strode toward his daughter. "What happened to you?"

"She's my wife." Stanford stepped between them and got right in the sheriff's face. "And you're leaving town."

"You'd best see this, Sheriff." Dr. Smith said. "Colonel Bennet is dead. Murdered."

The sheriff whistled as he hurried over to the body. "He sure is. And we have the bankers here who refused his loan the first time. They could be connected to this crime."

Peter grabbed Mary Beth's hand. "I'm taking my wife home. She's been ill and should be in bed."

The sheriff stopped him. "I was supposed to leave tomorrow, but I guess I'd best get enough facts to hand over to the city council." He gazed at Peter with narrowed eyes. "Plan on staying in town. I'm going to have questions for both of you."

"We'll be here." The bank didn't need any more bad publicity, but the dead man had insisted he and Mary Beth change loan policies. Surely no one in town would think she had a hand in his murder because they could foreclose on the house if Bennet's assets couldn't make mortgage payments.

MOMENTS LATER

Horrible scenarios ran through Peter's mind as he guided Mary Beth down the wooden sidewalk. Such an outing could make her far worse, especially if she were already with child. Peter kept his arm around his wife, supporting her as they came alongside the town bakery. They'd already walked two blocks from Bennett's house. "Do you need to sit down?"

"I would like that. Could we go in the bakery for a moment?"

Peter wanted to be alone before he had the conversation that nagged at him. The warrior in his soul tempted him to be cross with his wife, but in her weakened condition, she would get upset. Plus, citizens swarmed around outside, preventing privacy. But no one stood inside the bakery where a small table sat for customers who wanted to sample their breads. "Let's go inside and purchase a few dinner rolls. We can take home what we don't eat."

"Good idea, but it will be expensive." Mary Beth gazed in the window. "I've heard their breads are excellent, but Cook does such a good job baking, I've never tried them."

"This will be a special treat for us both," Peter said.

"You are very kind."

"It's not kindness, it's love." Peter grinned at her. "Reverend McCallie reminds us they are the same thing."

"I appreciate your love." Once seated with their selection, Mary Beth asked, "How did you find out where I was?"

"Ruth came to the bank when you left with Ida. I was terribly concerned, so I left immediately. Why didn't you send help rather than go yourself? The doctor wants you to rest."

"I was upset by Ida's condition, and I had to know what happened. She looked as if someone had beaten her, and I thought that might be related to whatever happened to Bennet. The problem is, I still don't know."

Peter huffed. "Ida's new husband is a brute. I saw the way he acted, shoving her about. He's the one who gave her that welt, and maybe he killed his landlord."

"I can't believe she would accept his proposal, or that her parents would permit her to marry such a man."

Peter shrugged. He cared about Ida as Mary Beth's friend, but he was much more apprehensive about his wife. "People change. I'm very troubled about your choice to endanger your health. You disobeyed the doctor's orders and placed yourself in a very emotionally charged situation."

"I'll admit to curiosity and boredom too." Mary Beth crumbled a bit of bread in her fingers. "I'm not accustomed to lie abed for days. Plus, I believe in sacrificing yourself for friends."

"If you must sacrifice yourself, then do it for me. Get well for me. I know you want a child, and so do I. I think we should pray about this together every night, in addition to taking care of your health."

"I like the idea of praying together."

Something about the gleam in her eye didn't convince him she would take care of herself if something exciting happened. But he had tried.

NOON

Her shoulders stiff, Mary Beth sat up in bed twisting a lock of hair. Her lunch, which consisted of soup and a biscuit, grew cold, but she couldn't bear to swallow a thing after what she saw this morning. She must get his grotesque face out of her mind.

"Yoo-hoo?" Jane came in wearing a crisp white apron. "Mary Beth, you've eaten nothing."

"I had rolls at the bakery, but the soup makes me gag." Mary Beth hoped she was with child, and the doctor would say he made a mistake. "I'm sorry. I know you're trying hard."

"Your husband wants you calm and relaxed, and I'm not succeeding in getting you there."

"Finding a dead body tends to be upsetting." Mary Beth handed her the tray. "And the sheriff said he wanted to talk to us, as if we are suspects."

"Utter nonsense."

"Not really." If only it weren't true, but she might be the prime suspect.

Jane frowned. "Where's the evidence?"

"First, I appeared on scene when he arrived, and Bennet did accuse me of spying in front of the head nurse. I also take care of all the Union patients at Mrs. McCallie's, and I set up the bank policies on not accepting fake legal tender."

"I'd think Mr. Grant would be a suspect first. Didn't he attack the colonel the first time he went to the bank?" Jane deposited the tray on the dressing table and sat on the bed.

"Yes. I was there, and his aggression surprised me. It was frightening having men fighting in the bank. Fist fights upset me."

Jane moved closer and touched her hand. "You are so tight. Any chance you might take a nap?"

"No." If only she could find relief in oblivion.

"Colonel Bennet was odd, you know." Jane ended by patting her back.

Since she worked at the bank and at Mrs. McCallie's, she didn't mingle as much with her friends at church. "Odd?"

"He slunk about the alleys and argued with everyone." Jane rose again and walked to the door. "He had altercations at the post office, the café, and at the printer's office."

"Hmm. Remind people that we've been trustworthy for many years. We need their business. I don't want them doing business in Cleveland."

"No one is going to take their banking to Cleveland. You are worrying about nothing."

Mary Beth closed her eyes. "Peter said two of our clients did yesterday."

Chapter Eleven

SATURDAY, AUGUST 1

Unbearable heat wore Peter down as he clomped down the sidewalk to the bank. His heavy footsteps sounded hollow, like a woodpecker hammering at a tree. A lady approaching him crossed the dusty street rather than pass him, and a man ducked into a store when he caught sight of Peter. Was it his imagination, or was the city rejecting him? As he stepped into the bank foyer, the jangling of the bell annoyed him.

Mrs. Teague rushed up almost bouncing, her hands clasped. "Oh, Mr. Chandler, have you heard?"

He sighed. If only he could get to his office before hearing the news of Bennet's death again. He would, however, be polite. "You have news, Madam?"

"Yes." She took a deep breath. Her eyes sparkled with energy. "I heard Colonel Bennet is dead, and the grocer is blaming Mr. Grant. Can you believe that? I've known that man all my life, and he's as gentle as a lamb."

Peter released a suppressed sigh and hoped no one thought of blaming Mary Beth. If anyone knew Bennet had accused her of spying for the Union, that rumor would circulate. The uproar over Mr. Grant had surprised him, and Peter hoped he did not have to fire his bank manager. His mother might never forgive him. "There's no accounting for what people might say."

"Isn't that the truth?" She nodded and lifted her chin.

Peter hurried up the steps before anyone else could corral him, but when he entered his office, his mother stood behind his desk. She jumped, as if she'd been snooping. "Mama? Did you need something?"

"Yes." She stiffened and touched her lips. "I withdrew some of my money. I plan to give it to Mr. Weston to manage. C&R Bank has become a dangerous place."

Mother wasn't meeting his gaze, and that worried him. What was she trying to accomplish? "Is there something you needed in my office?"

"I-I was going to write you a note. I shall drop by to see Mary Beth later this evening."

What did his mother have to hide? Was she behind the colonel's murder? The thought brought a wave of nausea. He hoped not. However, she always said she would do anything for her children, and the colonel had threatened Mary Beth. Would she go that far?

C&R Bank
Noon

Troubled by the news, Peter locked the front door and put up the closed sign. Events kept throwing suspicion on bank employees. Was he becoming too paranoid? Who could be behind such a conspiracy? How he despised doubting his staff, but he must consider the situation and think of every possibility.

He glanced around to ensure everything was put away for closing. On his right, Mrs. Phipps's desk was cleared.

She seemed a likely candidate, but he doubted she was clever enough to carry out such a plan. On the other hand, Evans had the brains, but he came with excellent references. Mr. Riddle had worked for the family for many years, but perhaps he had grown greedy concocting a scheme to obtain the bank. However, knowing Riddle, that seemed unlikely.

As Peter walked through the lobby, he noted the overstuffed chairs next to Phipps's desk sat in their proper place. The lobby was clear of debris. He moved forward to go behind the counter and grabbed a stray receipt on the floor before walking to Mr. Grant's office on his right. Grant sat at his desk, counting cash. "May I have a word, sir?"

"Of course." He pulled out a chair and gestured toward it. "Please come in."

Grant seemed open and unafraid, not like someone who had something to hide. Yet every scuffle at the bank involved him. Peter made eye contact, and Grant didn't avoid his gaze. "Where were you last night?"

Grant pursed his lips. "Last night? I had dinner with my mother and sister. Afterward I played chess with my sister and retired about ten. Why do you ask?"

"I'm sure you've heard about Colonel Bennet's murder." Peter wanted to be able to see Grant's face when he told him what he'd heard. "I understand the grocer is accusing you of murdering him."

Grant looked down, his lips closed and tight. "Yes. The sheriff talked to me, and I spoke my mind."

Peter remembered the time he confronted Colonel Bennet after he threatened Mary Beth. Anyone could say he was guilty too, and the sheriff might if he investigated. Grant did not act guilty. Mary Beth, however, had suggested Grant might have changed since he began courting Peter's mother.

Maybe he was a rival and planned to gain control of the bank by shifting suspicion for the murder to Mary Beth.

If only bank personnel weren't involved in all this.

THE NEXT MORNING

Mary Beth closed her eyes and tried to pretend the breakfast before her consisted of eggs and bacon, but the lack of fragrance wouldn't allow her imagination to enjoy the vision for long. Dry toast didn't appear as appealing. At least the doctor allowed her in the dining room. She could enjoy the vase of flowers Ruth brought from the back yard and the yellow tablecloth her late mother crocheted. Peter entered the room with his briefcase and pulled out his chair. "Sorry to keep you."

Mary Beth offered her best smile. Tardy or not, his presence excited her more than the meal in front of her. "I'm so thankful for the change of scenery."

Peter kissed her hand and offered grace.

Banging in the hallway stopped Mary Beth from her first bite. "What …"

Sheriff Campbell marched into the room followed by Sergeant Stanford who appeared dwarfed by the sheriff's size. Campbell's enormous frown rivaled the largest cannon the North owned. Stanford smirked. "There you are. I must talk to you both. Now."

Peter stood and placed himself between the sheriff and Mary Beth. "I'm appalled at the way you stomped—"

"Quiet." Campbell's bushy eyebrows lowered. "Police business takes priority. I want to know about the night you visited Bennet at the barracks beside the hospital. Witnesses say they heard angry voices."

Mary Beth dropped her head in her hands. What had Peter done?

"I thought you weren't sheriff anymore." Peter crossed his arms.

"That's not an answer," Campbell huffed.

"Bennet threatened my wife." Peter advanced closer, as if protecting Mary Beth. "I made sure he understood to stay away from her."

"Ah! I thought so." Stanford pushed his way past Peter and came toward Mary Beth. "Bennet must have given a reason."

"At the time, I was caring for Union soldiers at Mrs. McCallie's home, although I've not been there since my illness. Given the bank policy on loans and fake legal tender, he accused me of spying."

"Well, well. That sounds serious." Campbell's dark eyes bored into hers. "Stanford says you've been tormenting my daughter."

Mary Beth gasped. "What? I risked my health to help your daughter when she found the colonel's body."

"According to her husband, you've been interfering in their affairs, and I must insist you stop."

"Preposterous!" Peter said. "She's been sick. The first time she met him was at the wedding."

"Where were you all day yesterday and the day prior?" The sheriff continued to glare at her.

"At home in bed. Jane has been here caring for me, and Ruth has been helping. John came yesterday and helped Cook with dinner."

"I'll speak to them." Campbell turned to Peter. "And I need to know your whereabouts, Mr. Chandler."

"Me? Why?"

"You have a motive also." Campbell raised a bushy eyebrow. "Protecting your wife."

Peter sighed and rubbed the back of his neck. "I worked

in the office all day for the past two days. Afterward, I came here."

"Very well. I plan to make arrests tomorrow prior to leaving town." Campbell headed toward the door.

Peter met Mary Beth's gaze, "Who are you arresting? Who will serve as sheriff when you leave?"

"You'll have to ask the mayor. Good day." Campbell walked out.

Mary Beth did not like being a suspect in a murder case. She shoved aside the food and stood, but the room whirled about her. Peter grabbed her before she fell.

"Rest." He held her close and caressed her face.

"Nonsense." She pulled away as heat seared through her body. "We've got to untangle this mess, or Campbell will stick our heads in a noose."

Chapter Twelve

AUGUST 3

Mary Beth brushed her hair as she gazed in the mirror of her dressing table. She had lost weight, which would be hard to gain back. However, she felt much better after several days in bed. Using her mind would be the perfect cure. No more resting. Today she'd investigate.

Ruth knocked at the door and hurried inside. "Mary Beth, would you like me to start chopping dried herbs for cooking?"

"No." Mary Beth stood to look out her bedroom window. "The day is clear and sunny. Let's get fresh air. I'd like to visit Bennet's house after dropping by the bank."

"Yes! I'm weary of inactivity." Ruth clapped her hands.

Mary Beth gathered her parasol, flowery hat, and fan before meeting Ruth downstairs. "While I'm at the colonel's house, I'll gather information about his death."

"Why can't the sheriff make an arrest soon?" Ruth asked.

Mary Beth chuckled. "He decided to move rather than finish his job."

Mary Beth, Ruth, and John strolled through town. Mary Beth waved at Fannie's mother and Mrs. Haskell. Even the dirt drifting about from those passing didn't annoy Mary Beth. She enjoyed the fresh air and freedom. Once they reached the bank, Ruth and John stepped across the street to the café and climbed into a chair shaded by the building.

Humming a tune, Mary Beth opened the bank door— the tinkling of the bell sounded like music. Mrs. Phipps sat at her desk working,, and her perfectly-coiffured hair pleased Mary Beth. Being well enough to come back to the bank made her so lighthearted, she could float. Even the engraved wood around the teller windows brought a smile, although it needed some furniture polish. A customer came in behind her setting the bell ringing again, and Mary Beth turned. Since no one stood at the teller window, she extended her hand. "Good morning, Mrs. Jackson. How may I assist you today?"

Mrs. Jackson's lips bunched up. "I want to close my account right away."

Mary Beth swallowed hard, but she kept a smile on her face as she hurried behind the counter. "Just give me a moment to look up your account."

A quick nod was the response.

Mary Beth had to search a few minutes longer than she expected, which didn't appear efficient. Mrs. Jackson's gaze seemed to bore into her skin. When she found the Jackson ledger, Mary Beth's chest grew heavy. The total was quite a sum. "May I ask why you're moving your money?"

"Your reputation has suffered this summer, and I want to place my money in a safer bank." Mrs. Jackson's nose wrinkled as if she'd eaten lemons.

"I'll have to go to the vault." Mary Beth left to get the key, dreading the chore. How many more times would she have to do this? Her nightmare was coming true.

⚬⚬⚬

Ignoring her taut muscles, Mary Beth filled her lungs with hot, humid air as she, John, and Ruth strode to Colonel Bennet's house. Untangling the gloom over the bank would ease tensions and give her something tangible to do. She petitioned the Lord for divine guidance while she waved and greeted clients and friends. "We turn here at Poplar Street."

"I didn't realize the Campbell's lived so close."

"Yes. They also owned a farm in the countryside. I do not think they sold that." They turned a corner. "Here we are."

Mary Beth pointed to a two-story frame house with green shutters and a huge front porch. The windows shone in the sunshine. "That's the house. It's so pretty I can hardly imagine the tragedy occurring here."

"Oh, what's on that tree?" Ruth ran to the huge hickory beside the house.

John skipped to the tree and touched a dent in the bark.

"Uhm." Mary Beth hesitated to answer because she did not want to upset Ruth and John. "I'm not sure, but I'll take a look."

"May I go inside?" Ruth asked.

"Sure." Mary Beth wanted her out of the way, so she could examine the area, which she couldn't do the day Ida found the body.

As Ruth and John stepped on the front porch, Ida came out of the basement. "Hello, Mary Beth. Did you come to visit?"

Mary Beth's face warmed. Since the Sergeant had threatened her, she hadn't planned to drop in even though Ida was one of her closest friends. "I came to scrutinize the scene."

"What was it about the tree that Ruth was interested in?" Ida asked.

"She saw the dark spots." Mary Beth pointed. "Here and here. I think it's blood."

Ida blanched. "You mean from Colonel Bennet?"

"Yes." Mary Beth nodded and indicated the earth beneath their feet. "See the dark stains on the grass. The splattering blood made an outline of the upper part of the colonel's body."

"I don't recall any of that." Ida peered down. "How tragic."

"I wonder …" Mary Beth examined the bloody marks. "He was facing that way, toward the back of the property when the shot hit him. So, he wasn't going in the front door."

"Maybe he was hoping to talk to us," Ida said. "You'd have to face that direction to go to our little apartment."

Did the colonel know Ida's husband? Maybe they were working together to hurt the bank. Or maybe Ida murdered the soldier herself. Perhaps he knew something bad about her husband that she didn't want known. The thought made Mary Beth's stomach queasy, but she pushed it aside. "Interesting."

"That look on your face bothers me." Ida stepped closer. "What are you thinking?"

Mary Beth turned her attention to the tree. She wasn't quite ready to tell her friend she suspected her of murder. Besides, what motive could she have? "Something is wedged into the wood of the tree, and I wouldn't have seen that unless Ruth had noticed."

Ida came to her side. "Where?"

Mary Beth put her finger in the spot. "Here. See? That metal object split the wood."

"What do you think it is?"

"The bullet." Mary Beth pulled her drawstring purse off her arm and dug around in the bottom to see if she had anything hard she could use to pry the bullet out. A sound behind her startled her, and she turned around. Ida's husband approached scowling at her.

"There you are again, woman." He slapped Ida so hard she almost fell. "Tell her to leave you alone, Ida. You are my wife now."

Mary Beth had to hold back the contents of her stomach. "I'll leave the moment I get Ruth and John out of the house."

Surely the man wouldn't hurt the children. Did he play a part in the colonel's murder?

THURSDAY, AUGUST 6
NOON

Anna adjusted her hat at just the right angle and gritted her teeth as she gazed at the huge warehouse military officials had named Newsome Hospital. Soldiers of every size and rank scurried about the grounds of Cameron Hill overlooking the Tennessee River. She'd choose a suitable man and work her magic. Nothing would keep her from protecting her son and his business. If those soldiers in the barracks by the hospital had any clues about Bennet's death, she'd pry it from them with her fingernails.

A young soldier with a musket approached her. "May I see your pass, Ma'am?"

This boy might have a gun, but he was younger than Peter. Approaching him as a mother would work best. She donned a pleading look and moved closer. "Pass? Son, I live here, and I don't need a piece of paper to walk about the city."

His chin dropped, and his shoulders slumped. "You aren't one of the new nurses?"

"Oh, no." She patted him on the shoulder like his mother might do. "But I need ... information. Can you help me?"

"My provost marshal will be the one." He raised a finger with a twinkle in his eye. "I shall return."

Anna grinned as he scurried away. These young men carrying arms had less power than she possessed as a child. Moments later the boy hurried back with an older soldier, probably forty. He had a full, but well-trimmed beard of dark-brown and his gray uniform had several stripes.

He extended his hand. "I'm Lieutenant Cagle, ma'am, the provost marshal here. I understand you need information."

"Indeed." Dr. Smith had once commented a certain herb could make a man talk. She had purchased some in case her feminine charm did not work. Thinking of the herbal preparation in her purse, she offered him her hand, palm down for him to kiss, which he did. "I hate to take your time, sir, but it's noon. If I could, I'd prefer dining with you at the City Café across from C&R Bank. That way I can treat you to a sumptuous meal in exchange for what I can learn."

"Excuse me, ma'am?" He stiffened and stepped back. "You want me to have lunch with you?"

"I do." She raised her chin and managed to look down on him even though he was taller.

He pulled out a pocket watch. "I shall join you in a few moments."

"Very good."

An hour later, Anna Chandler sat with the lieutenant at the café. Her appetite succumbed to her anxiety about the bank, and she hardly ate a thing. However, she watched

Lieutenant Cagle devour mashed potatoes, fried okra, and fried chicken. Plying a man with food often produced whatever one wanted, especially if you added a certain preparation to his coffee. Leaning close, she fluttered her lashes. "What can you tell me about Colonel Bennet?"

The lieutenant stuffed a spoonful of potato in his mouth frowning. He narrowed his eyes and chewed for a moment. "I understand he graduated from military school with honors. His wife lived in Alabama, and he spoke of her often saying he'd like her to come here. He always managed to get what he wanted in the barracks, he mentioned he always succeeded on the battlefield or off."

Bennet wasn't here just to shoot Northerners. How interesting. She offered her most appealing smile. "What was his assignment?"

Cagle loaded his fork with potato. "Espionage I think, but …"

The café door opened, and Matthew Grant entered with Peter. Grant met her gaze, and his face flushed.

Peter ran toward her with a scowl. "Mama? We couldn't find you, and we worried."

Now the information would dry up.

Peter grabbed his mother's arm. He'd come in to get some lunch with Mr. Grant, only to find his mother with another man. How embarrassing to have her flirting with every man in the city. "Who is this man?"

Anna pulled her arm from Peter's grasp. "I am meeting with Lieutenant Cagle and chatting very quietly about his memories. However, you've brought on a severe headache. I think I shall retire to my bedroom at home."

He wanted to elaborate on what appeared to be foolish, but his tongue wouldn't move.

The door slammed behind his mother, and Peter turned back. Everyone in the entire café appeared to be looking at him. His cheeks warmed.

Mr. Grant touched Peter's shoulder. "My appetite is gone. I'll be in my office."

As Grant left the café, Peter closed his eyes and wished he could disappear.

"Sir, would you like to be seated now?"

Peter opened his eyes to gaze at the waiter before him. "Yes. But I won't require a menu. I want tea and pie. A large piece."

The waiter smiled as he motioned to an empty table. "What kind of pie?"

"A large piece. Any kind." Sugar was a great solution to his embarrassment.

"Yes, sir." He disappeared into the kitchen.

Peter dropped his head into his hands. He represented the bank, and he'd just allowed a family quarrel play out in public. What a disgrace. Maybe he should leave the city before he lost his reputation.

Chapter Thirteen

Mary Beth entered the simple room Dr. Smith's assistant directed her to. She sat down in the straight chair beside the open window. The examining table sat to her right, and across the room, a cabinet held bottles of various medications. A shelf underneath had disturbing instruments Mary Beth hoped he never used on her. She took a deep breath, imagined the doctor's face, and rehearsed another version of her speech. Today she hoped to learn a few facts about Bennet's death if the doctor would cooperate.

Dr. Smith entered. His thin face had the look of one who'd drained his inner resources. He ran his hand along his beard. "Mrs. Chandler, you look much better than the day I met you in the sheriff's yard."

She nodded ignoring the sweat beading up around her neck. "Ida came to me for help. I had no idea her husband was so volatile, or I would have taken precautions."

"I'm concerned about Ida." He nodded, raising one eyebrow. "If you see her again, tell her she can call on me anytime. I've dealt with family situations before."

She cleared her throat and swallowed several times to rally her courage. "I'm here to ask about Colonel Bennet.

Since there's so much talk about who caused his demise, I'd like to see all the bank employees cleared."

"My dear girl, what makes you think you can unravel that mess?" He recoiled.

"It's all so personal for us, doctor." She filled her lungs and noted the familiar smell of medication. "When I took food to the hospital recently, Bennet met me there and practically accused me of spying. Of course, I told Peter. He was so angry he proceeded to visit the man and scold him that same day. So, you see, we both look like culprits."

"This is a job best left to the authorities. It was murder." Smith wagged a finger in her face. "You should be attending to your duties at the bank and mixing medications."

"I thought the sheriff was leaving." She shrugged. "Who else will do it?"

Smith crossed his arms. "The city council will handle the problem with my guidance as mayor and town physician."

"At least tell me what time he died and the cause of death."

"I suspect you know both." He shook his head. "I saw you on the scene and you spoke about how he'd been dead several hours. Your nursing gave you wonderful observation skills."

"Yet you don't want me nursing again?"

"You'll have plenty of that once the children come." He moved toward the door. "Until then, stay away from murder scenes."

"He died of a gunshot wound to the back. Right?"

"And he died before he hit the ground." The doctor looked over his glasses. "I want you to behave, girl. I watched you grow up, and I don't want anything to happen to you."

Mary Beth wondered if the doctor had any reason to keep her from discovering the killer.

A FEW MOMENTS LATER

Mary Beth kept running her gaze back and forth along the dirt road that led to Bennet's home. She felt nauseated. If she took deep breaths, she could ignore the discomfort. She passed one frame house to her left where a lady sat on the porch. Two children on the lawn tossed a ball around while laughing. She waved at the boys and passed by several more homes with empty porches. The Bennet house would be on her right, but she slowed down, and examined each yard nearby. Ida's husband mustn't see her.

Several huge bushes bordered the lawn, and she hid behind them while she peered around to her left and right. When she was sure she was unobserved, she ran to the tree, digging in her purse for the pocketknife, hoping she could complete the job without hurting herself or being seen.

The blade was bigger and tighter than she expected, making it hard to open. When it finally popped out, she barely missed cutting herself. She reminded herself which side was sharp while she inserted the tip in the bark and pried at one side of the brown metal. The bullet didn't budge. When her hand cramped, she stopped and massaged the muscles. Using her left hand, she pried the other side, and the knife slid from her grasp. She groaned and searched several moments for the knife.

The bushes rustled and John peeked out.

"I am trying to pry metal from that tree, and I lost my knife."

John came out of the bushes and grabbed her knife from the grass.

He must have seen it fall.

"Thanks."

His gaze was serious as he hurried to the tree and pried. In a second, the bullet came loose. He handed her the bullet, closed the knife, and gave it to her.

"Amazing. Thank you."

"Friend." He kept his eyes on the ground.

"Yes, you are my friend." She touched his shoulder.

She jumped at a loud bang. A door slamming? Mary Beth rushed behind the bush with John. Her heart banging her chest, and her breath coming in gasps.

Ida's husband came around the corner. "When I come home, I expect my supper, woman. You'd best fix it quick."

Mary Beth vowed to stay away from the Bennet house from then on.

THE NEXT MORNING
C&R BANK

Anna turned away from the teller window and pushed aside the cash drawer and sack of money to look at Matthew Grant. "I can set up for the day without you hovering. My husband and I ran the bank together for years alone. Is something bothering you?"

"I need to know what you were doing yesterday at the café." Grant crossed his arms.

"I thought I explained that." She turned back to the drawer. "I rise to action whenever my son needs me. You shouldn't need more than that."

His eyes widened, and he stepped backward. "Unbelievable! You and I are courting, and I found you sitting in City Café with another man. That's unacceptable."

"If I need to accomplish something, I know how to flirt. I want to keep you and Peter away from the hangman."

Anna's pulse sped up as she rushed away from the teller window. "Why am I doing your job? You are the bank manager."

Matthew might be accused of murder, but not Peter. She'd see to that.

LATER THAT DAY
C&R BANK

Peter peered at the blob of metal in his wife's hand and tried to pay attention. The fine blush on her complexion reminded him of all the reasons he married her. "Let me see if I have the facts. You found that in the grass—"

"No." She grinned, and her eyes sparkled. "I believe that's the bullet that pierced Bennet's heart. I used your knife to dig it out of the tree trunk."

"You have my knife?" He patted his pocket and pursed his lips. "Yeah, I don't have it."

"Here." She pulled a wad of cloth from her bag. "Actually, John did the work, and he closed it for me. I wrapped it in a handkerchief."

Peter accepted the cloth and unwound it. "How did you do this? The tip is slightly bent from your efforts. I shall have to fix that."

She blotted perspiration from her face. "I barely missed Ida's husband. He staggered about like he was drunk and yelled at his wife about dinner."

"I don't like this." Peter placed the opened knife in the bottom drawer of his desk. He would fix the blade and hide it from his wife. "Stop trying to act like a sheriff or we'll be burying you."

"But the bullet, Peter. Can you tell what kind of gun was used by looking at this?"

Peter picked up the hunk of metal again and rolled it around in his hand. "It's so distorted. I'm not sure we can."

"Could we try? Especially since I risked my life."

"You what?" Peter's jaw dropped.

"I was teasing."

Peter wondered if she told the truth by accident. Knowing her, his protests wouldn't matter. "You'd best take care."

Mr. Riddle, Peter's secretary knocked and entered. "We have a lady downstairs who says she is Mrs. Bennet. She'd like to speak to you."

Peter's heart grew heavy, and he eased into his chair. "Please, send her in."

Mary Beth wrestled with a chair. Peter took it from her hands, positioning it to the left of his desk chair. "I don't look forward to this."

He extended her hand and pulled her close. How he loved her, and he was so thankful she stood by him.

Riddle knocked. "Mrs. Bennet is here."

The slender lady who entered had light brown hair swept up into a bun. Her complexion was fair, but her eyes reddened.

Peter rushed for a chair. "Ma'am, please sit down. We'd like to offer our sympathy."

"Here." Mary Beth stepped up. "A pillow for your back."

Mrs. Bennet sniffled and pulled out a handkerchief. "Thank you."

Peter sat on the edge of the desk and motioned for his wife to come closer. He was thankful she was with him right now. "How can we assist you, Mrs. Bennet?"

She covered her mouth, bent over, and sobbed.

Mary Beth moved close and put a hand on Mrs. Bennet's shoulder. "If we can do anything to help you, we'd be delighted."

Peter found himself tensing up in sympathy.

"Tell us about him," Mary Beth said.

Mrs. Bennet's tears dwindled, and she blotted her face. "He loved his job, and he wanted to stay in Chattanooga after the war. He thought the railroad could make the city into a transportation hub."

"What was his assignment here?"

"He didn't give me details, but he mentioned a collaborator. I'm not sure what he meant."

"What do you need from us?" Mary Beth asked.

"I wonder if it would be possible to cancel the purchase of the house here in town. Now that my husband is dead, I plan to stay in Alabama near my family."

"Your husband named you as his agent after his death?" Peter asked.

"He did." She reached into her bag and retrieved folded papers. "I believe that is what you need."

Peter gazed over the material she handed him. "This appears to be in order. I shall have my secretary prepare the papers. Once signed, I can reimburse the amount your husband had in his account."

"I'm taking my husband's body back with me, and I wish to leave tomorrow. Is that enough time?"

"We can prepare them in about an hour," Peter said. "Would you like to return?"

"I would." She stood. "Thanks."

As she left, Mary Beth turned to Peter. "But your mother insists we sell the mortgage. If we cancel it, we can't do as she asked."

"No. We own the house now, but we can rent. The income would replace some of the gold we gave Campbell.

"That means we'll have to convince Sergeant Stanford to give us money." She brushed the hair off her face. "I don't relish that."

Peter would ask Grant to handle that transaction. Since Stanford was aggressive, he'd tell Grant to be armed.

AUGUST 12
LATE AFTERNOON

Anna Chandler walked across Weston's sumptuous sitting room and sat in the Queen Anne chair by the window. From this position, she could see the sun setting on the river. If only her investigation produced more information. The dearest people in the world worked at the bank. She had to undo the bank's problems. Helping Matthew would please her too, since she assumed they'd marry. Weston would know what to do.

She heard a rustling sound and then a door shut. She rose. Weston must be home. His footsteps came toward her, she stepped into the hall. "Horace? I'm in the sitting room."

He came through the doorway dressed as usual in his dark suit, and he looked down into her face. "What a pleasure, Anna. What brings you here?"

"I have money for you to invest, and I need you to advise Peter." She plopped back into the chair overlooking the city. "He's made an unwise decision."

"You have money for me?" Weston lifted an eyebrow. "I'm accustomed to you asking for your allowance."

Knowing Weston, her actions would appear out of character, but he had no children. "I took some of my money from C&R Bank."

Weston puffed out his cheeks. "Why?"

"I'd like you to find an investment opportunity that will double it. Is that possible?"

He shrugged. "I can, but investments that pay the most are risky."

"I trust you because my husband did."

"What is this about Peter?"

"I worry about his handling of the bank." She paced across the room. Her stomach hurt, but her appetite had lagged for several days. "He's caught in a dilemma surrounding war politics. I don't want Mary Beth or Grant arrested for murder."

"Murder?" He rubbed his temple. "Do you want me to talk to the officials? I might be able to see how far the investigation is going. Or would you rather I offer my expertise to Peter?"

"Drop in on Peter and see if he'll open up. He could use advice."

"I can do that." He smiled. "I rather like your son."

"Thank you." She released a breath, and her leg muscles became wobbly. "Oh, and what do you know about Colonel Bennet?"

"Not much." He chuckled. "I've never seen you this tense, Anna. You don't usually ask for things, and now you've made several requests."

"I'd like to know more about him. If you run across something, will you tell me?"

"Yes."

She hoped she found the right information soon.

Chapter Fourteen

AUGUST 13
MORNING

The sun was coming up, and the air was cool as Mary Beth stepped onto the McCallie's porch and knocked on the door. Peter left early for the bank, and she had put together a basket of medication and a jar of soup for the soldiers. She hoped for a chance to talk with Ellen McCallie.

Ellen, dressed in a simple blue dress and white apron, opened the door. "Mary Beth. I have been concerned for you. Dr. Smith said you have been ill. I have just prepared tea and prayed for you. Please come in."

Mary Beth's heart was light enough to float away at the sight of her friend. "I bring supplies for your patients, but I would love some advice."

"I would enjoy a chat as well." Ellen stepped aside so she could enter. She led the way to the kitchen where biscuits cooled on the stove. "Working all the time wears you down, so we all need time to rest. Sit down and I will get biscuits and tea."

"Have I interrupted breakfast?"

"No. I'm using my good dishes for you and me. Grace is asleep." Ellen poured hot tea into pretty china cups. "Tom went to the hospital this morning. One of the soldiers asked for him, and he never refuses."

"As you heard, I have been sick." She shared the bank's situation and her problems having a baby.

Ellen patted her hand. "I am sorry about the bank problems. This house keeps me so busy I do not spend time with friends. Now I know how to pray for you. Please sit with me in church. I always feel alone with Tom preaching."

"Really? You feel alone?" What a perspective. She must not think of herself as the only one with challenges.

"I am set apart as a pastor's wife." Ellen laughed. "I know it all, or at least people think I do. And I must be perfect, and I am not. I get lonely. Often I want a friend to chat with."

All of this caught Mary Beth by surprise. She thought of Ellen as perfect, without problems. "Then talking to you about these things does not add to your burden?"

"No. I have prayed so hard for you to get well, and now I will take Peter and the bank to the throne of grace. You want a baby, which is a good thing. Sometimes that can be elusive, and oh, that is so hard. I ache for you."

Mary Beth explained about Dr. Smith and stress. "Is it possible to have less anxiety?"

Ellen took a huge gulp of tea. "It is easy to talk about feeling less anxiety, but I find it's much harder to do. We are living through war, and what woman likes that? My heart truly hurts for those soldiers I care for. War means pain and death."

"I know." Mary Beth thought back to her father's death, which almost brought tears.

"If I meditate on God's word, I find myself much more peaceful, but that takes focus and discipline. But I'm sure you've learned that."

Mary Beth nodded as she turned that thought in her head. "Your husband advised me to reflect God's love. I think of it as reflecting gold."

Ellen nodded. "That sounds like him. He always advises me to live as if I believe even during a tough time. As for not having a child, I have not suffered in that way. I cannot imagine the pain. I'm so sorry."

Again, Mary Beth blinked back tears.

"The Bible tells about several women who longed for a child and could not conceive. I honestly believe the Lord can make the barren have children. I will join you in prayer. We'll both believe God uses this situation for good. That's his promise."

"I could pray more, but I am a lady of action," Mary Beth pushed aside her tea. "Prayer seems like doing nothing."

"I understand that. We ladies make the family run, which means we must act, or nothing happens." Ellen smiled and pinched off a bit of biscuit. "Believe prayer is doing more."

"Prayer is doing more." Mary Beth inhaled as she pondered that thought. Talking to your creator had to be vital. She must consider how she might pray more consistently. "I needed to hear this."

"My husband often says the exact thing God wants me to hear. As his wife, sometimes I resent hearing it from him." She laughed.

How refreshing to hear the pastor's wife fought battles too. "Has the war impacted you?"

"Yes." Ellen nodded. "We have had the military complain about us caring for Union soldiers, but we tell them they are men who need Christ. Being in ministry means you care about others all the time."

"Banking means protecting our client's money. We only accept bills if we can exchange it for gold. We don't want broken bank notes, which are worthless."

"I know you will do your best." Ellen held up a finger. "Just be aware, you do not know God's plan. Wait for him."

What a big assignment.

About the Same Time
C&R Bank

Peter stopped beside the heavy metal door of the vault. He reached into his pocket for the key but hesitated at the sound of footsteps behind him. "Good morning, Grant. Do you need something?"

"I have a message." Grant came to the bottom of the stairs. "Yesterday a man who called himself Mr. Shaw stopped by. He commented that he knew you, and I asked if he wanted to meet with you. He said he wanted me to give you some information about a warehouse for storage."

Peter wasn't anxious to see Mr. Shaw, if he was the one Confederate official who tormented him last year. "Was he a large man with dark hair and heavy brows?"

"Yes." Grant nodded. "That describes him. I've been hoping to find a cheaper warehouse to store grain and cotton. Of course, it's best to sell it quickly in exchange for gold, but that is getting harder. Anyway, this warehouse offers much better prices, but I thought I would clear it with you first."

That didn't sound like the Mr. Shaw Peter knew, but he would need more facts first. After all, Shaw wanted to arrest him last year when he didn't agree to support the Confederacy. "Get the contract. We'll have to read it carefully and compare it to our present situation."

"I did, and Mr. Riddle has the contract for you to read." Mr. Grant turned and ascended the stairs again.

Peter had always considered Mr. Shaw a dangerous man. However, offering a warehouse space seemed an odd way to entangle the bank. They already had a warehouse where they stored corn and cotton that farmers used for payment. Mr. Grant kept track of those assets until they found a buyer. Perhaps he was involved too.

Noon
City Café

With Ruth beside her, Anna Chandler sailed into the café across from the bank wearing her latest creation, a light-blue, tiered dress with beige trim. Her hat sported a cluster of matching flowers, a gift from Weston. What a delight to show them off. Plus, she was elated her daughter wanted to have lunch with her. If only she would come home and wait a few more years before growing up, Anna would be thrilled.

As the waiter led them to a table, Anna gave Ruth's chin a gentle touch, a cue to watch her posture. She'd asked to be seated in the back since soldiers occupied the front, and their chatter filled the restaurant. As they passed men dressed in gray uniforms, she chose to ignore those who hunched over their meal as if they'd never eat again. Military service could bring out the worst in a man, and she thanked God the city council exempted her son from service.

Anna waited for the server to pull out her chair, but Ruth plopped down opposite her, seemingly forgetting all her instruction on posture and poise. That would be a lesson for later. "Ruthie, dear, I've hardly seen you since you left for Peter's house. I miss you terribly."

"Mary Beth is teaching me how to prepare herbal medicines, Mama." Her green eyes glowed. "Dr. Smith taught her during her father's illness. Now he allows her to do most of the medicines he uses. Isn't that wonderful?"

Anna restrained a sigh. She hadn't seen such energy from Ruth in a good while, but she intended to bring up education this morning. Her late husband provided money for schooling, and she wanted Ruth to take advantage of his preparation. "I'm glad you enjoy that my dear—"

"Not just enjoy, Mama. I adore doing it." She almost bounced in her chair. "Plus, I love Mary Beth. I helped about the house when she was ill, you know. I might even have the ability to nurse like she does."

That wasn't the news Anna wanted to hear. Nurses didn't enjoy the best reputations, unless they confined their efforts to family members. This new trend to train women and send them off to another city made her uneasy. "I'm quite fond of Mary Beth."

"But that's not all." Ruth flung her long hair over her shoulder. "John loves to watch Mary Beth's cook. He stayed around so much that Cook offered to teach him. Last night, he cooked fried okra that was very tasty."

"I'm proud of the way you've helped him, dear. His life will be much better because of your kindness."

"Well? Aren't you going to say 'but.'" Ruth narrowed her eyes.

"No. No. Not at all." She patted Ruth's hand, hoping to avoid an angry tirade. After Andrew's death, she hadn't dealt with her own grief well, much less her children's. Being a widow was most unpleasant. "I fear I wouldn't have reached out to him at all. I've focused on my sewing instead of youth. I do like making clothing for the needy."

Ruth rolled her eyes. "If I'd continued sewing, I'd probably have stabbed myself in the eye. I'm just too clumsy."

"Nonsense." Ruth appeared to avoid everything Anna enjoyed. She'd harbored the desire to have a close, almost sisterly relationship when her daughter grew up. However, the older Ruth got, the less likely that appeared. "You showed great progress."

Ruth snorted. "Are you speaking about the last blouse I made? I tangled the cuff into the shoulder seam."

The waiter came alongside Anna with menus. "There's a man at the door asking for you."

"Oh." She stood and looked toward the door. "That's Matthew Grant. How delightful."

"What?" Ruth shoved back her chair. "I'm not staying if he's going to sit down."

"No." Anna dreaded what Ruth might think or do. "He probably just saw me and wanted to say hello."

"Hello?" Ruth's cheeks turned pink. "Hello, I'm going to be your new stepfather. No thanks."

"You misunderstand." Anna reached for her hand. "I didn't tell him I'd be here."

"Well, now he's here, and I'm not." She scurried away without looking back, while throwing her hair over her shoulders.

Grant ambled up to the empty chair, scratching the back of his head. "Is Ruth coming back?"

If only Ruth would return.

Later that afternoon
Matthew Grant's home

Mary Beth took a sip of Mrs. Grant's coffee substitute and had to restrain a grimace. If only she could rush outside and spit out the infusion rather than swallowing. She sat, however, on a lovely sofa with green silk cushions. Matthew Grant's mother and sister, Mathilda, occupied chairs with green and yellow pillows. Mary Beth hoped to learn where Grant was the night of the murder, and his mother roped her into tasting her latest concoction.

A hopeful smile crossed the elderly lady's face. "What do you think?"

Mathilda wore a blissful smile as if she were drinking the finest coffee ever grown.

"Quite …" Mary Beth scrambled for a word that didn't sound derogatory. Poisonous sumac kept popping into her thoughts. Was this an opportunity to reflect God's love? She could care for these ladies even if she despised their recipe. "I can't seem to describe my thoughts. The flavor is so unique."

"Yes. I find it has a calming effect, especially if I drink more than one cup," Mrs. Grant said. She took a large gulp, seemingly proving her statement true.

"We've spent many hours perfecting the mixture." Mathilda grinned as she held her cup up. "You'll find the more you drink it, the more you like it."

Maybe Mrs. Grant and Mathilda had seared their taste buds. Poor dears. At least they were creative. "Really? I prefer tea. Since you're both so fond of this concoction, I'll leave you to drink the rest."

"You said you had something to ask when you arrived," Mrs. Grant said.

Mary Beth put down her cup, eager to change the topic. "I'm trying to clear up this dilemma surrounding Colonel Bennet's death. For the bank, you know. We want our reputations to remain excellent."

"Yes?" Mrs. Grant raised both eyebrows. "Is it really hurting business? I expected Chattanoogans to trust you more. You've lived here so long."

That made sense, but a few citizens in town kept spreading rumors. "I'd like to know where your son was the night Colonel Bennet was murdered."

Mrs. Grant stiffened. "Surely you don't suspect him."

"Not at all." Mary Beth made eye contact and smiled.

These ladies were sweet. "But I do have to convince the authorities. An alibi would do that."

Mrs. Grant's face brightened. "Oh. I see. All three of us were here. We had dinner and read poetry before going to bed."

"You are sure no one left?" Mary Beth had to make sure.

"I have no idea what happened after I went to sleep." Mrs. Grant chuckled.

Mary Beth turned to Grant's sister. "Mathilda?"

"I usually hear everything," Mathilda said, "But he could have left after I went to sleep. His bedroom is at the other end of the hall. I wouldn't hear him leave."

That tiny measure of uncertainty made Mary Beth worry.

C&R Bank
Peter's office

Peter hovered over a page of figures, adding and rechecking his numbers. He had a prospective client coming in ten minutes, and he wanted to complete his calculations so he could decide about giving the man a loan.

"Sir!" Mr. Riddle burst in with widened eyes and flushed face. "We need you downstairs. Now. They've come for Mr. Grant."

Peter's heart thumped in his throat. "What? Who?"

"The military. Grant's a suspect in the colonel's shooting." Riddle waved downstairs. "I thought you might be able to hold them off."

Muscles in his back and neck knotted as Peter headed toward the first floor at a trot. He should devise a convincing argument in Grant's favor, but he had no information to offer. Mary Beth promised to secure such facts today, but she hadn't come by with her findings.

The moment he stepped into the foyer, two armed men in gray escorted Grant from behind the counter. Several citizens huddled at the teller window, their faces frozen in fear. One lady held a hankie to her face, whimpering.

"Excuse me, sirs." Peter leapt off the stairs toward them. "If I may—"

"Don't interfere, sir." A third soldier at the door raised his rifle and came toward Peter. "We have orders to shoot if anyone resists."

Grant glanced back, his face devoid of color. A man on each side shoved Grant out the door as the third soldier approached Peter. "You'll have to take your complaints to the Provost Marshall."

"We are gathering evidence to prove his innocence," Peter protested.

"That's fine." The man lowered his rifle. "As I said, the Provost Marshall will handle the suspect from here."

Peter balled his hand into a fist. Whatever happened to innocent until proven guilty?

With Ruth beside her, Mary Beth hovered over a hot stove, stirring a new herbal preparation for Dr. Smith. Bessie had vacated the kitchen to shop in town, and Mary Beth had free access to the unused pots and pans hanging from the ceiling. Her mind turning over the facts. As the liquid became smoother, the information she had gathered failed to congeal the way she wished. It didn't make sense for Grant to shoot Bennet over bank policies even if his alibi was weak. The only weapon he owned was an ancient pistol, which was very inaccurate.

Ruth nudged her. "I have the jars ready. When will the mixture be ready to pour in?"

"Look." She pointed to the boiling liquid. "Do you see how smooth it appears? The grainy appearance is gone. We'll cook it until the liquid thickens. The mixture needs to cook longer and then cool."

A knock sounded on the front door, and Mary Beth missed Maud who usually answered. "I wonder who that could be?"

"If you want to get the door, I'll keep stirring." Ruth's eyes glittered. She appeared pleased to be left with such a vital project.

"Thanks." Mary Beth hurried to the door to find Mrs. Chandler there, wringing her hands. "Is something wrong?"

"Indeed." Mrs. Chandler brushed past her into the sitting room. "I don't know what to do."

Her stomach knotting up, Mary Beth edged onto a comfortable wing chair and waved her mother-in-law to the couch. "What happened?"

Anna Chandler sat and blotted her face with a linen handkerchief. "The provost marshal came by the bank and took Matthew Grant. I don't know when he'll return. I hate to think of them court marshalling him. Do civilians have rights when the military seizes them?"

Mary Beth groaned as she rubbed a hand over her face. The military might be harder to work with than the city council. Besides, she'd just decided she and Peter made better suspects. "I'm not sure the military has the right to arrest citizens." Mary Beth fingered her gold necklace. "We'd best contact Dr. Smith. He will know what to do."

"I know Matthew is innocent, but I worry we won't have a chance to prove that."

Ruth came in and closed the door behind her. "Of course, Matthew has no guilt. He just shows up whenever he's not wanted."

"Oh, dearie." Anna walked across the room and touched Ruth's face. "Don't be so cross, he's a nice man."

"Don't!" Ruth pulled away from Anna's touch. "How could you forget Papa?"

"I haven't forgotten." Anna moved closer to Ruth.

Mary Beth looked from one to the other and wondered what to do. All her life she had longed for her own mother, who died when she was a baby. Her heart told her she'd never harbor such anger at her mama under any circumstance, but Ruth saw Grant as replacing her father. And Mary Beth loved Ruth and Mrs. Chandler.

"Then what is all this fuss about Matthew Grant?" Ruth burst into tears. "I don't like him. He's too fat."

"He's a good man," Anna said.

"No!" Ruth ran from the room.

Chapter Fifteen

His limbs aching from being on his feet, Peter climbed the front steps to his house. Since he hadn't eaten lunch, his stomach also complained about his negligence, and he looked forward to the oblivion of sleep after dinner. Several clients had pulled out their funds to leave town after the military arrested Grant. Peter ended up working at a teller window most of the day as well as attending several meetings he couldn't cancel.

Mary Beth met him in the hallway. "Peter, you look so tired. Cook will have dinner ready soon."

He crumpled on the sitting room sofa and closed his eyes. "Indeed. We had one of the busiest days ever. I hope to stay awake long enough to eat."

"Mother came by and told us about Grant. She was quite upset about the military getting involved."

"Maybe they gathered facts we aren't aware of." Peter massaged his forehead. "You said he would protect the bank for my mother's sake. He may have an ulterior motive we don't know about."

"A lot depends on the gun that fired the bullet. Have you learned anything about the bullet I found?" Mary Beth lowered her voice.

"Why are you whispering?" Peter rubbed his eyes. "Are you worried Ruth might hear?"

"Yes." Mary Beth closed the sitting room door. "She lost her temper with your mother over Grant today. I think she's out back with John, but I'm being cautious."

"That reminds me. The bullet John pried out of that tree was a mini ball. The military now uses several rifles that shoot that ammunition. The aim is deadly because the rifle puts a spin on the bullet increasing its accuracy."

"That's good news." Mary Beth smiled and perched on the edge of the couch beside him. "That means someone in the military did the shooting, and they can stop searching amongst civilians."

Peter shook his head. "It's not that easy. An ordinary citizen couldn't obtain one, but all you'd have to do is go to a battlefield and lift one off a dying soldier. There are probably quite a few at Newsome Hospital."

"Grant's mother assured me the only weapon he has is a very ancient pistol that is difficult to shoot."

"What grown man is going to tell his mother about his guns?"

Mary Beth nodded. "I suppose you're right."

"Now that the military took over the investigation, I want you to leave it alone. It's risky getting in their way." He didn't think she'd listen, but he'd try to warn her anyhow.

"I'll be careful. I'm uncomfortable dealing with soldiers."

"Mary Beth, please stop. Now." She had no idea how unpleasant the military could be. He didn't want to see her in the brig.

"How's the bank? Are we still solvent?"

Peter sighed and sat up. "The stolen gold put us at risk, and a few customers have moved this week taking their funds. I fear we are close to the brink, which means we accept deposits only. However, we expect Mr. Field tomorrow."

"I assume he's bringing dividends?"

"Yes. I had to give Mrs. Bennet money today, but our investments have done well. We should be okay when Field brings gold."

They'd be safe if no one else pulled out their life savings.

AUGUST 14
MID-MORNING

Peter squinted in the bright sunshine as he left city hall with Mary Beth. The morning had grown even hotter since they began an unsuccessful search for Mr. Henderson, the city councilman, but Peter believed their search justified. So far, they'd been to Henderson's home, office, and now the city hall. Peter had visited several customers as they roamed down the city's wooden sidewalks, but he still wanted to appeal for Mr. Grant's freedom.

His wife grabbed her fan from her draw-string purse. "If we don't find him soon, we need to get some water. I'm exhausted by the humidity."

Peter glanced past her. On the curb across the street stood a lanky man in a dark suit. His face was turned away as he chatted with another couple. "Is that him?"

She inhaled sharply. "Yes. I believe so. Finally!"

"Come, let's catch him." He pulled Mary Beth across the dusty street as he hurried toward Henderson. However, the councilman moved in the opposite direction away from the couple he had spoken to. "Surely, we'll catch him. Mr. Henderson. Mr. Henderson!"

"Hello." Henderson turned and waved as a wide smile covered his face. "A pleasure, Mr. Chandler."

"We'd like to speak with you, sir." Peter let go of his wife's arm and broke into a trot following Henderson across an open lot next to the tailor's shop. The man had increased his speed, and Peter didn't want the councilman to get out of ear shot. "Mr. Henderson."

"Aye?" Henderson looked about, as if unsure where the sound came from.

Peter, out of breath, finally reached him and touched his arm. "I must consult with you, sir."

"Oh, oh, indeed." He chuckled and removed his hat, running his hand through his gray hair. "I supposed you were exhilarated because you saw me—a habit your offspring practice when very young. I'm sure you are aware. However, you possess none, so you might be unfamiliar with that behavior."

Peter's heart pounded like a racehorse. "Sir, I'm highly concerned. The military marched into the bank and carried off Mr. Grant yesterday. They wielded weapons and made threats as I tried to reason with them. I think he's a suspect in the death of Colonel Bennet, but they didn't make the charges clear."

Mr. Henderson's thin face shrank as he sucked in his cheeks. "How terribly foul. Totally unacceptable! Concern about ridiculous acts of force has been our greatest concern, that is, besides the ultimate safety of our citizenry."

Peter glanced behind him. His wife was catching up, breathing hard. She had the bulk of the facts to offer. "I tried to offer information, and one man aimed his rifle at me."

"No!" Henderson shook his head.

Mary Beth stepped up, huffing and puffing. "I actually saw the family yesterday."

"Indeed! What a travesty!" Henderson took a deep breath. "As my constituents, you may be assured I shall deal with this immediately and send you word. Such upstanding citizens should not be tormented like common criminals."

Peter's heart slowed a bit with the reassurance. He would also pray for the military to be reasonable. "If you need to reach me, I shall, of course, be working at the bank all day."

Henderson pulled out a pencil and a bit of paper. "Now, remind me of your name?"

CHATTANOOGA DEPOT
LATER THAT DAY

The train's horn bellowed as Peter pushed his way through the crowds on the platform through steam and smoke. The engine eased to a stop and people with trunks surged forward. A couple of porters ran alongside the train.

"Back up several steps so passengers can disembark," one porter yelled.

With a clang, the metal doors flew open, and passengers weighted down with luggage descended. At last, Mr. Field's round face and chubby figure appeared in the doorway. He toted two large brown trunks. Breathing hard, he placed one on the platform. A porter ran up to help him.

Peter waved. "Mr. Field. I'm here."

Field continued talking to the porter and didn't look his way.

Keeping his gaze focused on Mr. Field, Peter slithered through the crowd. Passengers getting off shoved him back and those getting on blocked his way. He looked over their heads, "Mr. Field!"

Two large men wearing black hats and long black coats elbowed their way to the place where Field stood. One knocked Field to the ground and ran off with his luggage. The other attacked the porter, he but failed to wrestle the trunk from him.

"Help! Thieves!" Mr. Field yelled.

"That's my friend!" How Peter wished for his rifle or even for the pistol his father stored in the bank office. "Let me through."

The throng parted enough for Peter to reach Field and the porter, who sat on the trunk panting.

A sharp whistle blew, and the second man melted into the crowd. The conductor ran up. "What happened?"

"My friend was attacked by two men in black." Peter was hot and angry. "They took one trunk and headed that way."

The Conductor blew his whistle again. "We'll get soldiers here to find them."

Peter wondered which piece of luggage held his gold, but he looked down at Field's limp body and shuddered. Field's life was more important than his dividend, even if the bank couldn't reopen tomorrow.

THIRTY MINUTES LATER
C&R BANK

Mary Beth's heart twisted as she gazed out the office window again. Peter was late. She gasped. Red-faced and limping, Mr. Field arrived at the bank with Peter following behind him. Two soldiers accompanied them carrying a trunk. What had gone wrong?

She flew down the bank stairs and threw open the front door. "Mr. Field, are you injured?"

"I've never in my life …" He panted.

"Come in and sit down. You can have Mrs. Phipps's chair, straight ahead. You need rest."

Peter directed the soldiers where to leave the trunk.

"Thank you." Field sighed and limped to the chair.

"Two men attacked Field after he got off the train." Peter's mouth and face were stiff. "I yelled for help, but it was hard to be heard over the crowd."

"Oh, no!" Mary Beth's heart pined for the lost income, but she recalled McCallie's words about reflecting God's love. Mr. Field had endured trauma, and he was more valuable than the gold their bank needed. "How terrible. I shall send for Dr. Smith."

"I'm terribly bruised, but I'm far more concerned about your interest payment." Field swiped his sweaty face with a chubby hand. "With all the military about, I had no fear of transporting that gold."

As he eased into the chair, she felt his pulse. She noticed he didn't refuse the doctor. She'd send for Dr. Smith after they'd settled in at home. "You'll be much more comfortable in our guest room. We'll take care of you. Would you like a damp cloth and some refreshment?"

Nelson's tummy bobbed with each breath. "Indeed, madam. You are an angel of mercy for a tormented soul."

"I'd best contact the sheriff, but then we haven't one anymore." Peter groaned and pounded his left hand with his fist.

"Perhaps Mr. Henderson?" Mary Beth said as she darted to the back room for water and a dampened rag.

As she reentered the room, Mr. Field had slumped over onto Mrs. Phipps's desk with his head in his hands. Peter paced.

"Here you go." Mary Beth handed the cloth to Mr. Field.

"Many thanks." Field buried his face in the dampness and then wiped his hands. "Wonderful. Just wonderful. At least I didn't put all the gold in one trunk. Perhaps the military will catch the man who took my other luggage."

Mary Beth whispered a prayer of thanksgiving for the gold they would receive. "I have water for you also, sir."

"I shall be fine for now, but your husband probably needs it." Field nodded toward Peter as he handed back the cloth to her. "Let's get your money in the safe. It's in the top of my luggage."

Mary Beth hoped they received enough gold to stay open.

Chapter Sixteen

FIRST PRESBYTERIAN CHURCH
WEDNESDAY MORNING

A desire for counsel and prayer brought Mary Beth to the church again in search of Reverend McCallie. When she entered the building, the smell of soap and furniture oil surrounded her, and pews in the sanctuary glowed with fresh wax. A boy in his early teens wielded a broom on the church floor, while an older girl dipped a mop in a large metal bucket and swabbed the platform.

The boy stopped sweeping. "May I help you, ma'am?"

Gazing into his face, Mary Beth realized he was only a year or so older than John. Doubtless he had a sad story, because her pastor had a way of seeking out needy people. "I hoped to see Reverend McCallie. Is he here?"

"He was called to see a soldier who is very ill, and he left in a hurry," the boy said.

"I see." Mary Beth longed for the comfort of hearing the pastor pray for the bank, however, she had petitioned God all day. "I don't recall seeing you at church before. What is your name?"

"I am George, and this is my sister, Sarah."

"Father was injured in the war and won't be able to fight again. But the pastor pays us to clean before the service so we can help Mama with bills," Sarah said.

"Good for you. We appreciate your hard work." Mary Beth wondered how she could show God's love to these two, but she couldn't think of any service she could render while they worked. She left the room and sat down in the foyer to pray. Before she enumerated her own concerns again, she lifted up the two young people and their family. What a good reminder that others experienced hardships during war also.

Peace filled Mary Beth as she descended the church steps.

However, a sudden movement caught her attention as she reached the sidewalk. A soldier hung back as if he were looking into a shop down the street. He was so far away, she decided to ignore him, but later, footsteps sounded behind her as she made her way to the bank. Was she imagining things? She looked back and recognized Lieutenant McDonald, who had created problems for the bank a year ago.

Was he following her?

WEDNESDAY NIGHT PRAYER MEETING

As the pastor requested, Peter bowed his head and lifted his heart in prayer. Soft organ music drifted through the sanctuary, and he relaxed, filling his lungs with air. As he listed the many difficulties he faced, he thanked God for the peaceful atmosphere where he could focus on God. His wife slipped her hand in his, and he prayed for her safety, especially with banking problems. How he'd longed for this quiet moment in the Lord's presence.

"Lemme have it!" a child beside him screeched.

He shifted his weight and kept praying.

"Sh-sh!" The lady's voice reverberated in the quiet room.

"No." A boy squealed. "I had it first."

He opened his eyes. Two boys tugged on the same book. Their high-pitched protests shattered Peter's nerves, and he thanked God he had no children yet. Right away, he despised his selfishness and prayed for the mother.

"Stop it." The lady moved one child. "That's enough."

One of the boys emitted a shrill wail, and Mary Beth left the room.

"See what you have done." The frowning lady grabbed one boy in each hand and escorted them out.

Quiet returned, but Peter worried about his wife, since she was still recovering from illness. He rose and walked out the back. The moment he stepped into the foyer, Mrs. Teague barreled toward him.

Her lips had disappeared into her frown, and her green eyes blazed as she approached. "There you are. What a mess you've caused."

"Excuse me?"

Mrs. Teague crossed her arms. "I came out here when I saw you get up. Someone revealed names of donors to the Newsome Hospital fund. How could you allow that information to leak out?"

Peter placed a hand on his burning stomach and wondered how much trust his fellow citizens would have in the bank once they heard the news. What a great way to lose more customers. At least Mary Beth didn't know. "I apologize, ma'am."

A movement to his left caught his attention, and he looked over. Mary Beth had been sitting beside the door, and now she was rushing outside.

"What are you going to do, sir?" Mrs. Teague waved a finger in his face.

Before he could answer, Mr. Haskell, who was ushering tonight, opened the door and waved from outside. "Peter, your wife is ill."

Ill? She hadn't been getting enough rest, but Peter had stopped urging her to get more since the murder. He'd been too busy and worried to think of it. He stiffened.

"You haven't answered me." Mrs. Teague hadn't moved.

"I shall look into the problem in the morning, ma'am." Peter made eye contact. "Thank you for your patience."

Mr. Haskell held the door open. "You'll find her just outside in the grass. I can take you home in my carriage if that would help."

"Thanks." Peter's heart galloped as he headed outside. He needed prayer time more than ever now. "I appreciate that."

"I shall bring my carriage round to the front."

Peter nodded and hurried down the front steps. Mary Beth lay in the grass beside the church. A lady held her hand and two boys darted up and down the sidewalk in front of the church.

The lady looked up as he stepped onto the grass. "She fainted after losing her meal."

"Peter?" Mary Beth's face was white. She sat up and offered a wry smile. "I'm sorry to trouble you. I had a terrible headache, but I became really ill when I heard Mrs. Teague."

"Trouble?" Peter wanted to scream at her for ignoring her health, but he must be gentle. "I'm going to see you home and call for Dr. Smith."

"I'll have to find out who released that information."

"Rest." He hoped she listened.

THE NEXT MORNING
C&R BANK

Mary Beth stood on the landing outside Peter's office and Mr. Riddle's. She gazed into the secretary's thin face hoping to catch any nuance of emotion as she questioned him. Of course, she still didn't feel quite normal after her crippling headache last night. The pain had left, but she was fatigued. However, this situation with Newsome was too delicate to put off.

Of all the bank employees, Riddle was the one she would trust until the sun went dark, but she still had to query him. "Have you had any dealings with the hospital account?"

Riddle raised an eyebrow as he shuffled the stack of papers in his hand. "I haven't. Is there a reason you ask?"

Mary Beth noted his demeanor seemed normal and explained the problem with Mrs. Teague.

"Ah!" Riddle nodded. "Yes, I can see her becoming irate over such a breech. Grant did most of the transfers, so he is the best person to ask."

"I wondered if some problem came up and the staff spoke about it during banking hours. Something that could be overheard."

"No." Riddle shrugged. "I hope you find the answer."

Mary Beth wanted some innocent explanation because she preferred to think someone made a mistake. "When you go downstairs, please tell Mr. Evans I'd like to speak with him in my office."

"I'm going there now." Riddle nodded in that direction. "I shall inform him immediately."

"Going where?" Peter came into the hallway. "Mary Beth, what are you doing here? Dr. Smith wanted you to rest at home today."

Peter's words brought back shards of pain in her forehead, and she massaged one temple. "I planned on speaking to Evans about the hospital account. We must find out how the public learned the information."

"I've already taken care of that problem. Mrs. Phipps told her neighbor. I fired her this morning." Peter turned to Riddle. "There's no need to speak to Evans."

Mary Beth's mouth fell open. The bank belonged to both of them, and Peter had never made such a huge decision without talking with her first. They'd already lost Grant because the military hadn't released him, and now they would be short two employees. "You did what?"

Right away, Mr. Riddle hurried downstairs.

Peter's eyes widened, seemingly shocked by her tone. "Come with me."

She followed him into the office and shut the door. "Why didn't you consult me before firing Mrs. Phipps?"

"I expected you to be in bed, recovering, not here." His face had hardened. "You were so ill last night that you couldn't walk. Go home."

Mary Beth stared at him as her stomach churned. "I want to be involved in decision-making."

Peter put his hands on her shoulders, "When your father was sick, you assisted him, right?"

Images of her sweet father flashed into her mind, making her long for him. His weak heart plagued him for months before he died. "Yes."

"Would you have scolded if he tried to work and couldn't?"

She nodded her head, knowing that's exactly what she did.

"Please understand my motive." He tipped her chin up and gazed into her eyes. "Please rest and get well."

How could she refuse his pleading gaze? She should never have questioned his motives.

Noon
General Bragg's Office

The small office where Peter sat was stifling. A tiny window occupied the wall across the room from him. When he tried to open it, he found it nailed shut from the outside. He sat in the only chair in the room, except for the one at the battered desk next to him. Sweat dampened his collar and ran down his back. Nevertheless, a slight tremor ran through his body as military men hurried by and guards with rifles marched past the entrance.

Yesterday, he'd heard the Union army was moving toward them again, so this wasn't the moment for a civilian to ask favors. Henderson, however, insisted Peter meet with General Bragg and demand the return of Mr. Grant. Henderson said the local government always held the right to investigate crimes, and so Peter waited. The work at the bank needed his attention, and he hated wasting time.

At last, a lieutenant entered. "Excuse me, sir, what is your errand?"

"I came to speak with General Bragg."

He frowned and shook his head. "You need an appointment."

How frustrating! His wife was annoyed with him, and now he had to wrangle with the military bureaucracy. "I had one, forty-five minutes ago."

"That's odd." The lieutenant scanned a small book. "Your appointment wasn't listed. Your name is Mister ..."

Peter wished he knew what the book contained and what kept Bragg busy. "I'm Peter Chandler, owner of C&R Bank. My city councilman, Mr. Henderson, made the appointment for me."

"What was the purpose of your visit?"

Peter wondered how safe they would be with such an inefficient military, but he explained the reason for his visit.

The lieutenant dipped his pen in ink and wrote on a sheet of paper. "Give me your name again, sir."

"Mr. Peter Chandler, owner of C&R Bank."

"Excellent." He rose and offered Peter his hand. "I shall see the General's aide de camp receives this message. You should hear from the General within the next few days."

If he has time, and if we aren't invaded.

Early Afternoon
Chandler Sitting Room

Mary Beth jerked into wakefulness when her head swayed left, causing a cramp. The book she'd been holding had slid to the floor. She massaged her neck as she bent over to retrieve it. Sleeping in a chair wasn't the best place, but she had rested until she fell asleep. Her head had improved, and she could tell her husband she hadn't been working. She leaned back in the wingback chair and yawned, flipping through the book Dr. Smith had loaned her on herbal medications.

"Mary Beth?" Ruth entered the room wearing an apron stained with herbs. "I'm going to need you to help me now."

"Very well." Mary Beth stood and stretched. Her neck protested, and nausea swept over her. If only she could shake this disease she caught from Mrs. McCallie's patients. She would rather be with child, but her doctor insisted she was not.

A knock on the front door interrupted the them, and Mary Beth groaned. Today she didn't feel up to visitors.

"I'll get that." Ruth scampered toward the hallway. "Mrs. Nelson from the General store promised to send more of those powdered herbs."

Moments later, Ruth led in Ida. Her face was red and one eye swollen shut. "I can't find the extra lace Mother gave me for her dress, and I can't recall if you returned it."

Mary Beth gasped. Whatever ailed her failed to compare with what Ida's husband inflicted. "You've been beaten."

"It's nothing." Ida sank onto the couch with a groan. "I made him angry. I've got to learn what he needs so he won't lose his temper."

"Nonsense. A man has no right to beat his wife." Dizziness forced her to grab the chair. She turned to Ruth. "Make a poultice with tea. It will shrink the swelling in her eye."

Ruth shuddered. "I can't recall how to do that."

Mary Beth steeled herself. "I'll do it. Take her up to the guest bedroom where she can lie down."

"No!" Ida screeched. "I can't do that. What if he finds out I've been here? I just need the lace. I thought I could sell it to replace a dish I broke."

"I thought you knew your mother asked me for the lace." A sigh escaped Mary Beth. She wasn't sure what happened to Ida's common sense. "Come into the kitchen. We'll do what we can."

Mid Afternoon
C&R Bank

At last, the bank foyer stood empty. Anna Chandler covered her mouth with her hand to suppress a yawn and shifted her aching feet. She'd been at the teller window since about nine this morning. Peter had built a brisk business, despite the war. While people hadn't stood in line, she'd complete one transaction and have another customer arrive.

Since she had a moment of silence, she hurried to Mr. Evan's office and found him bent over his desk. "Mr. Evans, I recall seeing a stool in here, but I don't see it now."

Evans looked up and rubbed his eyes. "My predecessor used that. I moved it to the storage in the back room."

"Would you mind staying up front while I fetch it?" Mrs. Chandler needed a break for nature anyhow. "I'm not accustomed to so many hours on my feet."

"I shall be delighted." He rose and piled up papers on his desk. "A change of scenery would be helpful for me also."

Anna hurried to the back room. She opened the door into the storage area. On her left stood a wall of filing cabinets containing records from the past. On the opposite side of the room, Peter placed extra materials on shelves. The stool she wanted resided next to the back wall, but an old desk Anna's husband used years ago blocked her way. She thought about asking Peter if she could bring it home for Ruth to use, until she realized Ruth lived with him. Life and the passage of time changed, and she didn't always adjust well to the shift. She and her husband ran the bank together when it first opened, and she never had to ask permission to use the furnishings.

Mr. Evans looked up as she walked back to the teller window. "Are you sure your break is over? It's been quiet."

"In that case, I shall go outside and cut a few flowers for myself. They'll add some color to my teller-cage."

"Go ahead." He chuckled. "I'm in no hurry."

Anna waltzed outside and cut a few dahlias and petunias from the large buckets around the front door.

"Anna?" Someone whispered.

Anna looked up to see Nellie, her friend from church. "Good afternoon. Are you a bank customer today?"

Nellie looked right and left before she leaned toward Anna. "What's all this about Angela Phipps?"

If only Anna had gone inside a moment earlier. She preferred not to answer this question. "Did you come to see her?"

Nellie frowned. "No. Oh no. I just heard a story that sounded unkind, and I thought surely you would know."

Unkind? Anna could feel herself growing warm. Angela wasn't a very efficient employee, but people shouldn't gossip over why Peter let her go. "I'd best get back inside. I'm working at the teller window today."

Nellie gasped and backed away. "Sorry, I didn't know."

As Anna hurried back inside, she pondered the situation. Perhaps Peter would need assistance getting the town folk to understand his decisions. She could take care of things and he didn't have to know.

Chapter Seventeen

Mary Beth stood at Ellen McCallie's kitchen sink with her sleeves rolled up and washed salve from her hands the way Dr. Smith had taught her. The room didn't look much like a kitchen right now. Ellen and Mary Beth had changed dressings, and they'd spread out rolls of bandages, various types of liniment and cotton on the worktables while water boiled on the stove. "Let me stay and put all this away."

Ellen shook her head as she wiped her hands on her apron. "You did most of the work anyway, cleaning those putrid sores Private Jones had. After being sick, you'd best care for your own health. Nothing here will take long, and I think the men will sleep now that they've eaten."

Mary Beth couldn't help thinking of all the work Ellen had with the extra soldiers who just arrived. "Maybe I could come back this evening and help you prepare meals."

"Tom's mother likes to do that, and I'm pleased to allow her to do what she can at her age. You come back tomorrow and check on the Union men. That's enough."

Mary Beth admired Ellen's pluck and unselfishness. "I can do that. Maybe I can take Grace out to play in the yard."

A huge grin spread across Ellen's face. "I'd like that."

A knock sounded on the door, and Ellen hurried to answer. She returned with two ladies dressed for visiting. The older wore a blue checked dress and the younger, who carried a huge basket, wore yellow. "Mary Beth, this is Mrs. Jones and her daughter. They came to see Private Jones, and I told them how you cleaned up his wound."

Mrs. Jones clasped Mary Beth's hand. "I appreciate you nursing him. The doctor insisted I leave it for someone else since I'm expecting again."

A stab of pain hit Mary Beth in the abdomen. If only she could conceive, but she wasn't getting the rest Dr. Smith prescribed, so she might never have a child. She managed a smile. "You are blessed."

Mrs. Jones lowered her tone, "You know the patient upstairs is not my real son. I'm John's second wife, and I wouldn't want to jeopardize the child I carry. His father wanted me to bring him a gift, and so I baked several loaves of bread."

Given all the work Mary Beth did for these men, she deserved a houseful of children. How unfair. Not wanting bitterness to set in, she managed a nod and hoped she looked sympathetic.

"The world is terribly evil, you know." Mrs. Jones tucked her chin. "Just today I heard about a widow getting fired from her bank job because she talked too much. Isn't that a shame?"

Mary Beth was hot now, and she wasn't about to agree with this lady. "Really?"

"Yes, it's a Mrs. Forbes, no Phipps, I believe. Such a shame in the middle of a war that an employer could be that hard. Everyone's talking about how terrible it is."

Ellen raised an eyebrow in Mary Beth's direction as she took Mrs. Jones's arm. "I do appreciate the baking. I assure you we will use it." Ellen removed the bread and returned the empty basket.

"We'd best be leaving now." The mother turned toward the door. "Give my best to Mr. Jones."

Mary Beth's stomach flip-flopped as she collapsed onto a straight chair by the table while Ellen showed them out. Mary Beth knew Peter was fair, but that left the bank vulnerable to the populace who didn't know the story.

Ellen placed a hand on Mary Beth's shoulder. "I saw you cringe, and I knew it must be the lady who worked in the bank."

Mary Beth nodded. She had related the story while they sorted clean bandages. "I don't know what to do."

Ellen sat down and pulled her into a hug. "Your husband is a man of character. He will handle this well."

She had to help her friend understand how dreadful the situation was. "A bank has to have trust to keep customers, and if everyone turns against us …"

"But you told me Mrs. Phipps leaked information. How can you trust someone who does that?"

"It didn't sound like Mrs. Jones knew that." Mary Beth entertained a longing to strangle Mrs. Jones.

"I've been a pastor's wife for several years now, and I have to battle anger too. If someone makes a sharp remark about his sermon or dislikes his looks, I find myself wanting to shoot arrows at them."

Mary Beth threw back her head and laughed at such an image of her gentle friend. "That doesn't sound like you."

"I can be vindictive if someone attacks my beloved." Ellen crossed her arms. "I've discovered the best thing to do is let Jesus have it. He truly cares about those we value, and he knows how to handle someone who is rude or impertinent."

"You have a fine husband."

"So do you." Ellen touched her hand. "Based on your illness, he chose to protect you so your health could be restored."

If only Mary Beth could bear a child, she wouldn't have to concern herself with banking issues as much.

C&R BANK
8: 00 A.M. OPENING

Anna sat another vase of flowers just inside the teller window and inhaled their subtle fragrance. Lovely. With plenty of blank receipts nearby, sharpened pencils ready, and her cash drawer arranged to her satisfaction, she was prepared for customers. She slipped off her shoes. The arthritis in her feet throbbed from standing too many hours. Plus, today she would use the stool most of the day. Across the room, a similar bunch of flowers decorated Mrs. Phipps's desk where Ruth would work today. In fact, she was already working—delivering a message to Peter from Henderson.

Anna glanced down to make sure her footwear was in easy reach, just in case. The bell tinkled and Mr. Grant walked in. Despite his crumpled clothing and disheveled hair, he made her heart dance. "Matthew! What happened?"

He shrugged. "The guard let me go this morning. He gave no reason, and I left before he could change his mind."

"Excellent." She abandoned her post to run into the foyer and hug him. "You'd best go home—"

"No." He slid from her arms and walked toward the counter. "I don't require sleep. I've missed too much work already, so I'll freshen up and do my job."

While she would prefer to mother him and make a fuss, she'd stay out of his way. A spineless man irked her anyhow. Matthew told her once he kept extra clothes in his office so he could keep his appearance pristine. "Peter went to the general on your behalf so his appeal must have worked."

Ruth entered the foyer from upstairs and plopped down at Mrs. Phipps's empty desk.

"I guess I'll spend the morning showing you what to do," Anna said, walking toward her daughter.

Peter would appreciate her help, that is, if he ever found out.

TWENTY MINUTES LATER

Mary Beth bustled up the front steps of her home and removed her bonnet as she stepped inside the foyer. The house was cool and comfortable compared to the hot sunshine outside. A dry mop leaned against the sitting room door with a dust rag propped on the handle. Odd. Maud was the only one who used those, and she'd left two weeks ago.

Mary Beth's basket held several purchases from the general store. She hurried back to the kitchen where she had left Ruth preparing medicines. "I'm home. Did you finish hanging up the herbs?"

The back door opened, and Bessie, the cook, entered. "Mrs. Chandler, I purchased eggs, cheese, and fresh vegetables for soup."

"Thank you, Bessie." Mary Beth peered behind the cook's plump body. "Did you see Ruth outside?"

"No, ma'am." Cook began to unpack her basket.

Mary Beth waved toward the pantry. "These are for medicines, and I'll leave them in here. Ruth must be in her room."

"Very good, ma'am." Bessie nodded as she unloaded vegetables on the counter.

Mary Beth turned to search upstairs and collided with someone taller. "Oof. Sorry."

Mrs. Phipps adjusted her coiffure. "I was going to tell you I was behind you, but you moved too fast."

Unbelievable. Mrs. Phipps? She didn't belong here and knowing her tendencies, she'd make a mess of the household. "What are you doing in my home?"

"Well." Mrs. Phipps drew herself up, lifting her chin. "You appear displeased, and I am offended. There's an explanation if you can contain yourself."

Mary Beth's body temperature rose for the second time today. She hoped she wasn't becoming an angry person. "What?"

"Mrs. Chandler hired me to work for you. We're going to tell everyone it's your idea, even though Mrs. Chandler will pay my salary. Oh, and she sent food also. Her daughter must have commented that you don't have enough."

"No." Mary Beth put a hand over her face. Her mother-in-law tended to manage Peter's affairs, and Mary Beth didn't want the chaos Mrs. Phipps brought. "No. No."

"Your house was filthy, especially the library. I've already mopped and dusted." She crossed her arms. "I'm a very good housekeeper."

That explained the mop and rag in the hallway. Maud never left them out once she finished her work. On the other hand, a housekeeper would help, especially since more soldiers had arrived at Mrs. McCallie's home. Besides, Dr. Smith now asked her to make almost all his preparations. He was busy with the hospital as well as his usual patients. However, Mrs. Chandler's interference was annoying. "I'd prefer to hire my own help."

"But you hadn't." The corner of Mrs. Phipps' mouth tightened into a smirk.

"Correct. I hadn't." She'd talk to Peter. He'd know how to handle his mother.

OFFICE OF C&R BANK

Peter beamed at his sister when she popped into his office waving a scrap of paper. She seldom walked anywhere, she bustled or bounced. He'd been trying to devise a way to solve the latest bank dilemma. "You have another message?"

She nodded, running her fingers through her dark hair. "A different man came with this."

His mother brought Ruth this morning, suggesting she fill in for Mrs. Phipps's vacancy for a few days. He'd agreed since having her here lightened the workload. Besides Peter and Ruth got along well, except for a short time after his father died. "Thanks."

"I like working for you almost as much as mixing medications." Ruth twisted a strand of dark hair while standing on one foot. "Do you need me to take a reply?"

Peter read the message his sister brought, while pacing the room. Henderson sent this message too. According to the missive, armed policemen at the depot found Mr. Field's suitcase in the brush just outside the depot area, but it contained no gold. As far as the bank was concerned, Peter must consider the gold lost and find other ways to increase the bank's holdings. Whoever accosted Mr. Field in the train station probably knew he was bringing money, or else knew he worked in the bank. "I might later, but you can return downstairs."

He must remember to give Mary Beth this news. She would appreciate knowing authorities found Field's trunk.

A glance at his watch told him it was time to move money to the vault. Hurrying downstairs to the foyer, his jaw dropped when he saw Mr. Grant behind the teller window, in his usual spot. Since they had no customers, Peter could express his delight. "Mr. Grant, no one told me you came in. How good to have you back."

"He just arrived." Ruth meandered up and slumped over the teller counter. "May I return to Mary Beth now?"

"I'd rather you stay the rest of the day, Ruth. Mrs. Phipps's chores are piling up." Peter wondered if his sister still disliked the bank manager because of his attentions to his mother. "Matthew, did they drop the charges?"

Grant shrugged. "They never told me, but I didn't argue when they said I could leave."

"I think I should speak to Henderson again and make sure you're in the clear."

The bell over the door rang and Mr. Weston walked in, looking impeccable in a sable suit with a gold watch chain hanging from the buttons of his waistcoat. He headed straight for Peter. "Hello, Mr. Chandler. It's good to see Mr. Grant back."

"Indeed, his absence left quite a void." Peter said. "What brings you here, Mr. Weston?"

Weston moved closer and lowered his voice. "I'm in town to deliver your mother's allowance, but while I'm here, I plan to open an account. You don't object to gold, do you?"

Peter shook his head. Customers never asked such an odd question. His mother probably engineered this visit. She shouldn't be telling anyone they needed gold, even if such information brought a new account. Their economic health shouldn't be discussed anywhere.

❧ ⟶ ⟡ ⟵ ⟢

170

A knock on the front door roused Mary Beth. She had dozed off in a plush library chair while reading on herbal medications—an attempt to rest. She left the library to answer the door, wondering who might call today. How she missed Maud. She never ignored visitors. Her breath stopped when she saw Ida's husband on her front porch. She had flung door wide open, making herself vulnerable to whatever he might do. "Mr. … uh, Sergeant. How can I help you?"

"You've been interfering with my wife again. She's been here. I know that." Stanford waved a finger at her as he came closer. "Anybody else would believe your innocence, but I don't. Standing there tall as if you ain't done nothin'."

"I believe you've done all the damage, sir."

Stanford's face crinkled into a scowl, and he reached for her.

"Argh!" She backed into the hallway. "Leave me alone."

"Who is going to make me?" He came closer.

She inched away, considering what she could use as a weapon, but the foyer had little to offer. The sitting room had lamps and framed photos. If she could ease into the kitchen, she could find many tools to whack her unwanted visitor.

He lunged for her arm. Mary Beth knocked the coat stand over between them as she moved further down the hall.

"Leave my wife alone." He grabbed her arm.

"Ouch! Let me go." She twisted loose but her forearm pulsated with pain.

Mrs. Phipps ran into the hallway and stopped short with widened eyes.

Apparently, she did not have sense enough to act. Mary Beth would have grabbed a book or a vase. "Do something!"

Angela Phipps nodded and bolted out the front door screaming.

Heart pounding, Mary Beth breathed fast, trying to devise a means of escape, while not taking her gaze from Stanford.

He moved toward her again, but this time Bessie slipped behind him from the dining room. In one swift motion, she splashed a bucket of steaming water over him.

"Yow!" He fell on the floor screaming.

Bessie dumped the remainder of the water right in his face.

While Stanford was howling, Mary Beth and Bessie rolled him onto the front porch. Once the door was closed, Mary Beth laughed. "How hot was that water?"

Stanford continued to screech and hurl insults.

"It be pretty near boilin'. We best be a takin' care of ourselves."

Chapter Eighteen

Peter shifted in his office chair. His head swirled as he glanced over the material Mr. Shaw had handed him. He glanced up at Shaw, a burly man with bushy brows and black hair. Today his dark eyes didn't appear to pose a threat. "If I'm reading this material correctly, sir, you are proposing that I invest in transporting goods to the Confederate military?"

Shaw's face broke into a smile. "You are correct. I pay in gold."

"That doesn't seem to square with our past relationship." Peter cleared his throat, choosing his words with care. "A year ago, you hounded me to lend money to the government. If I recall correctly, you even threatened me with jail time since my loyalties did not appear to lie with the Confederacy. Can you explain the change this represents?"

"Yes." Shaw slumped as he exhaled, and he sat for a moment looking down. At last, he met Peter's gaze. "I hated that job. My superiors put pressure on me to increase the government's income. The war was gearing up, and we didn't have needed supplies."

Peter rubbed a hand over his chin. "Are you saying you have a new position?"

Shaw bobbed his head. "Exactly. You are an honest man. That was clear from our interaction."

"I don't trust you."

"I guess if I were in your shoes, I would hesitate to trust someone who behaved the way I did previously."

What a dilemma. The man's mannerisms made Peter believe he might be honest after all. He pulled the papers toward him again and looked for detail. "Now you ask me to invest in shipping materials to troops."

"I am." Shaw scooted forward in his chair. "Although, I honestly don't expect it. I can see how you would imagine my character flawed."

Peter leaned back in his chair. "Explain your job to me."

"I oversee the movement of supplies. That includes weaponry, although another man manages that. I make sure troops have adequate food and medicine whether it's the troops who are training, on the front, or wounded in the hospital. The fact that the Union has been destroying bridges and railroads complicates things."

As Peter whispered a prayer for wisdom, an idea occurred to him. "What if I objected to sending food to troops engaged in battle or preparing to fight?"

Shaw rose and offered his hand. "I understand. Thanks for your time."

"Please sit down. I'm not finished."

Shaw's brows contracted for a moment, but he returned to his chair. "Yes?"

Peter couldn't imagine giving money to empower men to fight. He'd disagreed with slavery, yet the whole idea of the Union forcing the South to agree to their demands rankled. He'd chosen neutrality in this war. God commanded men to love the poor and downtrodden, so Peter could help the wounded. "What if I requested that any money I invest go to hospitals for food and medicine?"

Shaw scooted back in his chair, as if prepared to stay. "I'd accept once I reworked the contract."

Peter leaned forward. He was ready to negotiate. "What form of payment will you accept?"

Shaw's eyes lit up. "I can take gold, but I'll also accept money printed in the Confederacy. Because of my position, I have to."

Peter could invest a little of his own cash. If the man did as he asked, he would include money from the bank when he invested again. Receiving gold was the key. He scribbled numbers on a sheet of paper and slid it over to Shaw.

Shaw added a few numbers.

Peter liked the dividend he would receive. He handed Shaw the document and moved his ink stand toward his visitor. "Use my pen to alter the wording."

Shaw marked out the language Peter objected to and added his stipulations.

Peter signed and offered Shaw the cash. "I shall see you in a few days."

Shaw nodded. "You can count on that."

SATURDAY 12:30 P.M.

Peter had just closed the bank after a busy morning. His stomach growled as stepped onto the porch. His mind refused to sort the chaos from this morning. The war continued to alter his life, and last night worry over the bank kept him from sleeping. The latest newspaper he perused didn't include new troop movement. Perhaps the city would be safe a few days longer. Fatigue made his muscles heavy. How he longed for a good meal. Afterward, he'd settle into his library and read until he fell asleep.

When he opened the front door, the fragrance of food greeted him, and he hoped Cook announced lunch soon. He strode straight down the hall to his library at the back of the house. His huge leather chair called to him. He collapsed into its depths and closed his eyes. The investment he just made with Shaw popped into his thoughts. He seldom made snap decisions, and he hoped he hadn't made an error.

"There you are!" Mary Beth flew into the room. "Your mother. What are you going to do about her?"

Peter yawned and slumped forward supporting his head with his hand. "What's wrong?"

Mary Beth shook his shoulder. "Mrs. Phipps cannot do anything right."

"What?" He raised his gaze to her forearm, which bore a large bruise. "Did she hit you?"

"No." She waved her arms. "Your mother hired her to work for us."

If only he could rest, he might be able to handle another crisis. Facts. That's what he needed, and Mary Beth made no sense. He dragged himself from the chair and reached for Mary Beth's arm, hoping to get an explanation for the bruise. "Explain. And lower your voice."

She pushed him away. "Don't manhandle me. Sergeant Stanford has already done that. Mrs. Phipps is working here, and she annoys me. I could use Ruth, but I understand your mother took her to the bank."

"Wait." Peter held up a hand and peered at her face. "Who is Sergeant Stanford?"

"Ida's husband. He came here and tried to attack me," Mary Beth shouted as she gave details, including facts on his mother hiring Mrs. Phipps. "And I don't seem to be in control of my own life."

No. Heat seared through Peter's body. This was unacceptable. He rose to his feet and headed for the front

176

door. Ida's husband better keep his hands elsewhere. This had to be fixed. Now.

Mary Beth ran to the door and onto the front porch. She stared after Peter as he headed down the street away from the house. What had come over him? He ignored everything she said, and now he trotted down the street. Her life was collapsing around her, and he didn't seem to care.

With a huge sigh, she clattered back inside. Stomping down the hall, she headed into the kitchen. Dr. Smith had given her another recipe she must find ingredients for, and he needed the medication as soon as possible. She pulled her basket from the pantry on her left and headed for the back door.

"Excuse me, ma'am." A voice came from behind her.

Mary Beth paused and turned around. "Maud? What are you doing here?"

"I be wanderin' round here trying to find where Mrs. Phipps be a puttin' things."

"But why are you here?"

"I done thought you be a' knowin', honey child. Mrs. Chandler be askin' me to teach your new housekeeper. Course I agreed. Yous know I would be doin' anythin' for you, so long as I was home with my Billy, mostly. You know what I mean, bein' married 'n all."

Mary Beth was so peeved with Peter now, she could scream and hiss. But she didn't want to discuss that. "No. I had no idea."

"Well, I's here and my Billy says that I should stay mos' of the day, you know. To be sure Mrs. P. learns the job. I be hopin' you not be mindin.'"

Mary Beth was pleased someone cared about her opinion. Peter's mother did not. "Be my guest, Maud, and train away. I have to get some dried herbs."

"I be here when ya get back, now."

Mary Beth hurried toward the front door, and then realized using the kitchen door would be the closest way out. With all that was happening, her mind refused to work.

As she turned around to go back to the kitchen, Ruth dashed down the front stairs. Mary Beth looked up. "I couldn't find you. Where did you go today?"

Ruth paused halfway down. "Mother suggested I work at the bank since Mrs. Phipps left, and I like being there."

"Oh." Mrs. Chandler had every right to tell her daughter to work elsewhere, but Mary Beth wondered if either of them intended to inform her. "And where are you going now?"

"I heard you yelling at Peter, and I'm going home. To stay." She dashed down the steps and out the door before Mary Beth could ask if she got her clothes.

"Ugh." Mary Beth left by the front door, shoving it closed with her body. Must her life fall apart in just one day? She thought about her calendar, but it wasn't time for her monthly. Everyone was annoying her for some reason. How she'd love to lose her temper with Mrs. Chandler.

She marched into town, gritting her teeth. Jane waved to her from across the street, and Mary Beth nodded but disliked the effort. She'd explain her coldness later, and Jane would understand. Being gracious could be difficult at such a trying time. At least the streets weren't too crowded, and she avoided meeting many fellow citizens.

The vigorous walk had calmed her by the time she reached Nelson's grocery. Inside, straw littered the hardwood floor beside a crate with empty jars. Some shelves stood empty, while others still had plenty of goods.

"Well, look. Here's the newest Mrs. Chandler." Mr. Nelson stood behind the cash register at the counter on the right and handed money to a slender man. "Thank ya, sir. Mrs. Chandler's got some wind in her sails today. Her husband rushed by all red-faced a few moments ago. We'd best stay outta their way."

Blah. Mr. Nelson could even annoy the apostle John. Mary Beth headed to the back of the store where Mrs. Nelson kept dried herbs. Molly Nelson dusted shelves with a rag, and Mary Beth approached her. "Is your mother here?"

"I think she's in the storage room. We expect another delivery anytime. I'll get her." The girl dropped her rag and hurried to exit through a door to the left as Mr. Nelson approached.

"Whatcha looking for? Some herbal poison to use on that husband of yours? You would've been so much better off if you'd married my oldest son. Such a quiet boy. He's the heir to this entire store. All this could be yours. Even the empty shelves. What wealth." Nelson laughed at his own joke.

Mary Beth discretely moved away as her stomach churned from the smell of alcohol on Nelson's breath. Nothing about him was appropriate, but his words made her want to choke him. Despite being angry, she would be civil. "I need fenugreek."

"Where's a creek? We have the Tennessee River, but we can't sell that."

The grocer wasn't helping her mood. "No. That's not what I said."

"You're getting all uppity again. I can't understand why you thought you were too good for my son. He's a fine boy. My wife will get what you want. I must stay at the register." Mr. Nelson trudged back to the front.

Mary Beth stopped at a shelf displaying stacks of men's books. She closed her eyes and hissed, "Oh, God, help me hold my temper. I could kill him."

The door to the stockroom opened, Mrs. Grant meandered out glaring at a paper in her hand. She looked up.

Mary Beth strode toward her. "Mrs. Grant—"

"Excuse me." Mrs. Grant peered behind the shelf where Mary Beth had been standing. "Lily, have you been hiding again? You didn't make your bed."

A cobweb hung from Lily's hair as she slunk out into the open.

"How many times have I told you?" Mrs. Grant shook a finger in Lily's face. "You can't hide to avoid chores."

"I have come at a bad time." Mary Beth had thought of several other errands she could do to give Mrs. Nelson a few more minutes.

Mrs. Nelson frowned. "Not at all. I'm sorry to keep you waiting. As you can see from our half-empty shelves, we find it harder to get supplies. But a tradesman arrived, and I had to check the contents of his delivery. Molly's supposed to sweep, too, but I can see she hasn't. What can I find for you?"

Mary Beth handed Mrs. Nelson the list. "I need fenugreek as well as these other herbs."

"We keep herbs for the local hospital." She flattened her lips as she read. "It will take a few minutes to get the fenugreek. Molly can deliver all this to your home in about thirty minutes. Would that be all right, or would you rather wait?"

Mary Beth nodded. Molly had delivered items to her before. "That's very kind of you. Do you mind if I pay you?"

Mrs. Nelson nodded. "My husband is drinking today. He's impossible when he gets intoxicated. Let me tally this up."

Mary Beth gave Mrs. Nelson the money and checked her watch. If she hurried home now, she might get the recipe almost complete before Dr. Smith came for it. He spoke of an urgent need for the preparation and insisted he pay for it. She'd hurry.

Chapter Nineteen

Saturday Late Afternoon

Go away. Whoever was shaking Peter's shoulder should stop. There. The torment ceased, and he relaxed. Oblivion sucked him back into its smoothness.

"Peter? Peter!"

"Hmm?" He opened his eyes. Mother hovered over his face. He sat in his leather chair in the darkened library. His head was cocked at an uncomfortable angle, and he moved it about to relieve the pain. "What are you doing here?"

"I brought dinner."

"Dinner?' His stomach rumbled, and he licked his lips. The floor clock proclaimed it 6:05. "Why?"

"Where is Mary Beth?" His mother looked around the room.

Peter rubbed his face and yawned. When he left to find Sargent Stanford, Mary Beth had a bruise on her arm from his rough treatment. Peter had intended to have him arrested but wasn't successful. He'd left messages at the military base and with Henderson about Stanford's assault. Stanford had best keep his distance. Peter had wrestled in college and won several tournaments.

His mother shook his shoulder again. "Where is your wife?"

Closing his eyes, he filled his lungs and tried to bring his mind into the present. "Preparing medicines?" That seemed likely.

"She been a sleepin' upstairs, ma'am," Maud said from the doorway. "Dinner's ready, sir."

Maud? She worked for his mother now, and they didn't have a housekeeper.

"Come, Peter." His mother grabbed his hand. "Your food will get cold."

He stood, but an eerie unreality clung to him. His limbs were so heavy. But as he entered the hallway, the tantalizing smells of fried chicken met him. Hunger propelled him down the hall behind his mother. Turning into the dining room, he blinked at the bright lights. The table sparkled with the silver and crystal. Luscious aromas surrounded him from the covered dishes on the table. Mary Beth sat in front of an empty plate. Her face had no expression, and her eyes were glazed, as if she weren't awake either. "Where are you sitting?"

"I'm going home, Peter." His mother patted his back.

The inconsistencies didn't fit together unless he was still dreaming. His mother, Maud, and all the food didn't make sense. Facts. That's what he must have. "Didn't you say you brought this food?"

His mother offered a stiff smile and nod.

"It smells heavenly. But why?" Peter shrugged. "And why did you hire Mrs. Phipps without asking?"

Mrs. Chandler's mouth formed a thin line. "Ruth reported you cut back your own salary and served almost no food. How do you expect to give me a grandchild while doing that?"

Mary Beth gasped. "What?"

Peter's mother bunched up her lips, as if she were ready to give a sermon, and Mary Beth's eyes narrowed. If he didn't do something, the two women would clash.

"Mother, I know you like to help, but you must ask before you involve yourself in our lives. Why not stay and share this food with us?"

His mother stiffened and looked away. "I like to help when I can, but I'll leave you alone to eat."

Peter sighed as his mother left. He negotiated better when he was awake. When she dropped by the bank, he'd make another attempt at smoothing over the hurt she might feel.

Mrs. Chandler returned and leaned into the room. "Mary Beth, I forgot to tell you. Mrs. Phipps will wrap that painting of the Madonna and Child that hangs in the hallway. Peter brought it here by mistake after your wedding. I shall return for it later."

Peter spoke up, hoping to bring calm. "That was my mistake, Mother. It's been a full year, and I apologize for not resolving that earlier."

The tension about Mary Beth's face and mouth relaxed as his mother left. "What should we do about Mrs. Phipps?"

Peter took a gulp of iced tea before answering. "According to Mr. Riddle and mother, that decision upset a number of our fellow citizens since Mrs. Phipps is a widow. Why not give her a try? Have Maud train her and give her a chance. Later we could at least say she didn't turn out well."

"I suppose that sounds reasonable, but she doesn't inspire trust. Today she moved around all my herbal medications and the tools I use to make them." Mary Beth threw out her arms. "I could find nothing."

"Perhaps every woman has a different way of organizing." Peter spooned himself mashed potatoes from the nearest serving dish.

"I suppose I exaggerated my frustration." Mary Beth leaned forward to remove the lid from a dish in front of her.

"I wonder who cooked this?" Peter reached for another bowl of fried okra. "Hopefully, it will taste as good as it smells."

"Where did you go this afternoon after we talked? I worried because you were gone so long." Mary Beth took a bite of fried chicken. "Hmm. Good."

"I tried to have Stanford arrested for assaulting you. He must have been on patrol because I couldn't find him. I lodged a complaint with the military, and I left a message with Mr. Henderson. What did you do?"

"I prepared medicines for Dr. Smith, and then I returned to the bank to complete my audit." The inner side of her brows slanted upward. "The gold stolen from Field hurt us badly. I believe we should revert back to our old policy on loans to prevent your mother from pulling out any further cash."

Peter ground his teeth. "Bank policies should remain stable so that our customers know what to expect. I'm leaving things as they are now. I can find other technical reasons not to loan money should another officer apply."

"But Peter, your mother's threat hangs over us. In two more weeks, she'll withdraw more. At that point, we'll have to close."

"My mother doesn't run the bank."

The bank needed more gold to stay open. Peter would pray for guidance.

EARLY MONDAY MORNING

Mary Beth groaned as she gazed in the mirror. After sleeping late, she was still in her housecoat and slippers, and her hair was amuck—not ready to see her mother-in-law. If only Peter were here, he could handle his mother, but he'd left early for the bank. The last few days, her mother-in-law had created much frustration. Nevertheless, she must dress without delay and prepare to be polite.

The moment Mary Beth entered the sitting room, Mrs. Chandler offered a confident smile and pulled her into a sideways hug. "I've been wanting to chat ever since Saturday night, but we missed church yesterday. Ruth was congested, and I stayed home with her ..."

Mary Beth's mind tuned out as Mrs. Chandler continued chattering. Her self-assurance annoyed Mary Beth, and mothers should never irritate her children.

"All that to say, I'd love to chat about what you've found, since I've turned up very little. However, I must meet Mr. Weston shortly. He's taking the painting to have it appraised. Excuse me while I grab the parcel and leave."

Mary Beth cleared her throat. She longed to talk until they resolved their recent frustrations, but Mrs. Chandler appeared too busy. Mary Beth's emotions knotted even tighter, alarming her. Since she'd grown up without a mother, she'd always hoped Mrs. Chandler would fill that role. In many ways, she did. Who else would deliver a complete meal and worry over Mary Beth's diet? Perhaps she was too tense over the bank and overreacted. "I'll ring for Mrs. Phipps."

"Thank you." She came closer and placed a hand on Mary Beth's arm.

Mary Beth gazed into her eyes. She saw a softness in her mother-in-law's eyes and face. Perhaps all her actions came from a deep love for them.

Mrs. Phipps walked in. "Yes?"

"Mrs. Chandler came for the painting."

Mrs. Phipps frowned. "I could find no paper. Besides, I didn't think I could take it down without damaging it. The frame makes it quite heavy."

How frustrating. Mary Beth preferred to do as was promised. Mrs. Phipps seemed unable to follow directions here as well as the bank. Maud talked a lot but was very efficient. The contrast between the two women brought a rush of heat to Mary Beth's face. "Why didn't you ask about paper or go purchase some?"

"I stayed busy with other duties." Mrs. Phipps kept her eyes down. "Dust and dirt had accumulated everywhere."

"Indeed?" Mary Beth wondered why Mrs. Phipps did not meet her gaze. She might not be a good employee anywhere. "I shall obtain paper today. You may return to your work." Mary Beth waited until she left and then turned to her mother-in-law. "I apologize."

Mrs. Chandler nodded. "She's still new and unsure of what you expect. You always need a month or so to train someone new."

Mary Beth couldn't stop thinking of Mrs. Phipps's poor work habits at the bank. While she wanted to have compassion, the lady made her suspicious. "Is there any way Mr. Weston could pick it up here later today? If it's heavy, as Mrs. Phipps suggested, you wouldn't have to carry it."

"Excellent idea. You have a knack for solving problems." Mrs. Chandler headed for the door. "What time should I tell him?"

Mary Beth considered all she had to do. According to her watch it was nine. "I'll make sure it's ready by five this afternoon."

She had promised Peter she would rest, but now she didn't think that would work.

EARLY AFTERNOON

The afternoon seemed hotter than ever as Mary Beth hurried downtown. It hadn't rained in several days, and the street was extremely dry. Even the dandelions beside the road had shriveled. Their pitiful stems and scrawny golden flowers reminded Mary Beth how much the bank needed an influx of gold.

She'd just left Ellen McCallie's home where she'd changed dressings and checked her Union soldiers. The job took longer than usual, and now she had to hurry. After Mrs. Chandler left this morning, Newsome hospital had sent a message asking to purchase several of her herbal preparations. Since Dr. Smith had bought most of her inventory, she'd have to make more. Plus, she needed to find wrapping materials for Mrs. Chandler's painting.

Mrs. Nelson stood at the register with a line of customers when Mary Beth walked in. She wandered around looking for paper, adding several bottles of dried herbs to her basket. Since she couldn't find materials to wrap, she watched Mrs. Nelson and waited for her help.

After several minutes passed, Mrs. Nelson came to her side. "I apologize for making you wait. Business has been steady this morning. I'm concerned for my husband. He stepped away from the register about forty minutes ago to accept a delivery. If you don't mind, I'd like to check on him."

The distress on Mrs. Nelson's face bothered Mary Beth. She wondered if he'd been drinking again and passed out. "Go ahead. My purchases won't take long."

Mrs. Nelson's brow cleared, and she hurried through the door leading to the back.

Wham! Aaiee!

Mary Beth tensed all over. She dropped her basket and ran inside the storage room. The room was filled with wooden shelves from floor to ceiling. Many held merchandise or boxes. Toward the back of the room several large boxes lay on the ground as if they'd tumbled over. Mrs. Nelson stood beside them, looking down. She held her face in her hands. Her mouth hung open, and her complexion was white with shock.

Mary Beth hurried closer until she saw Mr. Nelson's motionless figure. He lay on his back, his mouth hanging open with a residue of bubbly saliva. His eyes were open and dilated. Both of those could indicate poison. Dead?

"Help him, Mrs. Chandler! Please!" Mrs. Nelson burst into sobs.

Mary Beth dropped to her knees and felt for a pulse, but found none. He wasn't breathing, and his face had a waxy appearance, as if he'd been dead awhile. "How long has he been missing?"

Mrs. Nelson collapsed on the floor, her face cold and pasty. Mary Beth stepped away from the body to help her. Rubbing Mrs. Nelson's hands and temples, she asked, "Is anyone else here? We need someone to go for Dr. Smith."

Five-year-old Lily eased in the room twisting a ruffle on her skirt. Her lips were stretched into a horizontal line and her eyes widened in fear.

"You may come in if you want. Your mommy is sick, and I'm trying to take care of her. I need someone to fetch a doctor. Is Molly here?"

"No. She's delivering." The little girl stared. "And my daddy?"

Mary Beth didn't have words. She shook her head. "I'm sorry. I can't do anything for him."

"I heard you the other day." The girl's voice was barely above a whisper. "You prayed you wouldn't murder him."

Chapter Twenty

Hot, stale air in the small storage room suffocated Mary Beth. She hovered close to Mrs. Nelson, who alternated between sobbing and sniffling. At times, Mary Beth worried the new widow would faint, since she was remarkably pale, but she'd refused to leave the room while Dr. Smith examined the body a few feet away. Mary Beth found a chair for Mrs. Nelson to sit on. If only she could get her to leave the room or drink cool water.

"Mrs. Nelson," Dr. Smith said, "did your husband take any medicines other than what I prescribed him?"

She shook her head. "I had a hard time getting him to take that syrup for indigestion, so I know he took nothing else. If he had avoided liquor, he wouldn't have needed that."

Mary Beth massaged Mrs. Nelson's shoulders, hoping to loosen some of the tension.

"I'm going to recommend you go home and rest." He motioned to Mary Beth. "Mrs. Chandler, will you accompany her?"

"Of course. I'll be delighted to." Bank worries could wait until later, but she'd have to work on medicines today to complete what the hospital required.

"Mrs. Nelson, you are fortunate to have an accomplished nurse with you. If she weren't here, I'd probably fetch her."

Mrs. Nelson stood, then swayed. "All I have to do is walk upstairs. The stairwell is behind us on the left. We've always lived over the business."

Mary Beth encircled her waist. "Let's move slowly. If you feel lightheaded, we'll sit down until you feel better."

"Please call me Betty." She offered a weak smile.

Supporting Mrs. Nelson, Mary Beth guided her up the narrow stairwell at the back of the room. The walls, covered with children's fingerprints, had no railing to hang onto. Plus, she had to turn sideways a little to make room for both of them. She was glad Dr. Smith ascended behind them in case she fainted.

"At the top, we'll enter the kitchen. We'll have to go down the hallway on the right. Our bedroom sits at the far end."

Mary Beth helped Betty Nelson into the sparse kitchen. A stove stood at the far end of the wall along with a sideboard filled with canisters and utensils. Under the window on the left wall a round table sat with a few random cups. Several easy chairs were gathered about a braided rug to her left. Her patient was out of breath. "How much further?"

"A few more steps down the hall." Betty's cheeks had a little color. "You can see it's roomier now that we're upstairs. We saved all the space for living area."

Mary Beth followed her patient down a long hall, passing several rooms with narrow beds. At the end of the hall, they entered a larger room facing the road. It contained a larger bed under the window. Mary Beth pulled back the thin yellow bedspread so Mrs. Nelson could lie down.

"Oooh. This feels good."

Dr. Smith entered the room also. "Where is your husband's medication?"

Mrs. Nelson waved to a black chest of drawers across the room. "On the left toward the back."

"May I get you some water?" Mary Beth fluffed the extra pillow and put it under Betty's head.

"Not now." She closed her eyes. "I'd like to rest."

"What is this?" Dr. Smith held up a jar with a printed label.

Betty opened her eyes and frowned. "I don't know. Where did you find that? That's never been there before."

The doctor motioned to the chest. "It was there beside the preparation I gave him."

Mary Beth took the jar. "That's the same type of jar I use, but I have no printed labels. Hmm. The instructions say to take a pinch in water twice a day. Where could he have gotten this?"

"As a grocer he buys and sells. It appears bits of this powder float in this glass of water he left here. I shall take this to my lab to see what it is. I suspect this is the cause of death. I need some water from the kitchen. I'll be right back." The doctor left the room.

Mary Beth turned back to the widow and took her hand. Her pulse seemed normal but what a tragedy to lose her husband like this. She couldn't imagine the sorrow she must feel.

A rustle at the door caught Mary Beth's attention.

Lily walked in with three uniformed soldiers carrying rifles. She pointed at Mary Beth. "She's the one who killed my father."

BANK OFFICE

Peter checked the paper with the list of customers and stuck it in his pocket. His father taught him to keep a good relationship with businesses who had borrowed money. He worked hard to do that. Today he would visit his clients to chat about business. Maybe he could give encouragement and offer to accept interest payments, saving them a trip to the bank.

Mr. Grant met Peter at the bottom of the stairs. His wrinkled brow concerned Peter. "Were you looking for me? I planned to see clients."

Grant tugged at his tie. "You might need to wait. Mr. Dempsey asked to close his account."

Peter's throat tightened. Dempsey was a great customer and had a large account. "I shall speak to him."

"Maybe you can talk him into leaving his money here," Grant said, turning back toward the teller window. "At least part of it."

Wearing his kindest smile. Peter walked into the foyer where the Dempsey stood wearing a light brown suit. "Good morning, sir. How can I help you?"

Dempsey ran his hand over his salt and pepper beard. "The wife and I want to visit my sister before we get too old to travel. The war and rumors of attacks has upset Mabel. I suspect we'll stay till the war ends."

"I see." Peter nodded. "Grant said you wanted to withdraw money. How much do you need?"

Dempsey looked down and shuffled his feet. "I reckon I need it all. I don't know if we'll be coming back, even though I hope to."

Peter swallowed to moisten his dry throat. He would need all the interest money today if Dempsey followed through. "You have been a wonderful customer, and we prefer to have you back."

"We are fond of you, Mr. Chandler. Your father was a fine man." He reached in his pocket and pulled out pencil and paper. "Let me do some figuring here. Maybe I can leave some money and tell Mabel we have to return."

"That would be wonderful." Was he selfish to hope Dempsey left a large sum?

Mrs. Nelson's Bedroom

Mary Beth's hands were clammy. Soldiers stood in the doorway holding rifles. They glared at her. She had prayed aloud, and Lily had heard. Why didn't she pray silently? She did most of the time. Could she explain her words?

The tall soldier frowned at her. His brown eyes pierced into her soul. "Ma'am, did you kill this girl's father?"

"No." Her hand flew to her throat, which seemed terribly dry. "I wouldn't ever—"

"I heard you say it." Lily pointed at her. "Are you lying?"

"No." She had nothing to hide. Why was she shaking? "I am a nurse. I would never—"

"I'm goin' to tell all my friends." Lily dashed from the room.

Mary Beth sighed. Who would bank with them if the whole town thought she murdered Nelson?

The soldier moved closer. "Why were you here?"

His rifle was too close. She imagined the cold barrel pressed against her face. "I mix medication for Dr. Smith. I needed some herbs from the store."

"And you were here just in time to kill this man?" His eyes narrowed as he pulled his rifle off his shoulder.

"No." Why couldn't she think? Say something convincing?

Dr. Smith appeared at the door. "What are you doing here? You are disturbing my patient."

"The little girl accused this lady of murder." He turned to the two other soldiers. "We need to summon the provost."

Mary Beth felt dizzy and the room faded.

LATER THAT AFTERNOON
C&R BANK

As Mr. Riddle entered his office with a stack of papers, Peter glanced at his watch and wondered where Mary Beth was. She'd promised to be here earlier, and he wondered what kept her. If only she was resting, but he knew her too well.

"I have letters for you to sign, and today's mail." Riddle placed the material on Peter's desk.

"Is Mrs. Chandler downstairs?"

"No. I haven't seen her today. Mr. Weston just arrived and would like to speak to you. May I send him in?"

"Of course." Peter cringed at his own words. He'd rather not talk to Mr. Weston when his mind was on Mary Beth, but perhaps Weston wouldn't take long.

Weston's brow was lined and his face solemn. 'I thought I'd drop by and offer my condolences. Is there anything I can do to help?"

Mr. Weston's words crashed upon Peter like an unexpected thunder. "What are you talking about?"

"Lily Nelson accused Mary Beth of murdering her father. It's all over town. Someone found Nelson dead this afternoon." He cringed. "I apologize. I thought you knew."

"No. No. No!" Peter pounded on his desk and reached for his pistol. He must protect his wife. Where was she?

"Excuse me, sir." Mr. Riddle reappeared, panting. "I've just received an urgent message from Dr. Smith. Your wife is with Mrs. Nelson. Apparently, they found Nelson's body in the storage room today—"

"Oh! I'm glad someone thought to give the news." Weston stomped. "Are you going to tell Peter his wife was accused of murder?"

Riddle cringed. "That wasn't … I don't … Dr. Smith said your wife … is distraught."

"I will see to her." Peter grabbed ammunition and headed out of the office. "Riddle, lock my office and make sure the bank vault is secure. Stay here until you hear from me."

Peter arrived at Nelson's grocery just as three Confederate soldiers ambled out the door and headed up the street away from him. He broke into a run and grabbed the doorknob.

One soldier turned and looked back. "The grocery is closed today. You'd best come back another day."

"No." Peter could hardly get words out. "My wife … Mrs. Chandler should be inside."

All three men stopped and stared. The tallest man tipped his hat. "So your wife is the murderer. Did you know she was violent when you met her?"

All three laughed as they walked away.

Peter fingered the gun in his pocket and gritted his teeth. What had they done to her? Was she still here? He rushed inside the store, but silence greeted him. The shelves were fully stocked, but no one appeared to wait on him. His shoes clicked on the hardwood floor as he walked toward the back. "Dr. Smith? Mary Beth?"

Heart pounding, Peter came to a door between two huge display shelves. Should he go in? He didn't want to invade the Nelson's privacy. On the other hand, the doctor had summoned him to come.

"Peter?" Dr. Smith called his name as he entered the store from the back room.

"I got the message and came to the store." He blotted his damp brow. "Is she hurt?"

"Mary Beth is upstairs in the Nelson's apartment, but I don't think she can make it home without help. She's in shock."

Mary Beth's head spun, and the light hurt her eyes. She tried to sit up but felt nauseated. Wasn't she still at the Nelson's? On the floor beside the dresser? Why? Her mind wouldn't work. How comforting to see Dr. Smith's bearded face and wrinkled brow. "Doctor. My head hurts. What …"

"You fainted. There's a nasty scrape on your head." The doctor held a cup up to her lips. "Drink this."

The acrid liquid made her cringe. "That's terrible. What is it?"

"A preparation to help you relax. Peter is here and will take you home."

"Mary Beth?" Peter leaned over her.

"But the soldiers. They accused me …"

The doctor had that no-nonsense look in his eyes. "A five-year-old girl stated her opinion. That's not proof."

"Is Mrs. Nelson—"

"I have her in hand." His bushy brows tightened.

Peter scooped her up, and she threw her arms around his neck. Dr. Smith and Jane scurried around the room. "Why is Jane here?"

"I sent for her," Dr. Smith said. Your husband will get you home."

"They accused me of murder. Lily promised to tell everyone." She tensed at the memory. "Will our customers leave?"

"Don't reflect on that." The doctor pressed his lips together and turned to Peter. "She's had enough for today. Take her home."

Chapter Twenty-One

The raucous sound of Peter's snores unnerved Mary Beth. His head lay on the pillow with his mouth facing her right ear. If only she could shift to her left side, but Peter's grip held her fast. At least he could sleep. Now that Dr. Smith's preparation had worn off, sleep eluded her. Images of the questioning soldier lingered in her mind. The five-year-old girl said she killed Mr. Nelson and left to tell her friends. What did the townsfolk think? If only oblivion would overtake her, but since she'd been heavily medicated, she'd slept most of the day.

Peter sighed and altered his position, freeing Mary Beth. She turned onto her stomach and pummeled her pillow into a ball, propping up her chin. Since she couldn't sleep, she could take inventory of her dried herbs or review the household budget. Her stomach growled, so a trip to the kitchen appealed to her. She eased out of bed, careful not to wake her husband. Perhaps she could locate a leftover roll while she perused her herbal supplies.

The cold hardwood floor caressed her bare feet as she padded downstairs by the moonlight. Once in the kitchen, she steered right to the pantry where the aroma of sugar and cinnamon greeted her. After her eyes adjusted to the darker room, she spotted a package of pastries wrapped in heavy paper. The smell told her she'd found a treasure. Surely this came from City Café. Hunger emboldened her to open the package. Her first nibble of perfect texture tasted like magic. She didn't want to swallow.

Thwack!

Mary Beth froze with the sweet roll inches from her mouth. Who else was in the house? She turned and jumped as a lighted oil lamp appeared behind her. The glare kept her from seeing who or what might be coming toward her. "Who's there?"

"I woke and couldn't find you," Peter said. "Sorry, I stumbled into the door frame."

Mary Beth's heart still pounded, but she released a sigh. "You scared me. I thought someone broke in."

He ran his hand over his rumpled hair. "I dreamed they threw you in jail. Then I heard something down here. Wake me up next time."

"I didn't want to disturb you. Since you're here, join me for a snack. I found these in the pantry."

"Yeah. A man from the café brought them by. I asked Mrs. Phipps to save them for later."

"This is later." She motioned to Bessie's worktable where she sat the sweet rolls. "Sit down and I'll make tea. We can decide what to do."

"Do?" Peter crossed his arms. "Dr. Smith wouldn't like such talk, and I agree."

"We have a problem to solve. Let's face it, everyone at our bank is under suspicion of some kind. That won't work. We'll lose customers." Mary Beth put the kettle on and pulled out cups.

Peter eased into a chair and picked up a sweet roll. "Correction. Two people are under suspicion. You and Mr. Grant."

"Okay. Be specific." Mary Beth put down a plate for a sweet roll like the one Peter just bit into. "But you are the owner and the employer. You could be next. Why not your mother? She's known for protecting you. See how easily the guilt can spread."

"You haven't mentioned Mrs. Phipps and Mr. Evans."

"Okay." Mary Beth pulled off a tiny piece of sweet roll and savored the flavor. She loved sugar, probably too much, and this tasted great even though the bun had less sugar because of the shortage. "Evans is our newest employee. Maybe he's not entirely honest. We fired Mrs. Phipps for leaking secrets."

"Evans had a great recommendation, and he's never caused a problem. Mrs. Phipps, well, I wonder if she's just inefficient."

"Or she's someone that can be bribed." At first Mary Beth didn't like her because she thought Angela might be flirting with her husband, but he didn't think she was. Either way, he wasn't interested.

"She does need money." Peter gave a yawn which melted into a sigh. "I don't want you in danger."

"I won't be if we work together. You'd be with me." The kettle whistled, and she got up to pour water over the tea leaves. She placed the pot between them. "We could scour the bank for clues."

"Wait. You and I did that once before when someone forged my signature on money. We had something to look for. What would we look for this time?"

"Anything irregular. I keep thinking all this has something to do with the bank."

Peter poured himself some tea. "This doesn't look right. It's too watery."

"It's still steeping." Mary Beth poured it back in the pot. "Have another sweet roll."

"I wanted to eat my pastry with tea." Peter leaned back in his chair. "If we went in early this morning, what could we do?"

"We can always clean up. Make sure things are where they belong. Did you close last night?"

"No. I asked Grant and Riddle to close together. I trust them both, but at the same time, neither would do anything with the other watching."

Mary Beth giggled. "That doesn't sound like trust."

"I don't like anyone closing except you and me." He put a spoon in his cup. "Is this ready yet?"

Mary Beth peeked inside. "Almost."

Peter yawned several times. "I can't abide going to work this early."

"Let's take breakfast and eat around your desk. An indoor picnic."

"You are determined." He pushed back his chair. "On one condition."

What on earth could he want? "Yes?"

"We close early."

"I agree." She whispered a prayer.

One Hour Later

Once Mary Beth stood in the foyer of the bank, her ideas shriveled up. Prayer seemed the best choice since some evil person had designs on their business.

"All right. We are here early, and therefore, whatever we do will be private." Peter held up his basket of goodies. "What shall we do?"

"We will move everything on your desk and have an early breakfast while we chat about the bank problems."

"Go." He motioned her upstairs. "I have the food, you clean off the desk."

Mary Beth chuckled. "You get the easy job."

Once in the office, they sat down to a feast of sweet rolls and lukewarm tea. Mary Beth grabbed a roll and took a tiny bite. "Mmmm. These are so good. I kept thinking we must have displeased a client. That person decided to injure us to get even."

Peter shrugged. "Or someone wants the money in the vault. I suspect an unhappy client would simply change banks unless our actions were against the law. The colonel who was shot was not pleased, not until we allowed him a loan."

"But doesn't that seem interesting?" She pulled apart a pastry. "This man demanded a huge loan when he hadn't been in town very long? Who buys a house in a city that's a target for an advancing army? I would wait until after the war ended because whatever property I purchased might be destroyed."

"You're forgetting his rank." Peter put down his tea. "I suspect he knew the Confederate's defense of the city and believed it would hold. He probably planned on using the house and thought he might as well purchase it. If that were the case, he'd be even more annoyed with a local bank that wouldn't extend credit."

"Do you think he would have destroyed our reputation if we hadn't loaned him money?"

"With his rank, it's more likely the Confederacy might have seized the bank."

"So, you agree with me the bank is a target?"

"Yes." He chuckled. "And we are here to find clues."

"Last time, I started going through desks." She inhaled as she considered. Staying in bed and trying to sleep might have been wiser. Nothing struck her as essential, but this was her idea. "Let's look in the filing cabinets. Maybe looking at client files will jog our memory."

"Do you mind searching alone? I didn't get much done yesterday."

"Sure." Her stomach churned. She hadn't thought much about yesterday impacted him. Plus, she got him out of bed much earlier than she needed to. Working by herself would be less interesting. She meandered downstairs to the foyer and turned left to go behind the counter, stopping at the filing cabinets in an alcove between the offices. As her fingers touched the files, her mind called up images of the customers. What was she looking for anyhow?

She closed the first drawer and repeated the process with the second. Peter would be thrilled when she acknowledged this was a waste of time. Nothing struck her as unusual. Perhaps she could snoop about in the vault, or better yet the offices. She focused on the office Evans used, a few steps to her right. Did he know anything helpful? But the last file drawer seemed to beckon. After all, she'd best complete the job she started. With a sigh she tugged, but the drawer didn't give. With a herculean jerk, she succeeded, but she couldn't read the tabs. An employee had packed the drawer full and nothing would move.

Part of her wanted to slam the drawer closed and hurry off to a more likely target. A mess like this, however, deserved a fix from the owner. She sat down and yanked out files, determined to transport a few to the drawer above. Once the files moved about, she pulled the drawer out all the way and reached to the back of the drawer. Her fingers touched something soft. Fabric? She got a firm hold and lifted out a gray bag.

She must see Peter. Now!

Peter pulled a sheaf of client reports, toward him as he settled behind his desk. Suppressing a yawn, he grabbed the nearest and poured over the numbers. The local printer continued to bring in adequate income and made the quarterly interest.

However, the grocer's report was not easy to read. Peter did a quick calculation, and the numbers didn't work. The man was either drunk or half asleep when he put together the document. Since Nelson hadn't paid the interest, Peter would need to stop by for a chat. With a groan, realization came to him. The grocer died yesterday, and the family wouldn't be in any shape to talk finances. Once the funeral was over, Peter could offer the widow some guidance. She might not want to continue the business in her husband's absence.

If only the bank had a more secure standing. He could offer her funds to tide her over, but he needed an influx of gold. Soon. Still showing kindness to the widow was vital. Certainly, he could offer food and provisions. Although, a grocer might have that.

"Peter!" Mary Beth rushed in the room holding a grey bag. "Look. I found gold."

He hadn't prayed or even considered sending a petition heavenward. This seemed too unlikely. For a moment he wondered if Mary Beth had hidden it herself. Did his wife have a secret, some mistake she needed to hide rather than admit a fault? She'd always had a problem admitting when she was in error. No. He refused to believe his wife would deceive him. "Where?"

"Bottom drawer of the filing cabinet behind the teller window. I could not move the files about, so I dug around in the back. And I found it."

"How much?"

She dumped the bag on his desk and the two of them counted together.

Peter pushed back his chair. Unbelievable. "That's the amount the thief stole from Mr. Field."

"Could this be his bag? Don't they use bags this color?"

"I don't know." His mind wouldn't even think of color. The larger issues bothered him. He had a pet theory regarding a person seeking bank funds or maybe even control of the entire bank. How foolish to conceal stolen money in a bank. "If this came from Field, how did it get here?"

"Mrs. Phipps."

"She's not employed here now. Besides, this is too recent."

Mary Beth pressed her lips together. "I do not trust her. Did you take her keys?"

"I did. Just in case she made copies, the locksmith comes today to change the locks."

"Your mother? Ruth?"

"Mother might hide money on the premises, but I know she wouldn't steal money from Field. Plus, Mother would never threaten Father's bank. This was his life's work, and she's proud of what he did."

"What about Ruth?"

Peter chuckled and shook his head. He understood his sister when she was younger, but not anymore. Her moods baffled him. "You know her better than I. She'll even tell you her secrets."

"Knowing her, she might store money here without telling us, but I don't think she has this much."

Chapter Twenty-Two

Mary Beth hadn't visited Dr. Smith's home office often. She wasn't sure whether to sit at the desk by the door or the chair by the examining table. Peter asked her to come and consult with the doctor about the gold they found, even though they believed it to be the money stolen when Mr. Field visited. Suspecting their employees bothered her, but they seemed the most likely culprits.

She stepped to an adjoining door that stood ajar and noticed herbs hanging from the ceiling, a mortar and pestle, and a huge metal table. This must be where he prepared medications and did autopsies.

Footsteps sounded behind her, and she turned. "Doctor, Peter and I need guidance."

"Oh?" His gray eyebrows shot upward. "I assumed you came by my request. I wanted you to examine Nelson's medications with me. Go on into my lab and I shall show you what I mean."

"I will." She was eager to see what he found.

He led her to the metal table and pulled out three bottles of medicine and opened one. "Nelson often complained of headaches. This is a powder I gave him."

Mary Beth swirled the contents of the bottle. "It's willow bark and fennel seeds and it looks fine to me."

"I agree." He opened the second small bottle. "Here is chloral hydrate. A patient can overdose with this, but I made sure Nelson knew how to use it. He only needed help sleeping if he was trying to stop drinking, which I fear didn't happen often."

"I've never seen this one." Mary Beth gazed at the clear powder.

Dr. Smith nodded. "It's rare here. A German doctor developed it. I don't think Nelson used much. The last one is the concern. I want you to look carefully at the contents."

She looked at the third bottle which contained dark powder with fragments of red. "Again, I don't recognize anything."

"This is the one I suspect. The major ingredient seems to be ground licorice root. Plus, you can see bits of red shell."

"I do see that. What is it?"

The doctor opened a glass cabinet and pulled out a box which he handed to Mary Beth. "I believe it is rosary pea, a medicinal plant grown in Florida. However, dosage is crucial because a lethal dose is minute."

The box contained six red oblong balls the size of a blueberry. Each had black around the end. "These are rosary peas?"

"Yes. The contents of one would kill a man. Nelson bought and sold herbs, and someone offered the preparation to Nelson as a mood enhancer. He was often depressed and might try it for himself. He probably took it the night before since it is slow acting."

"But surely there were symptoms."

Dr. Smith straightened. "His wife said he complained of nausea all day, but that was common when he'd been drinking too much. I need to question her more closely and find out what he ate. Sometimes your diet can delay the action of certain poisons."

She thought back to Nelson's body in the storage room. "The residue of saliva around his mouth—"

"He probably had a seizure as he was dying."

"Despicable! So now to find the culprit."

"No. It will be enough to clear your name." Smith rubbed a hand along his gray beard. "Search your medicinal supplies in case the perpetrator tried to implicate you."

"That would mean I talk to Ruth. She works alongside me now."

"Very wise." He nodded. "Now what question did you have for me?"

"Peter and I found gold hidden in a filing cabinet." Mary Beth sighed at the irony of the situation. "The amount matches what was stolen from Mr. Field. We would like advice."

"Hmm." The doctor crossed his arms. "You want my opinion as mayor, I assume. I'd say you have a dishonest employee who would know when a dividend was coming."

"We suspect Mrs. Phipps. She seldom does what we ask, and we are beginning to think it's deliberate."

"Have you considered your new employee?"

"He came with such good references."

"Did you contact the people who wrote them?"

"Yes. We never heard from them."

AN HOUR LATER

Mary Beth hurried into her kitchen pantry where she kept jars of powdered herbs. She wanted to open each jar and examine the contents to make sure no one contaminated her work. However, she must work fast. Cook would be here soon to start the evening meal.

She examined the order of the bottles for tampering. Ruth had helped her organize by alphabetical order, and that appeared unaltered.

A noise behind her caught her attention, and she pivoted to see Mrs. Phipps.

"Sorry to bother you, ma'am. You have a package of herbs from the grocer, and a lady who called herself Ida is at the door. Her clothes are dirty, and she looks beaten. Do you want me to send her away?"

"No!" Mary Beth ran to the front of the house hoping her friend wasn't as bad as Mrs. Phipps made her sound.

Ida had collapsed on the floor of the foyer and was trying to pull herself into a sitting position. The bodice of her dress was torn, her swollen lips bled, and bruises covered her face and neck.

Mary Beth harbored a desire to whack Stanford with a piece of firewood. "What happened?"

"I upset him again." Tears leaked down her bloated face. "And I think I'm with child."

Mary Beth thought about the nursery, and she knew what she must do. "I have a place for you to stay. If he continues to beat you, you might lose the baby."

"If I could stay here until I get well, I would be grateful." Ida wiped away tears with the back of her hand.

"Of course. Let me give you some liniment for those bruises. I have a beautiful lavender jar you can take some home with you in, but right now I want you to rest."

"I'm so grateful, and I promise not to stay long."

Mary Beth realized she wouldn't have time to care for Ida and go through the medications before she met Peter at the bank.

Relieved, Peter sprang to his feet when Mary Beth entered his office carrying a pitcher and cups. She had promised to be here ten minutes ago, and he was on edge after Ida's husband had threatened her. Besides, he needed to consult with her on their next move. Every choice mattered when the bank's funds were so low.

"Maud made some fresh tea before I left home. I wish I had her in my employ instead of Mrs. Phipps." Mary Beth deposited the pitcher on his desk and poured him tea. "Tea makes life look and feel tolerable."

He took a large sip and praised God for refreshment. "Another family came to close their account, and we need to discuss several items."

"Dr. Smith says we need to suspect our employees and especially our newest. Did you ever receive an answer from Atlanta about his references?"

"No, and this bank isn't the one we usually deal with. I sent a telegram. In addition, I plan to interview each employee to see what they knew about Mr. Field's visit."

"I could help with that. Then we can compare notes."

"Mary Beth, I want you to rest more. Here's something else I considered. Would Matthew Grant have orchestrated Nelson's death since Nelson accused him?"

"Matthew Grant?" Mary Beth groaned. "We've known him for so many years I cannot see him acting that way."

"He can be aggressive. We've seen that recently."

"But I have news. The doctor found the source of Mr. Nelson's poison—a plant from Florida."

Peter shook his head. "Grant would not have access to something from there unless he had an accomplice."

"Who could that be? Mr. Evans?" She shrugged. "Dr. Smith wants me to check my medicine to make sure someone didn't set me up."

"Good idea." Peter sat and rubbed his temples. "In light of the problems here at the bank, I plan to stay up all night and do an audit of every account, not the partial one you do. We can't be sure how much we have until we count it."

"I shall stay with you," Mary Beth sipped some tea.

"I'd rather have you at home resting. Then you could take over for me while I sleep."

Mary Beth shook her head. "I won't be able to sleep without you. Tell me where we will start."

THE NEXT MORNING

Her stomach rumbling, Anna hurried down the street alongside Ruth. Both of them had stayed with Mrs. Nelson and her children overnight, not something planned. Anna's heart had ached when she saw the widow's tears, and she'd do anything to ease her burden. Despite the early hour, the morning was already humid. Not many stores had opened, but she hoped the café had. She wasn't sure because she had never eaten there this early. Today, however, Ruth had been talking about food since she woke, and Anna was hungry too.

"Mama, I don't see why we couldn't eat with the Nelsons."

Anna glanced over at her daughter. The girl shouldn't have to suffer for her mother's urge to ease grief. While Mrs. Nelson's pain bit deep into Anna, her baby suffered for her choice. She chose to ignore Ruth's frown to admire her growing beauty. Her shiny dark hair reminded Anna of her late husband, and Anna loved her. "The Nelsons no longer have their father, and I worry about how much food they can afford. On the other hand, I am wealthy enough to buy whatever we need. Come along. The café is just ahead, across the street."

Ruth squinted. "Are they open?"

"Someone's there." Anna sniffed the delightful fragrance of baking bread. "They are baking."

"Oh, yeah." She nodded, her eyes glowing. "That aroma. I want to eat it all."

Anna raised an eyebrow as she reached for the café door. "Remember your manners. A lady doesn't wolf down her food."

"What a delight, Mrs. Chandler!" The café owner greeted her. "I have just prepared a basket of bread and rolls for the bank. I saw your son and his wife enter as I came to work. I'm sure they'd enjoy a morning snack."

"Is there enough for us too?" Ruth spoke up. "We stayed with the grocer's family last night."

"Indeed." He handed Mrs. Chandler a large basket covered in a cloth. "I'll bring by a pitcher of fresh coffee too."

Anna sighed. Coffee was so expensive she only had one cup each morning now. "How can we thank you?"

"Take care of yourselves." He waved and stepped backward. "We need our bank."

Ruth tugged on her arm as they walked across the street to the bank. "Hurry, I'm hungry."

At the door, Anna shifted the heavy basket so she could reach her drawstring purse. She needed the bank key.

"Mama! Careful." Ruth frowned. "I'm almost faint with starvation."

The basket was slipping, but she almost had the key.

Mary Beth opened the door from the inside and lifted the parcel from her hands. "Peter and I saw you from the office."

Lines between Mary Beth's brows bothered Anna. "Is something wrong?"

"Yeah, I may die from starvation," Ruth rubbed her stomach.

"We have a few questions for Ruth."

The tone of Mary Beth's words bothered Anna, and her mothering instinct rose within her to protect her youngest child. "I'm sure I can answer anything you might need to know. Besides she's hungry."

Mary Beth frowned and motioned to Anna's daughter. "Come upstairs, Ruth."

Anna followed. If anyone questioned her daughter, she would be there.

Chapter Twenty-Three

Mary Beth entered her husband's office and deposited her mother-in-law's basket on the table by the window. Peter came to her side as she pulled out a chair for Ruth. Mrs. Chandler followed, and Mary Beth hoped she didn't create barriers because they needed answers now. "Please sit down. I want you to think carefully as I ask questions."

Ruth pulled her brows together as she sat down. "Is something wrong?"

"Poison killed the grocer." Mary Beth crossed her arms. "And many poisons come from plants."

Ruth's eyes widened.

"That child would never hurt anyone, and besides she's hungry." Anna walked toward Ruth and placed a hand on her shoulder. "Come—"

"In a minute, Mother." Peter shook his head. "This is important."

Mary Beth nodded. "Very important. Ruth, do you recall seeing any herbs missing from those we were drying?"

"No." She shrugged. "But I haven't been there for several days."

"What about the herb garden?" Mary Beth sat down and leaned toward her. "Was it intact?"

"I-I cannot remember anything different."

Mary Beth pulled a box from her pocket and opened it, revealing small red berries. "Have you ever seen these?"

"No." She gazed into Mary Beth's eyes. "Why? I want to know what happened."

Mary Beth sighed. "This is called Rosary Pea or Abrus Precatorius, and it contains the poison abrin. Dr. Smith and I found bits of this in Mr. Nelson's medication."

Ruth's face went white. "How? Who?"

"Now you've scared her." Mrs. Chandler's voice rose. "I insist you leave her alone. She hasn't even had breakfast."

"No, Mama!" Ruth turned to her mother, eyes blazing. "I helped prepare medications, and I need to be aware of dangerous herbs."

Mrs. Chandler turned to Mary Beth. "You cannot believe she did this, so why the interrogation?"

"Because I have been accused of murder, and since your daughter helps me, she might be a suspect too."

Once his family left, Peter hurried into the office across the hall and flipped through employee files for Evans's recommendation. After the bank audit turned up nothing suspicious, he moved to the next item he and Mary Beth agreed on. He found the file and a copy of the query he sent. Possibly the post office lost the reply. Today he would send a telegram requesting information.

"Excuse me, sir." Mr. Riddle entered the room. "Mr. Shaw is here waiting for you, and he seems quite happy."

Peter hoped Shaw had a large dividend waiting. "Very good. Give me a moment."

"Is there something I could help you find?" Riddle peered into the filing cabinet where Peter stood.

Peter glanced into his secretary's face and remembered his faithful work, especially during the time Peter lost his father. He explained enough of the situation for Riddle to act. "Please find the recommendation for me and write up a query letter for me to sign."

"Right away, sir."

Peter headed toward his office hoping Riddle didn't guess his concerns—yet.

SAME TIME

Accompanied by Ruth and Mrs. Chandler, Mary Beth clattered down the wooden sidewalk toward home. As she turned down Maple Street, she saw Mrs. Phipps standing on the opposite corner with a man. No. Mary Beth held her breath. Her arm was linked with Lieutenant McDonald. Unthinkable!

"Isn't that your housekeeper?" Mrs. Chandler touched Mary Beth's elbow.

Mary Beth nodded. "Indeed. I'm speeding up to catch her, but she seems unaware I caught her when she should be working."

Mrs. Chandler raised an eyebrow. "We may have learned why she doesn't get her job done."

"I never liked that man." Ruth rolled her eyes.

Mary Beth would prepare a sermon for the housekeeper, but she continued toward home rather than confront her in public.

Once inside her house, the luscious smell of baking bread met her. Cook would be working, so this wasn't the best time, to prepare medications.

Maud met her in the hallway. "I bein' so glad to see ya. That dear lady upstairs bein's sick and all. I been a worryin' all mornin'."

"Ruth, head to the kitchen and start looking through the herbs. I shall look in on Ida."

217

"Dear me. Ida? The new bride?" Mrs. Chandler frowned and shook her head. "You don't need someone contagious here because you might be with child."

"I doubt she's contagious. She shows signs of a beating, and she told me she's probably pregnant."

Mrs. Chandler grabbed Mary Beth's arm and propelled her to the stairs. "Dear woman, let's see what we can do for her. That husband of hers should be shot."

Mary Beth hoped Stanford didn't find out where Ida was staying, or he might shoot them all.

A Few Moments Later

Anna's heart galloped, and she was breathless as she reached the doctor's gabled home on Cameron Hill. Mary Beth had asked her to fetch the doctor right away, and visions of Ida's injuries propelled her to go as fast as she could without running. However, the incline seemed even steeper than ever today. How she grieved for the young girl she saw grow up. If only Anna could inflict damage on that lousy soldier-husband for his behavior.

Just as she reached the sidewalk, Stanford scowling with his hands clasped in fists, bolted out Dr. Smith's front door and marched toward the road.

Unable to catch her breath, Anna stopped and leaned against the stone entrance by the walk. She wondered if fury and exhaustion got the best of her as a wave of dizziness made her unstable.

"Anna?" Greta, the doctor's chubby wife came out to the porch. "Are you ill?"

Anna shook her head. In a moment she'd be fine.

Greta disappeared inside, and Dr. Smith ran out, grabbing Anna's elbow. "Mrs. Chandler, let me help you inside."

Anna waved him off, but she stumbled.

Dr. Smith scooped her up, carried her inside, and placed her on the sofa. "Rest for a moment and let me take a look."

"It's ... Ida ... not me." However, she did feel more comfortable.

"Hmm." The doctor's bushy eyebrows went up. Greta handed him a stethoscope, and he listened to Anna's heart. "You have a heart murmur. I want you to stay right here while I see to Ida. I assume you mean Ida Stanley?"

Anna nodded. "She's at Mary Beth's."

"I've been concerned about her." The doctor rubbed his salt and pepper beard. "You came here to see me today, understand?"

"Please ... don't tell."

Smith winked at her. "I have no idea what you mean."

The doctor left, and Anna closed her eyes, imagining ways she would like to punish Stanford. What a terrible man. Maybe he robbed the bank.

Sunday Morning

Watching, Anna stood in the church foyer facing the open double doors to the street. Bright sunshine streamed inside, and the room grew warmer as more people entered.

She needed to see Ruth but not Dr. Smith since he had advised her to keep resting today after her episode two days ago. He didn't understand her body's resilience. Besides, she had several situations to manage—for everyone's benefit.

Ruth had stayed overnight at Peter's home. She was assisting Mary Beth to review and update her supply of medications for Newsome Hospital and Dr Smith. Anna approved of both and enjoyed thinking she took part in such ventures by lending her daughter to Mary Beth. However, her daughter still needed a mother since she was prone to slouching or bouncing rather than walking.

At last Anna caught sight of Peter and Mary Beth coming up to the church steps. Mary Beth turned to speak to Mrs. Teague who looked away with a scowl. Peter waved at Mr. Cravens who turned as if he did not see. Dreadful. This rudeness stemmed from Peter's change in bank policy allowing loans to be paid in paper money. If only she could convince him to change his policy back to his father's, this impossible situation would resolve. They must come to realize the value of her experience.

Mary Beth met her eyes and smiled. How thin and tired she appeared. Anna often worried about her because she worked too hard. If Mary Beth were with child, Anna would insist she rest more. Perhaps sending Maud back would help.

Ruth appeared from behind Mary Beth and ran to her. "How was your evening, honey?"

"We got through all the medicines." Ruth beamed.

"Very good." Anna patted her head. "I think you should stay a few days longer."

"Why?" Ruth flipped her long hair over her shoulder and wrinkled her brow.

"You are good medicine for anyone." Peter and Mary Beth must understand Anna wanted to help them, cooperate. They needed what she had to offer.

Later That Evening
Chandler Library

Peter heard heavy footsteps coming down the hall toward his office, which must mean Dr. Smith had completed his work. He'd called him to check on Ida's condition and examine Mary Beth. Peter leaned forward in his heavy leather chair to put his book on the desk. He'd tried to read, but the words faded into the paper because he was too worried about his wife.

The doctor knocked on the open door and walked in carrying his black bag. Peter noted Smith had no rigidity to his thin face. Maybe he could offer good news.

Peter stood. "What can you tell me?"

"Mrs. Stanford has improved significantly with rest and medication. She has experienced a lot of trauma and needs several weeks to fully recover. I applaud your kindness offering her a place to stay."

Peter crossed his arms. "We put ourselves at risk to have her here, but we could do nothing less."

"Further beatings could harm the baby or take its life." Smith cleared his throat. "Mrs. Stanford must decide what to do about her husband. She can leave or ask the city to charge him; however, given the threat of invasion the military won't be inclined to jail him."

Peter would allow her to stay as long as she required a safe place to live, but he refused to report Stanford for assault. He didn't want to clash with the military—his other complaints had not produced change. "What about Mary Beth? After church tonight, we discussed the bank situation, and I explained our primitive investigations have given us nothing. She cried. I believe she's weary from all the stress and work, but I wanted your opinion."

"I'm leaving a tonic for her." Smith reached into his bag and pulled out a bottle. "Have her take this twice a day."

"You explained that to her?"

"I did." He nodded. "I know you both are experiencing a lot of stress with bank issues. Make sure she sleeps, and we will pray for the best."

Peter took a deep breath. "But will she conceive?"

"I don't know." The doctor shrugged. "In his wisdom, God made our bodies complex, and even self-healing. I attempt to use the limited tools I have to save lives and improve them. God must do the rest."

Mary Beth would be devastated if she could not have a child.

Chapter Twenty-Four

THE NEXT MORNING

Mary Beth woke almost the moment Peter rose, but she kept her eyes closed, hoping she'd go back to sleep. She listened as he poured water into the basin to shave and ran his razor across his face. Her stomach growled, and she realized she couldn't sleep more, and she had plenty to do. Her energy had returned. Maybe the tonic worked?

The bank needed income. She should visit the sheriff's house and prepare it for renting, and Ellen McCallie would require medications. Once she got to the bank, she must interview employees to see if anyone knew when dividends were due to arrive. However, before all that, she must check on Ida.

Now that her mind buzzed with a myriad of thoughts, she'd best rise and start her chores. Throwing back the cover, she sat up and rubbed her eyes.

"I was trying not to wake you." Peter crossed the room and kissed her forehead. "Why not take a nap, and I'll ask Maud to bring up breakfast?"

"I think Maud left last night." Mary Beth giggled at the thought of asking Mrs. Phipps to bring up a tray. She'd think it beneath her.

"What was the joke?"

"The difference between Maud and Mrs. Phipps." Mary Beth hurried around the room dressing so she could accompany Peter to the bank. "I suggest we have breakfast together. At least Cook does her job."

As Peter and Mary Beth headed down the stairs to the kitchen, Mary Beth spotted Ida stumbling toward the front door. "Ida, where are you going?"

Ida turned, displaying the fading bruises on her face. "I cannot continue to burden you. I have an aunt who lives nearby, and I thought I would stay with her."

"You are hardly well." Mary Beth rushed to her side. "I doubt you've even had breakfast. You can't leave without your medicine either."

Peter came up behind Mary Beth. "I agree with my wife, Mrs. Stanford. Stay here while you recover, and we will see that you get to your aunt's in due time."

"I cannot." Ida wrung her hands. "I've already been too much trouble. If my husband finds me here, all of us may die. I cannot have that on my conscience."

Mary Beth put an arm around Ida and guided her to the kitchen. "I insist you have breakfast, and then I will go with you."

Peter nodded. "I shall accompany you also. You might need protection, and the bank can wait."

Peter fingered the loaded gun in his pocket and kept his gaze roving the streets as he accompanied his wife and her friend into town. He had devised a plan to protect the women should they meet Ida's husband. His heart pounded, and he whispered a prayer. Mrs. Cole passed them, and Mr. and Mrs. Teague crossed the street before they reached him. If only he could convince Chattanooga citizens he wasn't dangerous. "We are going by the bank so I can sign some papers this morning," Peter said.

"I am still inconveniencing you," Ida said. "Let me go alone. You'll be safer."

"Nonsense." Mary Beth said. "We enjoy having you with us."

"I endanger your lives."

Peter kept his eyes roving as they neared the bank. He looked forward to getting out of the public and devising a plan to move Ida in secret.

As he stepped into the bank, Mr. Riddle hurried to him. "Mr. Chandler. We are awaiting your signature."

He left the ladies to follow his secretary.

Mary Beth intended to follow Peter, but she looked back, and Ida wasn't behind her. "Ida? Ida?"

Mr. Grant stood at the teller window. "A soldier took her outside."

Mary Beth went to the bottom the stairs and called up to Peter before heading back outside where she came face to face with Stanford. He had his wife's arm twisted behind her. Ida was weeping.

"Mrs. Chandler! What a pleasure to see you here."

Mary Beth's heart lurched. "You are hurting your wife."

He came toward Mary Beth with a scowl and slapped her face.

She recoiled, almost falling backward from the blow. Her face burned, and she tasted blood. "What was that for?"

"Stop lying, woman. How many times do I have to tell you to stay away from my wife?"

"Leave her alone." Ida had pulled away and started running. "You want me, not her."

Stanford caught her, punched her in the face and escorted her away.

Mary Beth almost lost her breakfast.

PETER'S OFFICE AT THE BANK

Peter finished signing papers and glanced up from his desk as Mary Beth stumbled in. He was horrified by his wife's disheveled condition. Her cheek was swollen, and a trickle of blood ran from her mouth. "What happened to you?"

She sank into the chair before his desk and covered her face. "Stanford found us, and he was angry I had assisted his wife."

"What? Here at the bank? Where?" He hopped to his feet and pulled out his rifle.

"Yes." Mary Beth leaned back in the wing chair and closed her eyes. "He caught her as she entered the bank. Now he knows she was with me."

"Unbelievable!" He stepped to the door. "Mr. Riddle send for Dr. Smith. Now!"

Peter was angry with himself. He should not have gone to the bank first before getting Mary Beth's friend to safety.

His wife was probably in shock, and he was at fault.

AN HOUR LATER
CHANDLER BEDROOM

Sitting on the edge of her bed, Mary Beth's heart kept a lively rhythm as Dr. Smith prodded her body and listened to her chest. Peter paced, and Jane hovered nearby. Her limbs were heavy with fatigue, but at the same time she longed to see Stanford behind bars. What a brute!

"Doctor, what do you think?" Peter moved toward the bed, placing a hand on her shoulder.

"She took quite a blow, and I want her to rest at least twenty-four hours." His eyes met hers. "Do you understand, Mary Beth?"

"Yes." How could she spare the time? So much depended on her.

"I am lodging another complaint against Stanford." Peter squeezed her shoulder. "As mayor, can you see that through?"

"I shall urge the military to deal with him, but they are not always cooperative." Dr. Smith pulled out ointment and placed it by the bed. "Put this on your face three times a day. It will sooth that irritation, and I will visit tomorrow. I want you here, in bed."

Mary Beth nodded. She reclined on the bed, and Jane adjusted the covers. Right now Mary Beth wanted to sleep for days and forget all her troubles.

Dr. Smith left the room, and Jane followed him.

"Dearest, please do as the doctor asked."

"I shall. However, Peter, let me do something with my mind. I'll even stay in bed. With two murders, I believe there's a plot against the bank. See if one of our employees knows when dividends come in."

"I already talked to Evans and Grant, but they both claimed ignorance." Peter leaned over and kissed her forehead. "Devise plans to find information from the bedroom."

"I do have an idea about the sheriff's house."

"Please don't plan on going there." Peter shook his head. "You know who lives in the basement."

"You can do this while I stay right here." Mary Beth patted the sheets. "Get Grant to hire some men to clean it up, so we can rent it. Ask them to bring anything renters can't use to the bank for us to dispose of. We could rent to military staff since the house would be nicer than their barracks."

"Excellent idea." Peter nodded. "I'll get that process started as soon as I get to the bank. Maybe being confined will give you more great ideas."

Somehow, Mary Beth would devise a way to talk to Nelson's family about his medicine.

Chapter Twenty-Five

Two Days Later

Mary Beth relaxed at the breakfast table, inhaling the aroma of the fresh bacon Mr. Weston sent with wishes for her recovery. The price of bacon made it a rare treat. How pleasant to return to a normal routine and eat in the dining room with her husband. Stanford's brutal attack had caused spasms in her neck and shoulders, and she had rested as ordered. While enjoying the breeze coming through the open window, she took a sip of tea. "I've been thinking it's peculiar that Stanford waited for us at the bank. He doesn't have an account there. Does he?"

"That's easy to establish," Peter said. "And I think we should."

"Thank you." Mary Beth sliced a bit of bacon. "Could he have befriended Ida because she was my friend?"

"To learn more about the bank?" Peter sighed. "I suppose that's possible but hard to prove."

"If only I could ask Ida, but I can't go near her now."

"Please don't. I'm beginning to wonder if Nelson's death was another attack on Grant's character rather than yours." Peter took his last bite of biscuit.

Mary Beth massaged the soreness in her neck. "Why?"

"Think about it. If Nelson's daughter hadn't heard you mumbling about her father, no one would have suspected you. And Nelson was the one who accused Grant of killing the colonel."

"True." Mary Beth savored another slice of bacon. "But what about the tainted medicine. That does appear to implicate me because the jars I use are the same."

"But the label was printed, and you have no typewriter."

"That's true also." Mary Beth nodded.

"Finding the poison testifies to your cleverness. Who wouldn't expect a grocer to have exotic items in his home? Merchants offer him all sorts of items to sell. Didn't you say his symptoms were similar to his alcoholism?"

"Yes. Alcohol can upset the digestive system, so in his case, it did seem the same." Mary Beth leaned back in her chair. "I'm feeling well enough today to ask some questions of the family and servants. Maybe I will find something useful."

Maud came to the door. "Reverend McCallie is here to see Mr. Chandler."

Peter looked toward the door. "Where is Mrs. Phipps?"

Maud groaned and shook her head. "I wished I'm a never. She be a courtin' that Lieutenant feller in the backyard. I be tellin' her she better watch herself cause you ain't be toleratin' such."

"She needs you to fill in for her, Maud." Peter looked at Mary Beth. "I don't think she can do any job well. We might need to fire her."

Mary Beth nodded. "Yes. But I wanted to give her a chance especially since people were talking about us."

"You are so sensitive, but you cannot always do what others think you should." Peter turned toward Maud. "Send in the pastor."

Reverend McCallie entered and clapped his large hand on Peter's shoulder. "Good morning. It's good to see you both."

"We'd be pleased for you to join us for breakfast or at least for tea." Mary Beth reached for the bell.

The lanky pastor patted his stomach. "Ellen fed me well this morning, but I would love some tea."

"I invited you to come and pray with us because we find ourselves in a dilemma due to the events surrounding our bank. Church members appear to be shunning us, as if we are responsible for the murders." Peter sighed. "I guess we need to ask for guidance too."

McCallie's long face crinkled. "Your mother reminds me of the situation every week, and of course, I am saddened."

"Oh, does she?" Peter shook his head.

"She's attempting to be helpful." Mary Beth patted Peter's hand.

McCallie nodded. "However, I think you should keep attending services, and I will ask my wife to have you for dinner one evening."

Mary Beth placed a hand on her throat. "Oh, but Ellen has those soldiers to care for, and I have not been able to assist her in a long time. Won't this add to her burden?"

"We have visitors almost every night, and I daresay you'd come offering help." McCallie chuckled. "Let me speak with her."

"You are kind." Mary Beth smiled.

"No. I am called to serve just like the rest of us. Remember I told you about reflecting God's love. Once we know his grace, that's what he calls us to do. But let's pray. Oh, Heavenly Father, I pray for the Chandler family. Uproot the evil that threatens to destroy their business, and I pray the evil men will be caught in their own snare."

His words grabbed her attention. Maybe more than one man plotted against the bank.

━━⚬ঞৎৡঌ⚬━━

The Next Day

Mary Beth dropped off medications at the McCallie's home and changed bandages for two soldiers, and she arrived at the grocer about eleven. As soon as she entered, she realized her investigation would take longer than she'd planned.

On the right, a crowd stood in line at the register where Mrs. Nelson, who had dark circles under her eyes, waited on a customer. Lily sat on the floor across the counter, hugging a doll. A tradesman, looking bored, stood nearby with a crate.

What better time and place to reflect gold? Mary Beth leaned over the counter. "Mrs. Nelson, may I run the register while you see to this gentleman?"

Mrs. Nelson's face beamed. "Oh, yes. Thank you."

Mary Beth stepped behind the counter for the next lady waiting in line. "I will add up your purchases, ma'am. We want Mrs. Nelson to put away her supplies because those vendors who bring goods to us are quite important."

The lady frowned. "Some are odd, if you ask me."

"I thought he was mean," Lily shifted her doll and left the room with her chin raised.

Mary Beth wished she could find out what Lily meant, but she might not be the best witness. She stopped adding up the prices to listen carefully. "Did you see someone unusual here?"

"I'll say." She lowered her voice to a whisper. "And he made such ridiculous promises that would make a clever person suspicious."

"Do you recall what those promises might be?" Mary Beth matched the lady's conspiratorial tone, hoping she might learn something.

"Saying such things with a child present. Humph! A proper lady would never discuss such, so if you'll just tell me how much I owe, I shall be on my way."

"Yes, ma'am." Mary Beth told her what she owed with pleasure. She thought she'd found a clue. She waited on the other customers and then wandered into the storage room where Mrs. Nelson was flipping through records.

"Mary Beth." Mrs. Nelson looked up from her paperwork. "I appreciate what you did. I'm training my oldest daughter, Molly, to help me, but she's not feeling well. Her monthly is so unpleasant. Is there anything I can do for you?"

"I would like to question your cook about what your husband ate that day.

"Josey is upstairs now. Why not go and talk to her?"

"I shall. First, I have another request. I'm wondering where your husband got some medication Dr. Smith found in his room. Do you have records of vendor deliveries?"

"I do. However, I wasn't here that afternoon. I am not sure if that man brought merchandise or just samples. We typically like to try new products before carrying them." She pulled out a book and flipped pages. "Here. My husband took a sample, but the name is terribly hard to read."

Mary Beth bent over the book and tried her best to decipher the name, but all she could see was the date, which Nelson wrote. "I cannot read it either."

"Molly was assisting that day and has a good memory. Mine worsens every day, so perhaps you can return when she feels better." Mrs. Nelson smiled and extended her hand.

Mary Beth took her hand in both of hers. "I am so sorry for your loss and for the hardship you face without your husband. I shall be delighted to come again and bring you lunch."

A few tears ran down Mrs. Nelson's cheek as she nodded.

Mary Beth prayed God would help her find the culprit who took Mr. Nelson's life.

Mary Beth made her way up the narrow steps above the grocer to the kitchen. As she climbed, she met the aroma of baking, and the temperature grew warmer. In the kitchen, a slender lady with her hair in a bun threw coals into the stove on the left of the room. "Josey?"

"Yes'm." She stood and turned, wiping her hands on her smudged apron. "What can I do fer ya?"

"I am Mrs. Chandler. I serve as apothecary for the hospital. Dr. Smith and I are trying to unearth the cause of Mr. Nelson's death. Can you tell me what he ate that day?"

She sniffed and shook her head. "Near as nothin'. I made fried chicken the night before, and he was sure jolly while he wolfed it down."

"And the next morning?"

"He woke queasy, or at least he be sayin' that." She crossed her arms and pulled a frown. "Of all the moanin' and groanin' as the day wore on. I tells Mrs. Nelson, and she says offer him broth. When he were a drinkin' that was soothin'."

"Did it help?"

"No." Josey shook her head. "I thought maybe he had some whiskey in his room because he was very tipsy. About midafternoon he came a roarin' in here saying he be lookin' for his wife."

"Shortly after that we found him in the storage room. Is that right?"

"Yes'm. I think so."

Mary Beth thanked her and hurried back to the storage room. She located the ledger Mrs. Nelson had shown her and checked the date. The stranger delivered the poison the day before Nelson died. Whoever brought the poison knew Nelson was an alcoholic who was often depressed. Nelson probably took a dose with glee, which would explain Josey's description of his mood.

Who added the poison and why?

Chapter Twenty-Six

C&R Bank
Earlier That Day

Anna had not slept the night before and woke with a headache, but she had no one to call. She always hated being alone in the house. Maud and her husband were staying with Peter while Maud trained Mrs. Phipps. Ruth had spent the night with friends from church. In addition, Grant had not invited her out for the last couple of days, and Anna worried he had misunderstood something she said. Worst of all, Peter had not abandoned his new bank policies. Unacceptable.

Today, she would gain control of her life, and she would start by talking to her son. This time her wording would change also.

She dressed in shades of blue, including a hat decorated with a huge flower, and had breakfast at City Café. Once she entered the bank, she found her son in the vault counting and recording cash. He didn't look up when she entered, but she launched her speech anyhow. "Peter, since you have not returned to your father's bank procedures, I must remove another large sum of money."

Peter looked up, his eyes blazing. "Mama, as I told you before, I structured the new policy for Colonel Bennet.

Since no one else qualifies, I shall not grant any such loans again. So, I haven't changed anything. I'm still on the gold standard."

"But your father—"

"Excuse me, sir." Mr. Riddle, the pencil sitting on his ear, walked in holding a telegram and frowning. "You heard from the bank in Atlanta where Evans claimed he worked."

Peter snatched the telegram from Mr. Riddle and blanched as he read.

No. Anna and her late husband founded the bank together. Was this the end? Pain slashed through her stomach. "What does it say?"

Peter handed it to her.

"Never employed Evans," Anna read. Her son should have checked references sooner, and this proved he needed her guidance. "This is terrible. He could be the murderer."

"Evans said he worked at that bank." Peter turned to Riddle. "I want to speak to him. Now."

Riddle said, "Evans isn't here today."

Anna gasped. She could envision him stealing money and leaving town. If Andrew were alive, he would be livid.

Peter's lips tightened. "Did he send a message?"

Riddle shook his head. "He has never missed work and never been sick in the ten months he has worked for us."

Peter ran a hand along his neck. "I must speak to Mary Beth. Has she arrived?"

Riddle nodded. "I shall fetch her."

Anna knew Weston had offered to give Peter banking advice. She hoped her son would turn to him in this crisis.

Mary Beth arrived as Peter was climbing the stairs to his office. She had been thinking about reflecting gold, and the Lord brought to mind the fun times they'd shared together, in spite of all the banking chaos they had endured. She thanked God for Peter as well as God's provision to solve those mysteries they'd lived through. However, she believed she should let Peter know how much she appreciated him. "I don't think we've ever climbed these stairs together."

"Uh, no." Peter shook his head. "I remember the time I chased you up here so you couldn't investigate my office without me."

"I said walking up together." She giggled. "Chasing doesn't count."

"Oh, yes. It counts. I recall tickling you until you begged me to stop. That was more fun than walking together."

They'd reached the landing, and he waved her inside.

"I'm glad you're my husband, Peter. I don't tell you that enough." She turned to look at him. "And I found useful information at the grocers."

"Let's discuss that later." He closed the door and engulfed her in a passionate kiss.

When he let her go, she stepped back and grinned. "You learned something?"

He nodded and handed her the telegram. She sank into the chair in front of his desk as she read about Evans. "What a nightmare."

"Evans did not come to work today, but in light of this news, I fired him. Ask Mr. Riddle to send a letter to his home with that information. I want you to clean out his desk and change the locks."

"What are you going to do?"

"I shall get the facts, and to do that, I shall take the night train to Atlanta. The bank may have further information about him." He closed a ledger and straightened his desk.

"Atlanta? I don't feel comfortable with you gone." She placed a hand on her chest.

"I will not be gone long, honey." He came close and caressed her cheek.

Under normal conditions, she carried out the investigations, but Peter had said she needed to do more thinking than working. "Does the bank have enough gold to stay open?"

He nodded. "We received gold from an investment I made with Mr. Shaw, so the bank will be fine for couple of days unless Mother pulls out more cash. I am going home to pack."

Her mind raced with possibilities. "Do you think he could have orchestrated these murders?"

"Once I talk to the bank, I should have a better idea about his character."

TEN MINUTES LATER

Mary Beth ambled downstairs and turned right at the counter to enter Evan's office. She found his desk uncluttered. Several handkerchiefs sat in the top drawer, along with a cheap comb. He had no pictures or letters, and the writing materials belonged to the bank.

She stopped to gaze at the simple desk, recalling it happened to be the same desk Mr. Gustav Sadler used for years. How she adored him as a child. He had carried candies in his pocket for her. However, he'd died last year after she discovered he had embezzled the bank's money. How ironic that two dishonest people worked here. Evans too had deceived her. He appeared to care about the bank. Yet he betrayed her trust.

Trust. A five-letter word that held such importance.

Mr. Riddle walked up carrying a crate. "Mr. Chandler said to bring you this for Mr. Evans's things."

Mary Beth shook her head. "He left little here. Something smaller would work. Maybe he knew we would find out he lied."

"Which reminds me, Mr. Grant had the sheriff's house cleaned out. We have a crate with materials for you to sort through in the storage room. I shall look for a small basket for Mr. Evans." Riddle walked away.

Mary Beth opened the last drawer on the left and found a pile of receipts from C&R bank. They belonged in the cash drawer, but she dug back further and found gold.

Mr. Grant walked up. "I have the morning deposit for the vault. Shall I take it upstairs to your husband?"

Hot all over, Mary Beth wanted to scream at Evans. She paused and took a breath, "I shall open the vault. Peter has left for Atlanta."

Grant's eyes widened. "When?"

"He wants to visit that bank Evans supposedly worked for."

"I assume this relates to the telegram?"

"Yes. Emptying his desk, I found a pile of receipts from C&R Bank and gold." She grabbed a pencil and added up the amounts shown on the receipts. Then she counted the money. "The amount matches. Twenty dollars in receipts and twenty in gold. When customers brought in money, he was stealing it. If we didn't have a receipt, we wouldn't find it missing."

"That would work until a customer complained." Shaking his head Grant examined a receipt. "That total would buy a couple suits."

"Yes. Or a typewriter." Mary Beth gathered the receipts and handed them to Grant. "Credit these to the proper accounts. I hope this represents all the money he took. We must be able to trust our records or else we fail completely."

As she walked to the vault, she considered how much Evans knew. He was acquainted with security procedures, the bank routine, when dividends came, how the offices were laid out, when customers paid their bills, which citizens had money, and which people owed money. Evans could steal or blackmail more easily, threatening the safety of the money people entrusted to them. C&R Bank needed its customers, and many were already losing faith.

If Mary Beth could not trust their banking procedures, how would Chattanoogans trust them?

THAT EVENING

The sun was low in the sky and the temperature still warm as Mary Beth stood on the porch waving. Peter returned her wave and walked through the gate of their picket fence down the street carrying his briefcase and trunk. The house felt empty already, and she realized how much she appreciated him and his kindness. Lately, he had petitioned the military several times on her behalf. She would pray for his safety, while she tried not to worry.

So much had happened, she could not quite take everything in. Of course, she hated that an evil man had targeted Nelson with poison, and someone had taken the colonel's life. How could Ida's husband beat her until she bled and not feel terrible about himself? Evans's actions seemed so personal. How could he act like a friend? The event brought back all the betrayal Sadler created even though that happened over a year ago. Evans had lied to them and pretended honesty while taking their livelihood. She and Peter had increased bank security, but apparently, they still needed more.

In Peter's absence, she must decide what to do. Right now, she wanted to learn about the circumstances around Mr. Nelson's death. If she found the guilty party, she could remove suspicion from the bank. She needed time to do that. Perhaps Mrs. Chandler could fill the empty place at the teller window. She came to the bank daily anyhow. Ruth could mix medicines with little supervision, freeing up Mary Beth's time.

Another thought came to mind. If Mrs. Chandler would work at the teller window, Mary Beth could ask Grant to talk to her about leaving her money. That would solve another problem.

After a quiet prayer for guidance, Mary Beth also felt she should initiate a conversation with her mother-in-law. With grace.

She hoped she could sleep.

EARLY THE NEXT MORNING

Mary Beth woke as sunshine seeped through the curtains, kissing her bedroom with light. She turned to see if her husband was awake. Smooth sheets and his empty pillow sent a pang through her body. How she missed him. This morning she wanted his arms around her to reassure her they'd overcome the obstacles, but she must rely on God for that. She closed her eyes, picturing him sleeping in a hotel in Atlanta, and she whispered a prayer for his safety and success.

Noises came from downstairs, which probably meant Cook had come in to prepare breakfast. She rose and dressed in pale pink gingham, taking extra care with her hair to brighten her mood. Stomach growling, she bustled downstairs. While eating, she would start a list of chores to finish in Peter's absence.

Once downstairs, Mary Beth strode toward the noise, which came from the kitchen. She entered the room and gasped. Lieutenant McDonald held Mrs. Phipps in a passionate embrace. "Excuse me!"

The couple continued.

Mary Beth cleared her throat. "Mrs. Phipps, I do not recall assigning this chore."

Mrs. Phipps pulled away, breathing hard. Her bodice was partly unfastened in front, and her dress wrinkled.

McDonald threw his head back and guffawed. His coat wasn't buttoned, and his shirt was untucked.

The sight turned her stomach. Such behavior should not happen in her home. How she hated the numerous problems men created. Certain men rated exemptions, like her husband and Dr. Smith, but they were rare. She stiffened her hand to slap him but managed to stop herself. "McDonald, you may leave now."

"We were only saying goodbye," he said. His green eyes reminded Mary Beth of a scolded dog. "And we promise to stay outside next time."

"Leave now." Mary Beth should have brought Peter's gun downstairs in case the soldier refused. "And you, Mrs. Phipps should go with him."

Mrs. Phipps gasped and giggled. "What? I get a day off?"

"You are fired." Mary Beth looked right into her eyes.

"Fired?" She stepped back and covered her mouth. "Why?"

"For kissing?" Lieutenant McDonald puffed out his chest. "I cannot believe this."

"I am addressing Mrs. Phipps." Mary Beth pointed toward the door. "You should be gone."

He shuffled toward the door. "What an impossible employer you must be."

Once he left, Mary Beth turned to Mrs. Phipps who was trying to repair her disheveled bun. "You have ten minutes to take anything that belongs to you."

"But—"

"Go."

"Why?" Mrs. Phipps sounded like a child.

Mary Beth could think of plenty of reasons, but all of them wanted to rush past her lips at the same time. Mrs. Phipps continued to need guidance from Maud much longer than she should. And despite the new brown paper Mary Beth placed in the pantry, the painting Mrs. Chandler wanted still hung in the hallway. "I have caught you twice with the lieutenant when you were supposed to be working."

"Ma'am? The lieutenant has only been here for a moment, and he was about to leave."

"Please be excusin' me, ma'am." Cook entered behind Mary Beth. "but I be overhearin' this. I can be a helpin' this lady out. You be comin' with me now."

Mary Beth covered her mouth to hold in laughter until Mrs. Phipps was outside. What a relief. Now she must have the locksmith rekey the locks in case either one of the lovers decided to take revenge.

Chapter Twenty-Seven

An Hour Later

After a meager breakfast of tea and toast, Anna stepped out of the dining room and spotted Maud in the back hallway to her left, donning her hat. Several days had passed since she had interacted with her housekeeper, since her husband, Billy, kept up the chores. Yesterday, Anna had noticed he appeared fatigued. "Maud, where are you going?

The black lady stopped and turned. "Oh, yes'm. I be a goin' to Mrs. Mary Beth's to be helpin' the new girl to be knowin' what to do."

Anna recoiled. Assisting at the bank, making Ruth several new dresses, and preparing for another church social had occupied her time. "Mrs. Phipps cannot manage alone yet?"

A knock sounded on the front door.

"I shall be a gettin' that Ma'am."

Anna followed Maud to the door wondering who might call right after breakfast.

"Good mornin,' ma'am, I just be a tellin' Mrs. Chandler I was goin' to yours home. Please come in."

Mary Beth walked in carrying freshly cut roses in a vase. She appeared rested, and the pink dress she wore accented the color of her eyes. She extended the flowers to Anna. "These are for you."

"How kind. And they are lovely." Anna had always thought Mary Beth a beauty, and even more so today. She caught a whiff of the flowers and felt transported to heaven. "What brings you here so early?"

"I thought I'd best update you on several situations." She smiled. "May I come in?"

Anna was thrilled Mary Beth trusted her with her concerns. Maybe she came to announce she was with child. "Of course. Let's go to the sitting room. Would you care for tea?"

"No, thanks. I've just eaten. We are still finishing the bacon Weston sent."

Anna led her daughter-in-law to the sitting room on the left and guided her to the blue brocade sofa. Anna deposited the roses on an occasional table and seated herself in a matching wing chair across from Mary Beth, the best place for giving advice. "Isn't Weston marvelous? Especially in tough times."

"Indeed." Mary Bath adjusted her skirt and sat with perfect posture. "We are grateful."

"I know he has offered Peter advice and even offered to buy into the bank," Anna said.

Mary Beth lowered her brows. "I wasn't aware of that, but he has been kind."

"How can I help you?" Anna felt quite generous and ready to offer anything to help her son's wife.

"I thought I'd best tell you I fired Mrs. Phipps." She raised an eyebrow. "On several occasions, I caught her with Lieutenant McDonald when she should have been working. She never did wrap up that painting for you, and I heartily apologize we've had it so long."

"Never mind, dear child. Maud will see to that, but oh my, what a terrible man. I daresay Mrs. Phipps will get herself into trouble." Anna shook her head and sighed.

"I have never liked him. Too artful by half."

What good sense her daughter-in-law had. At one time, Anna thought Mary Beth might be in love with the lieutenant, but she and Peter made the perfect couple. "Would you like my advice on replacing her?"

"I have some ideas, but I wanted to ask to use Maud another week ... while I search, if you don't mind. Please."

Anna nodded. How sweet of Mary Beth to request rather than demand. "That sounds reasonable."

Mary Beth scooted forward. "And I really could use Ruth a couple days a week to mix medications."

"Of course. I don't think there's a problem."

"Except that you had her working at the bank. Of course, you have the right to give her instructions, but I would like to coordinate more so I know when I can have her assistance."

Anna massaged the sudden ache in her temples. "I did send her to the bank, yes. That's true. After Mrs. Phipps left. What a quandary that lady has caused. But if you need Ruth for medications—"

"I do." Mary Beth stood. "Peter went to Atlanta to unravel the situation with Evans, so I must stay close by to sign papers. And I wondered, do you know anything about Stanford, the man Ida married?"

"No." She shook her head. "Why?"

"I thought it odd that he met us at the bank while Ida was staying at my house. I wonder if he has designs on the bank. Could you, perhaps, ask a few questions?"

Anna was delighted to be useful, especially to her husband's bank. "I can. What else?"

"Do you realize Peter longs to please you? He set up things with Bennet so he would leave bank policies intact except for that one exception."

Anna stood and embraced her daughter-in-law.

LATER THAT MORNING
C&R BANK BEFORE OPENING

Mary Beth paused outside Grant's office to consider her exact words. This morning she had dealt with her mother-in-law's interference with as much kindness as she could—reflecting gold. Now she wanted to ask if Grant could help.

"Good morning, ma'am." Grant appeared in the doorway. "I was headed for the teller window. Did you need me?"

"Indeed." She looked toward the front door but didn't spot her mother-in-law. "I prefer not to be overheard."

"Of course!" Grant stepped aside so she could come in.

She chose to speak softly rather than close the door. "My mother-in-law has threatened to withdraw more of her gold from the bank."

Grant groaned. "She has not informed me, but I hope she does not."

"That could create unpleasantness, because if our gold reserves drop too low, I may have to close the bank while Peter is gone. I spoke to her at home early this morning and communicated Peter didn't intend any disrespect to her. I sense she responded. If the topic comes up between you, would you reinforce that Peter had to deal with a difficult situation?"

Grant let out a heavy sigh. "I suppose I could try, but I doubt my influence."

Mary Beth eased out the door. "I understand—"

"Mrs. Chandler." Mr. Riddle waved and hurried toward her. "Evans has disappeared from his boarding house. Since your husband indicated he wanted to file charges, I sent a message to Henderson."

"Excellent." Mary Beth walked toward the secretary. "Are there any appointments today?"

Riddle shook his head. "Not until this afternoon. However, the locksmith is here, and he reported someone tampered with the lock on the vault."

"What?" Mary Beth clenched her teeth. Surely this was Evans at work again. If only the government scourged criminals like they did years ago. Evans deserved a beating. "Stealing from customers at the teller windows must not have satisfied Evans. I want that man in jail."

Riddle nodded. "Perhaps Henderson can locate him."

Mary Beth stomped her way upstairs to Peter's office. The vault door cost the bank a large sum, and they had little to spare for repairs. Most citizens thought of them as wealthy, but they had no idea how close they came to insolvency.

Peter, armed with his briefcase, arrived at the Atlanta bank, hoping to discover more about Evans. He had expected the bank to be large, but the brick building and embellished entry impressed him. He scanned the room looking for the two officials who had agreed to meet him in the lobby. Four teller windows faced him, and several people waited in line at each one.

A young man wearing a pin-stripe suit approached. "Good morning, sir, are you Mr. Chandler?"

"I am."

"Very good. The vice president will speak with you in the conference room. Follow me."

Peter followed him to a room at the rear of the bank and sat down at a long table.

A chubby gray-haired gentleman wearing a dark suit entered. "Mr. Chandler, I am Mr. Simpson and serve as bank vice president. Share your concerns."

Peter pulled a long document from his briefcase. "A man calling himself Mr. Evans gave me this recommendation using your bank's name and signatures of those he claimed worked here. What do you know of him?"

"Indeed." A wrinkle formed on Simpson's brow as he studied the material. "I am unfamiliar with several names. Excuse me."

Peter's heart rate accelerated as Simpson returned with two distinguished-looking men. A balding man with a goatee entered first, and a shorter one came next. "Sorry for the delay. Let me introduce the bank manager, Mr. Fox, and comptroller, Mr. Beasley."

Peter rose and shook hands with both. "I appreciate your time. We sent a letter when Evans first applied to work for us, and we never heard back."

Mr. Fox, the balding man stepped forward, "We cannot vouch for this man's identity and cannot be held accountable for any unlawful actions he may have committed."

"You misunderstand me, sir." Peter kept his tone friendly so the bank employees would not feel threatened. "I am here merely to gain information. When I received this, I mailed the bank asking for your confirmation. I received no reply."

Beasley, the shorter man, frowned and shook his head. "I am sure I answered. I always do, but mail gets lost these days."

"So, of course, we cannot help you." The manager crossed his arms. "I trust we have settled this satisfactorily."

Peter worried he would be dismissed with nothing more. "I hoped you might have some information about him."

"But without identification," Fox raised one eyebrow. "how could we—"

"I daresay we can assist more than this," Beasley said.

"Not if we never hired him," Fox said.

"What did this man look like?" Beasley asked.

"He's about five feet, sandy blond hair with brown eyes, and a scar on his chin." Peter ran a finger over the left side of his chin to demonstrate the placement of the scar.

"Except for the scar, that sounds like Charles Dixon," Beasley said, pursing his lips. "Dixon worked here for three months, which is our probationary period for new employees."

"I shall find that employee file," Simpson said, as he left the room.

"This man called Dixon may or may not have forged signatures," Fox said. "I fear, Mr. Chandler we have given you all we have."

Beasley held up a finger. "Dixon could be the very man. He was not a good sort. If I recall correctly, he was married with children, but he was deeply in debt from gambling. We hired him after a large acquisition, which added extra work for the bookkeepers. However, he often arrived late for work, so we did not keep him on."

Fox shook his head. "We have still not established Evans is Charles Dixon."

"I am grateful for any information you find," Peter said.

Simpson entered the room with a file in his hand. "I have Dixon's file. Inside I found the date hired, a list of days tardy, and the date his employment was terminated."

"We need an address," Beasley said.

"I see one, but someone marked it out," Simpson said.

"We have done enough speculation gentlemen, so I bid you good morning, sir." Fox said and left.

Beasley hung back, and after the manager left, he turned to Peter, "I would be so grateful if you would forward me Evans's current address."

Peter relaxed and his heart rate slowed. "I will. I cannot express how grateful I am to you for taking my side in this situation."

Chapter Twenty-Eight

Mary Beth put aside last month's general ledger and rose to find the next. She had been editing Evans's work since he had broken their trust. A year ago, she had discovered discrepancies in another employee's work a short time before he died, so she now suspected Evans could have hidden something else. So far, however, she had located nothing irregular.

A knock on the door broke her concentration, and Grant stood there with the cash drawer from his teller window. "We have had a busy morning, so I thought you might want to move money to the vault earlier than usual."

Mary Beth nodded. "Good idea."

Mrs. Chandler popped into the office with her cash drawer too. "The bank is quiet, so I brought mine as well."

"I'd prefer someone stay down there." Mary Beth's heart sped up as she took Mrs. Chandler's drawer and prepared to count the cash.

"Riddle is in the lobby." Mrs. Chandler smiled. "I wanted to have a word with you as well."

"Oh?" Was her mother-in-law deliberately flouting Peter's rules? He wanted an employee at the teller window all the time the bank was open.

Mrs. Chandler arched a brow. "I recalled some information after you left this morning."

Mary Beth stopped. She could not count money and converse at the same time. "Yes?"

Mrs. Chandler raised a finger in the air. "Mrs. Campbell commented that Stanley courted Ida from the moment he arrived in town. She thought their engagement too brief, but her husband wanted to move out west——"

Ruth and John came barreling into the office. Both were panting and sweating. Ruth's brown hair hung in tangled ringlets.

"Mary Beth, your kitchen is burning," Ruth screamed.

"What?" Mary Beth gasped. "Are you sure?

Ruth ran her fingers through her damp hair. "John and I were going there to work on medicines. We saw smoke. Cook ran out of the house, screaming."

THE CHANDLER'S HOME

Mary Beth's side ached from running all the way from the bank, but she did not stop. She kept picturing herself as a child following her father around the house, and the tea parties they had in his library. His bedroom sat above the kitchen. Was it already damaged? All her mother's sewing would be destroyed. She had died after Mary Beth's birth, and Mary Beth clung to those remaining bits of her love. What about the pictures? Mrs. Chandler never got the painting she wanted to take back. Surely the medication would not survive. All that hard work would be lost.

When her house came into view, she released a groan. Black smoke billowed from the kitchen area, and the smell made her want to wretch. Neighborhood men passed buckets of water to pour on the fire. Coughing and tearing up, she slowed down to a trot, wondering if the men wasted their time and water. She needed to get in and see what she could salvage.

"No, ma'am." A muscular man whisked off his straw hat and held her back. Ash covered his overalls, and his round face wore smudges. "We cannot allow you to get closer. The fire is raging. It's dangerous."

A spasm of coughing kept her from replying for a few moments, but she cleared her throat. "The house belongs to me. I must get in."

He blotted his face with a limp handkerchief and pointed behind her. "The military are sending men to empty as much as they can. That building is no place for a lady. If the rain gets worse, it will be a blessing."

"What rain?"

"Ma'am, it's drizzling. You are getting wet."

Mary Beth was damp with sweat, but a fine mist also fell on her arms. Tinged with soot, she'd be a sight if she stayed outside. "Yes, I see. Praise God. What is your name, sir?"

"George. My land backs up to yours. I was a friend of your father, and I was working out in the field when your cook started screaming. My wife and I mobilized the neighbors."

"How can I thank you?" She realized she was shaking, and she had no idea what she could do to pay this man back for his kindness.

"You should get out of this weather."

The sound of horses caught her attention, she turned to see two large wagons approaching, driven by military men. One drew up alongside her and stopped.

George rushed over and spoke to the driver. "Miss, he's going to take you to safety."

Rain fell harder and she did not argue when George lifted her up to sit by the driver. "We own the large gray warehouse by the river. Use that if there's anything worth keeping."

"Very good, ma'am. I hope we won't need to. This sergeant is going to take you to the nearest neighbor. You will still be able to see us working."

Mary Beth coughed into her handkerchief as she tried to consider what to do next.

That Evening After Dark

Mary Beth didn't feel courageous as she stood at the threshold of her charred home. The heavy smoke brought on a coughing fit, and she worried about making her way through the remains with only an oil lamp. Would she fall through the partially burned floor? What if the fire was only smoldering and flamed up again? She could lose her life. But she must save a few articles of clothing for herself and Peter.

At the front door where she stood, the front stairs appeared intact except for a few places along the foyer. She looked down at the floor and believed it would hold her weight. She crept in, testing before each step. The temptation to go left of the stairs and peek into the kitchen where the fire had raged overcame her. She was being careful. Inching along, she managed to make it to the kitchen door behind the stairwell. Parts of the floor had gaping holes, which she avoided. The contents of the kitchen appeared charred.

But what was this in the foyer behind her? She put down her lamp, turned carefully and reached for the broken jar. With a handkerchief she rolled it up and thrust it into her pocket. Why would the lavender jar she gave Ida be here after the fire? Of course, it was broken. The heat would do that. Later in daylight she would examine the contents to see if she had made the preparation.

Here was proof that either Ida or Stanford had been here.

Now she would head upstairs and see what clothing she could salvage.

Anna held the lantern aloft as she inched inside her son's home. The hallway floor was charred, and she had to watch where she stepped since parts of the floor were gone. The overwhelming smell of smoke made her want to gag, but she had come to fetch her daughter-in-law. She truly ached for the poor girl. How would she have handled this upheaval if Andrew had been traveling? "Mary Beth? Are you here?"

"Yes." A reply came from upstairs.

Why would Mary Beth come here in the dark after the fire? That dear girl needed a mother, and Anna knew how to do the job. She swung the lantern toward the stairs, which seemed to be intact. "I am coming up."

One step at a time, Anna eased upstairs. The wall to her right appeared very black, so she clung to the railing on the other side of the stairs. If her daughter-in-law could get upstairs, she could also. At last, she reached the landing. A breeze came in through a hole in the ceiling and smoke engulfed her making her wheeze and cough. "Where are you?"

"Come left. I am in the first room."

Anna headed toward the sound until she saw a light in a room to the left and Mary Beth's back. Her dirty hair fell to her shoulders and her dress was soiled. She would need a warm bath and clean clothes. "What are you doing?"

"I am packing clothes for Peter and me."

"Do that tomorrow. I came to take you back with me."

"No. I had to see the house after the fire was out. The heavy rain helped even though the roof leaked. The kitchen cannot be used, but the bedrooms on this side of the stairs are unharmed except for the smell and dampness." She turned revealing a soot-covered face. "Jane asked me to come stay with her, and I agreed."

"Ruth is worried about you. She wanted me to check on you, and I spoke to the neighbors first."

"We lost all the medicines." Mary Beth sniffled. "But my garden appears unharmed, so I shall make more."

Mary Beth was not thinking clearly, probably in shock. Poor child. "When will Peter be home?"

"He might be back tomorrow." Mary Beth shivered. "I hope so."

"Do you need me tomorrow at the bank?"

"Yes." Mary Beth sighed. "Peter will need assistance at the teller window if we have a busy day again."

"Perhaps I should offer to assist with hiring. However, I shall go home now. Are you sure you won't come?"

"No. Jane and her father will arrive soon for this trunk."

As Anna made her way back downstairs, she heard Mary Beth weeping.

AN HOUR LATER

Mary Beth trembled as she situated herself by the fireplace in Jane's room. She had just bathed and washed her hair. Few occasions presented themselves to build a fire in the summer, but the weather had cooled after the rain. Besides, Mrs. Haskell insisted, and she was grateful for her kindness.

So much had happened today. Just managing the bank alone would have been challenge enough, but watching fire devour her home hurt. What would her father think to see his home so damaged? Then again, he was in a better place and might not value the physical world as much. Seeing the damage to his bedroom made her heart ache. Part of his library was destroyed too. How she loved that room where she and her father used to sit in the evenings. Peter had no idea what had happened and had left no address. He planned to be home soon. Would he go to their charred house or to the bank first?

Jane knocked and entered. "I wanted to make sure you were comfortable."

"I am. Thank you." At least Mary Beth would enjoy her visit with Jane. They had been close growing up.

"What are you going to do now?"

"I am thinking of that too." Mary Beth ran a hand over her mouth. "I must consult with Peter on repairs. Plus, I need to return to the grocer's home and ask a few more questions."

"Do you think the fire could be related to the attack on the bank?"

"Possibly, but I wonder if I angered McDonald because I fired his girlfriend." Mary Beth chuckled at the thought. "We were too patient with her. She does not know how to work."

"I am glad the men spared as much as they did."

"Oh, I owe a debt to George. I cannot imagine the damage if he hadn't gathered men to help."

"I am glad you can be grateful at this horrid moment." Jane fluffed a bed pillow. "I suggest you retire early. You have much rebuilding to do."

"And investigation. We must learn what Evans hoped to accomplish."

Chapter Twenty-Nine

Early the Next Morning

As Peter trudged out of the Chattanooga depot at dawn, he could not recall being so tired. A few people milled around the Crutchfield House, which sat across the street, but few citizens came out this early. His hometown never looked so good—despite the humidity.

His trip to Atlanta had been hasty, but he had news to share with his wife. He couldn't wait to collapse into his own bed. Every time he had closed his eyes in the Atlanta hotel, he recalled how Mary Beth did not want him to leave.

However, when he turned onto his street, an odd smell greeted him. He paused to sniff. Smoke. Something had burned recently. He strolled on until he passed the huge curve and could see his home. His heart pounded at the sight of the charred roof.

Forgetting his fatigue, he broke into a run. His wife couldn't reach him because he was unsure where to stay in Atlanta. Questions filled his mind. What caught fire? Was his wife okay? How much did they lose?

A voice called his name. He turned to see Mary Beth running toward him from the Haskell's home next door.

Mary Beth was relieved to see her husband. His shirt was wrinkled, and his face was covered with a day's stubble, his hair was mussed, but he was home. "Peter."

He grabbed her around the waist. "Dearest Mary Beth! I saw the house and worried. Are you well?"

Mary Beth ran her hands through his hair. How she'd longed to see him, to have him hold her. It seemed as if months had passed since he left. "The fire was horrid. I wanted you all day."

"What caught fire?" Peter's blood-shot eyes gazed into hers.

"I believe it was arson." Mr. Weston walked up, holding his hat. Anna Chandler came up beside him. "The culprit pulled down your wife's drying herbs and set them afire. They burned slowly. The kitchen and that side of the house sustained damage. The other parts of the house were damaged by water and smoke, but I believe it can be salvaged."

The intrusion annoyed Mary Beth. What made Weston feel he could walk up and take over the conversation?

Anna patted his arm. "Mr. Weston was kind enough to visit last night and again early this morning to assess the damage—at my request, of course."

Peter released Mary Beth to shake his hand. "I appreciate your concern, sir."

Mary Beth held back her anger. She admired her husband's diplomacy because this should have been a private moment between the two of them.

"Weston will have dinner with us tonight, just the four of us." Mrs. Chandler waltzed over to Peter and touched his cheek. "Dear one, I'm so glad you returned. You will come back home?"

Peter kissed her hand. "Maybe. I am working on accommodations already, but we will come to dinner."

Mary Beth longed to applaud her husband. He handled his mother so well. On the other hand, she had prayed and sought the Lord before she approached her mother-in-law yesterday.

Right now, she wanted Peter to hold her.

SEVERAL HOURS LATER
C&R BANK

After he had shaved and rested, Peter entered his office to find his wife working a ledger at his desk. She held a pencil in her mouth and had scribbled numbers on a paper beside her. He had told Riddle they needed privacy so they could talk, which his mother prevented earlier. "Dearest, I have returned and feel much better. Your idea of napping at the Haskell's was genius."

She looked up and smiled. "You appear more relaxed. Tell me about your trip."

"I believe the man we know as Evans was Charles Dixon, and he needed a great deal of money." He gave her a summary of what he learned.

"Apparently he intended to obtain gold from us." Mary Beth put down her pencil. "He made no errors in the ledgers. Instead, he took the money and receipts before anyone wrote down the transaction. The locksmith thought someone tampered with the lock on the vault. However, before he left, he said the original design included a defect. It's now fixed."

"Have you changed all the locks?"

Mary Beth nodded. "I intended to have our house done as well since I fired Mrs. Phipps. The fire occurred before I had a chance."

"You fired her?"

"I found her in McDonald's embrace, and that made up my mind."

"Good for you. I shall locate another lady for the job. Mr. Haskell is looking for a house for us to rent. Several of his clients plan to move as soon as we work out an agreement."

Mary Beth chuckled. "Which means we will be here when the Northern armies arrive."

"We will have a place to live until we must leave. Our evacuation plan remains in place. I never intended to give Evans any money," Peter said. He did not want to alarm her, but he believed she would be happier in their own house rather than staying with his mother.

"I am so uneasy."

"And my trip did not help." He walked across the room and massaged her shoulders. "I apologize."

"I am wondering if the poisoning of the grocer is related. Everything about his death seemed to indicate poison, and they would check what he took."

"And the potion?"

"I have never made that, nor did I have the herbs, but the authorities did not know that. And of course, someone could say the house fire fits in. The person who started it used my drying herbs, which appears to implicate me. One other thing, I found an unusual bottle from the potion I gave Ida for bruises. Could it be Stanford?"

Peter gave it some thought. "Did he ever come to our home?"

"Yes." Mary Beth rubbed her temple "Remember that time you saw a bruise on my arm? Bessie and I threw him out."

"Yes." He nodded. "I remember now. Evans took a short break every day."

Mary Beth's eyebrows lifted. "I never knew that."

"He was never gone long," Peter said. "And I don't recall him having a break for a meal, so perhaps that's when he ate."

"Would he be gone long enough to go to our house?"

"Probably not. But maybe he met someone."

"How many people do we think collude to get our bank?"

"Think about it," Peter said. "First the colonel was shot. Didn't we assume that was evening? Evans wasn't working in the evening. The grocer took poison in the evening."

"But someone brought it to him during the day," Mary Beth said.

"Evans could get to the grocer from the bank on a break," Peter said.

"What about the house fire?"

"Evans was already gone. He could have started it."

"But so could someone else. Maybe McDonald or Stanford. Their duties do not keep them busy all the time. They hang around town during the day," Mary Beth said. "There are too many possibilities."

THAT EVENING

Peter relaxed as he locked the bank door. At last, the workday had ended. The full moon gave enough light to see the other businesses along the street. He and Mary Beth had gone over documents and audited records several hours past closing. He threw his arm around his wife, who stood beside him. "How I long for sleep."

"Yes. I've never been this tired, ever." Mary Beth nodded. "But first we have dinner at your mother's house."

"At least I know the food will be wonderful."

"Will your mother understand if we don't stay long after we eat?" Mary Beth touched his face.

"Her sympathy is boundless, especially for me." Peter kissed her hand. "She won't be angry."

"I am surprised we failed to learn anything tonight. What kind of thief takes money at the teller window and leaves it in his desk?"

"If we keep looking, we will find facts. Let's trust the Lord to guide us." He didn't feel as confident as he sounded, but he did believe God would look after them.

"I feel forsaken now. Right now, when I long to be in my own bed, I don't have a home anymore."

Her voice sounded flat, and that bothered Peter. "Life has been stressful, but God has not forsaken us."

"I know. We both learned that in the past, but how do I stop feeling this way?"

Peter hugged her but had nothing to offer. His insides were hollow, and the world seemed cold. "We are almost there. Let's focus on having a good meal."

Peter walked inside and guided his wife to the sitting room. He realized once he was inside, he hadn't knocked like he often did.

As he entered the sitting room, Weston rose from the sofa. He wore a tweed suit with a gray handkerchief in the outside pocket. "Hello, Mr. Chandler, Mrs. Chandler. How are you?"

"Good evening, sir." Peter offered his hand. "Thank you for your help in the last few hours. Discovering the cause of the fire meant a lot."

Weston smiled and looked down. "Anna requested it, and I am so fond of her. I intend to marry her if I can persuade her to accept. She's still in love with your late father."

"Right now she's enamored with Mr. Grant," Peter said.

"Yes," Mary Beth said. "That might present a problem."

"No." Weston laughed. "Grant poses no threat to me. Your father trusted me, and I believe Anna will also."

Peter sank into the overstuffed chair across from the financier and closed his eyes. He did not want a stepfather, and his need for sleep overwhelmed his desire to understand this man. Banking involved many difficult people.

God help me.

Chapter Thirty

AT THE SAME TIME

Anna stepped into the kitchen to see how the meal progressed. The aroma of roast, garden vegetables, and chocolate cake surrounded her. Tonight would be delightful. Ruth, Peter, Mary Beth, and Weston had arrived for dinner. She loved nothing better than having her entire family under her roof, and Weston was dear too. Better yet, Peter and Mary Beth would stay overnight for months while workmen repaired their home.

Plus, Weston could guide her son with his financial wisdom. Who could argue with a man who made his own fortune? "How much longer, Cook?"

"We are ready to serve, ma'am."

Anna swished into the sitting room where Weston and Peter occupied armchairs while chatting, and Ruth sat on the sofa with Mary Beth. How Anna adored them all. She clapped her hands. "Dinner is served."

Weston rose while still addressing Peter, "I am rather surprised the North has not taken Chattanooga already."

Peter nodded, while walking. "I agree. The railroad makes our city strategic."

Anna could not abide talk of war. At least their opinions coincided, because she hated men debating each other. "I do hope you both like roast beef."

"Yes, Mama." Peter nodded. "And your cook makes the best."

As they entered the dining room, she pointed to their chairs, which she had been considering all day. Weston and Peter must sit near each other, which would allow Weston a chance to give his input. "I am at the head of the table, and Ruth at the foot. Mary Beth you sit on the left. Peter and Weston will be on the right."

She sighed with satisfaction as Peter and Weston sat together.

Billy and Maud entered with plates of food, which Anna passed around.

"Peter, Ruth tells me John has become quite good at portraits, and he can sketch them quite fast," Mary Beth said.

"Wonderful. That might be a particularly useful skill." Peter placed his napkin in his lap. "We might ask him for assistance."

Mary Beth grinned. "My thoughts exactly."

"Is John the young man I see with Ruth occasionally?" Weston asked.

"Yes." Ruth took some mashed potatoes and passed it to Mary Beth. "He seldom speaks even though he is very smart."

"This talent might become income for him." Weston took a slice of beef. "I am happy to hear he has useful skills."

Anna could not abide talk of this young boy tonight. She placed Peter and Weston in the same room for a reason. What better time to change the subject. "Weston, have you shared with my son how you obtained your fortune?"

Weston wiped his mouth as he chuckled. "No. That endless story would dominate the conversation."

"Nevertheless," Peter said, while cutting his meat. "I would love to hear that account. We can learn from each other, and I confess I have plenty to learn."

Anna smiled. What a fine son she had, and he would be perfect if he would listen to her.

"You are kind," Weston said. "And I am interested in what you are doing. Should you need cash, I could assist you by buying in. You are talented enough to succeed, and I would like to share in that success."

"Really? I have not had many offers like that one since the war started," Peter said.

"I am sure you have not," Weston blotted his face with his napkin and laughed. "With the Union breathing down our throats, more and more people are leaving."

The men continued to converse about the various types of weapons the two sides used, and Anna grew restless. If only she could get them back on banking.

As the meal came to a close, Weston rose. "I have a long way to drive, so I'd best be on my way. Anna, thanks for the lovely meal."

"Of course. We shall have you come again soon."

Weston had not done her bidding, and she was not pleased, but perhaps he did not want to be too forceful.

Peter put aside his napkin and got up also. "Mama, thanks for dinner. As usual, the meal was perfect. Will I see you at the bank tomorrow?"

Anna filled her lungs. "You aren't going to stay? I had Maud prepare a room."

"No." Peter leaned down to kiss her cheek. "Mary Beth took our clothes to the Haskell's, and Mr. Haskell is assisting us to locate a house to rent."

Her plans for the evening had failed.

THE NEXT MORNING

After breakfast at the Haskell's, Mary Beth watched from the dining room window as her husband accompanied Mr. Haskell into town in their carriage. How fortunate to have such dear friends in such uneasy times. While her husband worked at the bank, she must work to restore her stock of medications.

Jane, dressed in a lovely silver frock, came to stand at the window beside her. "Shall I show you the basement where Papa said you could work?"

"Yes. Please."

They walked downstairs to the Haskell's daylight basement.

"You can see we use the room for storage." Jane pointed out trunks and old furniture occupying a portion of the room. "The servants cleared a section by the window. "You can work on that wooden table."

Mary Beth noted a few cooking tools, and woodstove that was vented outdoors. Her mortar and pestle had been destroyed. She'd go by the grocer for a replacement. She would also need to buy certain herbs right away, labels, and more bottles. "This will do nicely."

Hinges on the door upstairs squealed, and Jane looked up. "Is someone up there?"

"Mary Beth? It's Ruth. Mrs. Haskell said you were down there."

"I am."

The sound of footsteps followed, and Ruth came to her side holding out sketch paper. "Look what I have. John has been drawing."

Mary Beth gazed at drawings of Evans, Mrs. Phipps, and Stanford perfect in every detail. "These are wonderful."

"I had him do several for practice. All of these have been troublesome. Besides, I think you might require them."

A Half Hour Later

Armed with John's photos in her shopping basket, Mary Beth entered the grocer. She needed herbs and supplies, and Jane accompanied her to pick up items for her family.

Mary Beth noted the smell of wax and cleaning supplies as she waved to Molly who worked at the register. Since the mortar and pestle might need to be ordered, she headed to the back where Mrs. Nelson stacked jars on the shelves.

"Good morning, ma'am." Mrs. Nelson extended a hand. "We are always glad to see you."

"I have a list of things I need." Mary Beth put a scrap of paper in Mrs. Nelson's hand. "And I would like to speak to Josey and your youngest daughter while I wait."

"Of course. I think I have all these, although the prices are rising. Please make yourself at home while I gather them. You know where to go."

"Thank you. How is your health?" Mary Beth saw more lines around Mrs. Nelson's face and mouth.

Mrs. Nelson blinked hard. "I am fine. Most of the time."

"I am sorry." Mary Beth ached for her. "Call on me should you need something."

One hand over her mouth, Mrs. Nelson nodded.

Mary Beth patted her arm and headed into the stockroom to go upstairs. She found Josey sweeping the kitchen. "Good morning, Josey. I have a quick question for you."

"Yes'm?"

Mary Beth held out the sketch of Evans. "Is this the man that brought medications to Mr. Nelson?"

Josey took the paper. "No. Not 'im."

Mary Beth held back a gasp. She'd expected a positive answer because evidence pointed that way. How could they be wrong? At least she had John's other drawings. Next, she handed Stanford's picture to Josey. "And this man?"

Josey's face lit up. "That looks more like 'im."

"Are you sure?"

"I ain't sayin' no more, ma'am. I could be wrong, and Mrs. Nelson be a gettin' mad."

"Thank you." Mary Beth offered her a smile. "Where might I find the youngest Nelson? Lily?"

"She be playin' in the hallway." Josey turned away.

Mary Beth hurried down the hallway where the little girl rocked a battered cloth doll. "Hello, honey. Can you look at a picture? Do you recognize these men?"

The girl widened her blue eyes as she looked from one photo to the next. Finally, she touched the picture of Stanford.

"Did he come to talk to your daddy?" Mary Beth asked.

The girl met her gaze for a moment. Then she mumbled something to her doll and walked away cradling the stuffed toy close.

Chapter Thirty-One

CITY CAFÉ

Peter gazed at his wife with admiration. Mary Beth sat across the table from him chatting with her friend, Jane. Mary Beth had her hair in the usual bun, but she was even more attractive with the curls around her face, especially when she smiled. They expected his college friend from Cleveland to join them for lunch, so Peter was determined to enjoy himself. The café owner had placed flowers at each table and tall ferns sat around the room. Why not forget the untoward circumstances and relax?

Mary Beth leaned close. "You will be interested in what I learned today."

Peter winked at her. "I love anything you say."

Mary Beth cocked her head and frowned, seemingly not understanding his tease. "Josey, the Nelson's maid, recognized Stanford as the man who dropped off the tainted potion, not Evans."

"She actually said that?" Her news intrigued him, submerging his playful mood. "I assume you displayed the sketches. Were you there, Jane?"

Jane shook her head. "I was shopping for Mother."

Mary Beth held up a finger. "And the youngest Nelson daughter picked Stanford out when I asked if she recognized either photo."

"How old is she?" Peter thought of his motto, get the facts. Emotions could lead one astray.

Jane squinted. "I think she's five."

"That young?" Mary Beth turned toward her friend. "I thought she was older. If that is true, I am not sure she could be a witness. However, I expected them to identify Evans as the one who brought the tainted medicine."

Peter was surprised Mary Beth would speak so openly around Jane, but they had been friends for years. He leaned toward being cautious, while his wife took chances he would avoid. "That's interesting, dear, but not exactly proof. What do you think, Jane?"

"At only five, I doubt the girl's testimony could be used in court."

"I am confident this information rules out Evans as the poisoner." Mary Beth said.

The waiter brought Rob Hatcher to the table. He wore a suit, but his bow tie hung loose around his neck.

"Here's Rob." Peter stood and offered his hand.

Rob's face broke into a welcoming smile, and he threw an arm around Peter. "Great to see you again so soon."

Peter motioned for him to sit in the chair to his left. "Let me introduce my wife, Mary Beth."

Rob bobbed his head "Great to meet you."

Mary Beth extended her hand to shake. "I have heard lots about you, and most was funny."

"Guilty as charged," Rob ducked and laughed.

"And her friend, Jane Haskell."

"Good morning, ma'am.

Jane smiled as her face turned pink.

Peter thought he saw Rob's eyes light up, and Jane gaze at Rob with admiration. However, Peter never succeeded at matchmaking. "Rob and I were great friends in college, but we drifted apart afterward." Peter slapped him on the back and flicked Rob's open collar. "He manages to escape tradition and still accomplish things. We had some great times."

"Indeed. The pranks ... but your wife may not want to know." Rob laughed.

Mary Beth cocked a brow. "If you are the same age as Peter, I am surprised you haven't been drafted."

Peter swallowed hard. What a topic to bring up with a new friend, but his wife tended toward being spontaneous. "My wife has served as a nurse to the military hospitals in town."

"Very commendable, ma'am. I tried to join when the war started, but I have a heart murmur, and the doctors refused my application." He puffed out his chest. "But I feel great."

"And you look wonderful," Peter said. "You and I need to practice baseball."

Rob laughed. "I am sure I would win."

"We have a puzzle for you, sir," Mary Beth said.

"Yay. I love solving riddles." He elbowed Peter. "Remember, we used to figure out who played jokes on us."

"We need to identify a man who offered a tainted preparation to our grocer. The grocer died afterward."

"Ooh. Find the murderer? I advise you to call the sheriff."

Peter sighed. His wife's boldness still surprised him. Would Rob think she gossiped?

Mary Beth reddened. "Ours moved away." She explained what she had done and showed the sketches.

"I am impressed." Rob's eyes widened. "You married a clever woman, Peter."

"My wife can do anything. She has served as nurse, bookkeeper, seamstress, and pharmacist. And my close relationship with you emboldened her to trust you completely," Peter said giving his wife an indulgent smile. "Please consider all this information as privileged."

"Of course." His eyebrows relaxed, and he nodded. "In the absence of law enforcement perhaps the four of us could work together."

Mary Beth's eyes sparkled. "Wonderful."

Jane nodded, and her cheeks grew darker red.

Peter gave his friend a gentle punch. "How long do you plan to be in town?"

"I have a couple jobs here, and I plan to stay for the foreseeable future." He made a fist of his hand and stuck out the pointer finger, simulating a gun. "We may all have to leave eventually unless we want to paint cannons."

"That sounds marvelous." Peter grinned at his friend. He would enjoy having Rob here. "Where are you staying?"

"Crutchfield House," Rob said.

"Then team up with us, Rob. However, ladies," Peter injected, "before you do anything. Let us know your plans." Peter determined to keep his wife alive.

"Tomorrow there is a party at church with food and croquet," Mary Beth said. "What a great opportunity to ask questions."

"I shall escort Miss Haskell to the event and use those sketches to see what I can learn. I am a popular man at parties. People will talk to me more freely than they would you," Rob said with a nod toward Jane. "With your permission, of course."

"I would enjoy that. Thank you." Jane said.

Peter laughed. Rob could create the wildest schemes, but his tactics usually worked. "We shall follow you around to see what you learn. This should be amusing."

NINETY MINUTES LATER
OUTSIDE CITY CAFÉ

"I enjoyed getting to know you, Rob." Mary Beth shifted her bundle from the grocer and squinted against the bright afternoon sun. Jane, Rob, and her husband stood with her on the sidewalk outside the café. Jane carried a package of supplies too. "We should do this again soon."

"We will. I am glad you will be here in town," Peter said. "But I need to get back to the bank."

"I must cut herbs to dry," Mary Beth said.

Rob offered his arm to Jane. "And I should escort Miss Haskell back to her home. She should not have to carry this heavy package. Besides, these days you never know what dangers she might face."

Jane accepted his arm, and they went down the street together.

Mary Beth reached for her husband's hand. "I think we might have started a romance."

Peter shrugged. "Neither of us planned that, but I should be a gentleman and take your packages."

"Excuse me, sir. Are you Mr. Chandler?"

Mary Beth turned to see a short, chubby man dressed in a suit and carrying a briefcase. "Yes. My husband is Mr. Chandler."

"You are Mr. Beasley?" A line formed between Peter's brows. "From Atlanta?"

"I am." The man smiled. "I hoped to see you as I passed through. May we speak in private?"

Peter led the way inside the bank and up to the office. "You may speak freely in my wife's present. We work together."

Mary Beth couldn't wait to hear what he had to say. She grabbed a chair and motioned for him to sit. She and Peter took seats next to each other opposite him at the desk.

"I have been worried ever since you came. You see I cannot speak of Dixon around the bank employees."

Mary Beth pulled out her sketch. "Is this the man you speak of?"

He took the paper and gazed down at the face. "Yes. That is Charles Dixon. I cannot understand why he was hired because his history seemed unsavory. Perhaps he had the other employees in his power. Yet he was fired so quickly. It makes no sense."

"What else do you know?" Peter asked.

"I liked the man. He was a polite, diligent man, and he did not appear to fit the history we had." Beasley pulled a handkerchief out of his pocket unfolding and refolding it over and over. "I wish I could tell you more."

Mary Beth wished that too.

Chapter Thirty-Two

THE NEXT DAY

Bright sunshine, hot weather, and cloudless skies greeted Mary Beth when she arrived behind the church for the afternoon social. Being outside felt wonderful. Several ladies were setting up wickets for croquet on the lawn, while others set tables for food and refreshments. Mary Beth brought fried chicken the Haskell cook had prepared and John's sketches. Today she hoped to enjoy herself and gain information regarding the activities of Evans and Stanford.

She approached Mrs. Jones, who oversaw the meal. "Where should I put this chicken?"

"The large table beside the back door, right there." Mrs. Jones pointed. "Thank you."

Mary Beth left the food there and turned to ask where else she might help.

Ruth came up to her. Today, she wore her dark hair up and John, dressed in a simple shirt and top, trailed behind her. "Hi, Mary Beth."

"Hello." Mary Beth hugged Ruth and waved to John, who preferred not to be touched.

John handed her several slips of paper.

She put a hand on her chest. "For me?"

He nodded, and she accepted more sketches from him. "These are very good, John."

"I explained you were using his drawings," Ruth said. "And he did more."

"John, you have McDonald and Stanford together in this picture. Did you see them this way?"

John looked away.

Ruth spoke up, "I think so, but I will ask him when he is less nervous."

"Are you going to play croquet?" Mary Beth pointed to the wickets and mallets.

"I shall if John does."

"You are such a good friend." Mary Beth squeezed her shoulder. "I saw all the herbs you hung to dry in the Haskell's basement, and I appreciate your hard work."

"I am quite fond of Ruth too," Mrs. Teague walked up. "She and John bring me flowers."

"Good for you. That is sweet," Mary Beth said to Ruth. She nodded toward John, but he did not meet her eye. She turned to Mrs. Teague with the sketches of Evans, Stanford, and McDonald. Mrs. Teague had been kind to John, so perhaps she would praise him. "See what clever work John does?"

"Oh, quite good. Although I do not like either man," Mrs. Teague said.

Elated Mrs. Teague spoke to her, Mary Beth asked another question, pointing to the picture of Stanford and McDonald. "Have you seen these two together?"

"I think I have, but my memory is poor. You might ask others," Mrs. Teague said.

Mary Beth's heart skipped a beat. Not only had Mrs. Teague broken her silence, but she had also provided useful information.

Mrs. Teague wondered off, talking to others.

Mary Beth glanced around for Peter or Rob. Rob finally arrived with Jane, but the two kept to themselves. Mary Beth did not want to interfere with their budding romance, instead she chatted with friends and asked questions of them.

"Mary Beth?"

She turned to see Ida standing on the outskirts of the property. "Why not join us, Ida? I doubt your husband would come here. There are so many people, he would not dare hurt you."

Ida shivered. "I would be safe ... until he got me home. I cannot stay long. I overheard my husband talking to another man last night outside our apartment. Something about Colonel Bennet looking for a spy when he came to Chattanooga."

"That is helpful. I've been thinking about the loan. It seems odd Bennet would want a loan for a house that could be damaged in the war. Perhaps flushing out a spy was his real motive." Mary Beth put her arm around Ida.

"Ouch." Ida pulled away and backed into the trees bordering the church land. "My shoulders are sore."

Mary Beth wondered how Stanford bruised her shoulders. She followed Ida. "Leave your husband and go to your aunt. He's going to kill you."

"And I am worried about you. Spies could be after the bank, so I had to warn you." Ida backed away.

GUEST ROOM HASKELL HOUSE
EVENING

The fluffy pillows and soft bedspread were comfortable. However, Mary Beth did not think she could sleep until she talked to Peter. He was still consulting with Haskell in the library and had not come to the church event. She eased herself into the chair beside the bed and tried to push aside her fatigue and think. Ida's face kept appearing in her mind. The fear on her face probably came because of the beatings she endured. What if Ida was correct? If a spy targeted the bank, that could explain the murders. However, she worried about who might be next. The thought of someone trying to kill Peter made her nauseated.

At last, Peter entered the bedroom, running his fingers through his hair. He slipped off his coat, and his shirt bore many wrinkles. "We have worked out a rental house, and we have a carpenter to work on our house. We can start moving furnishings sometime next week."

"You look exhausted." Mary Beth rose and picked up his jacket. "We are comfortable here. Is there any reason we have to move right away?"

"Yes." He collapsed on the bed. "It is my responsibility to provide for you. Not Mr. Haskell."

"I wish you could have come to the social." Mary Beth rubbed a hand over her mouth. "Rob spent all his time with Jane. I thought he was going to help us."

"Rob probably forgot. I suspect Jane is on his mind. I should have made it my job in the first place. Perhaps he can help us in the future. I can trust him, and he's resourceful."

Mary Beth told him about Mrs. Teague's information and what Ida said.

"Two men from the military might talk to each other. I am not sure that will help. However, the information about spies might be important."

"I worked on medications all morning. I can drop off a fresh supply Monday and discuss the situation with the military."

"No." Peter got up. "Let me approach the military. Do not put yourself in danger."

MONDAY MORNING

Anna stepped outside to walk to the bank and found the August morning to be less oppressive than she expected. The coffee Horace Weston brought her last night gave her extra energy this morning. The substitutes used these days never had the robust taste she loved. Besides, she wanted to arrive before Peter, since today she would withdraw the last of her money. She would refuse to listen to any argument. After all, her dearest Andrew left her the money to use as she pleased. Weston had invested much of her gold, but this time, Anna planned to keep the money at home, handy for emergencies.

When Anna arrived, Grant was setting up his teller window, and the rest of the bank appeared empty. She waved in his direction. "Good morning."

"Good morning."

Since he seemed preoccupied, she wrote up a receipt for herself and found the account ledger where she changed her account to zero. As much as she cared for Grant, she didn't want him to know what she was doing because he would object. Next, she hurried to the safe and used her duplicate key, which the locksmith made the day he set up the safe.

Her purse bulged with coins, and she decided to take her money home for safekeeping.

Now she was no longer under the control of her son's sloppy management.

ABOUT THE SAME TIME MONDAY

The provost marshal sent Mary Beth and Ruth to the office of the signal corps. The room held a table and two chairs and a few filing cabinets. Mary Beth and Ruth had arrived at eleven in the morning after delivering medications to Newsome Hospital. She decided to ask her questions, so Peter wouldn't have to come. Mary Beth hoped to learn about spies. However, the staff left them alone in the room.

"Do I hear footsteps?" Ruth said.

Mary Beth cocked her head. "That does sound like someone walking, but they are not close."

"I wish this man, whatever he is called, would show up so we could leave." Ruth twisted a strand of her hair. "Going to the hospital fascinates me, but this room is stuffy."

"We have been here about forty minutes." Mary Beth shook her watch. "Unless this has stopped working."

"My stomach is growling. I want to get lunch."

Mary Beth's mind reeled with possibilities. She did not know much about the military, but she had a great imagination. "Maybe the man who heads up the secret service bureau is busy."

"Or else he wants you to go away."

A sudden idea came to Mary Beth. She could have Ruth watch the door while she sifted through the files. "Crack the door and peek outside. Do you see anyone coming?"

Ruth opened the door and looked both ways. "It's deserted."

"Good." Mary Beth opened the first filing cabinet.

"What are you doing?" Ruth's face grew red.

"The information I need could be here, and we won't have another chance. So, I'm looking through these instead of just sitting."

Ruth's eyes lit up. "In that case, I can help."

Mary Beth shook her head. "Someone needs to act as look out. Watch out for soldiers who might come in here."

Ruth returned to her place at the door while Mary Beth worked as fast as she could.

"Sh-sh." Ruth held a finger to her face.

"Is someone coming?" Mary Beth hurried back to her chair.

"A man walked by as you closed that drawer. I thought he could hear you, but he is gone."

"Oh, good." She returned to the cabinet. "I shall keep looking."

Mary Beth worked for another forty minutes but found nothing useful. She was not sure where else to look.

Chapter Thirty-Three

Pouring over materials in his office, Peter stayed late to close by doing an inventory of gold on hand. His numbers kept showing several hundred dollars less than closing on Saturday. He rubbed the back of his neck. "I cannot seem to balance. This total is much lower than I expected?"

Mary Beth walked in the room. "Was that meant for me?"

Peter looked up. "No. But my numbers are wrong."

Mary Beth handed him a receipt from Mrs. Chandler's window. "You will find the answer here. Mama Dearest took out more cash."

"She put us in crisis." He sat back, rubbing his chin. "We could close the rest of the week since we are moving into the rental house."

"What about your idea of staying open for deposits only?"

"In light of the two interest payments this week. I shall stay mornings in the office while we wait."

"If your mother asks how the bank is doing, what shall I say?"

"Ask her to come see me. And if anyone else questions you, tell them we are moving into a rental house."

Mary Beth inhaled to fill her lungs. Peter was clever. He would find a way to stay afloat.

21 AUGUST 1863

Peter urged the horses forward, and the loaded wagon inched along the dirt road. Packing had taken longer than usual, which meant he might need to borrow the Haskell's horses again tomorrow. He turned to Rob, who sat beside him. "Did we pack too much furniture?"

Rob shook his head. "The road is better in the city. We'll get more speed there."

John, who was between the two men, made a clucking sound while bouncing up and down.

An hour later, Peter pulled up the horses when they reached the rental house, a small white frame in the downtown area. "Whoa."

Mary Beth hurried out to meet him by the fence. "We will be late to the prayer service. Remember, President Davis called this a day of prayer and fasting for the nation."

"Oh, no. We got busy packing up furniture, and I forgot." Peter ran his hand along his neck.

"I have clothes for you. If you hurry, we can still participate." She motioned them inside.

Rob looked down and pointed to smudges of dirt on his trousers. "I cannot go like this. Let me stay and look after the horses."

Peter threw the reins over the picket fence. "I shall help. The two of us can move faster, then you can see if anything I have fits you."

"I like that idea." Rob nodded."

As Peter and Rob turned toward the horses, a huge blast shook the town.

The horses snorted and stomped around nervously.

John covered his ears and ran inside the house.

Mary Beth screeched.

"That sounded like artillery." Rob ran toward the horse nearest him. "Calm down, fella."

"That was." Peter hurried toward the other horse and rubbed his neck. "Easy boy. We picked a bad day to move."

Another blast rattled the furnishings in the wagon.

Mary Beth ducked and ran indoors.

What a problem. Peter was moving into a house they would probably need to evacuate soon.

Mary Beth huddled in the dark basement listening and praying. The Bible promised trials, but having cannons shoot at your home fell into the category she called a nightmare. A year ago, the Union had fired on the city, but Mary Beth lived several miles from downtown in relative safety.

The city remained quiet, but Mary Beth worried. Last year the shooting went on much longer. Where were the men? What about John? If she knew Peter, he would scout the area and even talk to city officials. She prayed all of them would be safe.

More blasts shook the ground, but they seemed further away. Nevertheless, Mary Beth's heart pounded like a freight train running for safety.

Peter and Rob came into the basement with John. "Mary Beth, I checked out the situation. Union soldiers set up their cannons across the river. They chose the exact same spot from which they pelted the city last year."

"Their guns are doing very little damage," Rob added.

Another cannon exploded closer, and Mary Beth jerked. "I want to leave."

"Let's go stay with Mama," Peter pulled his wife closer. "She will be much happier during this barrage."

"I am worried about getting there." Mary Beth snuggled closer to Peter. "Besides, most of our clothes are still at the Haskell's."

"Based on the angle of the guns, you will be safe if you go away from the city," Rob said.

"I can take us around the back to the Haskell's home," Peter said. "Mary Beth, is there anything you need here?"

"No. But we will be leaving a lot of furniture here." She worried the guns might blow up what they had moved in. All of this belonged to her father, and she loved each piece for that reason. At least she had not moved the tablecloths her mother had made.

Rob spoke up, "I can stay here to look after the house and the horses. Since the Crutchfield House sits right at the railroad, it might be dangerous to go there."

"I would appreciate that," Mary Beth said. She wanted to cry and hug him. "But I do not want you injured either."

John grabbed Mary Beth's hand, and she wondered if he would go with her.

"I can take care of myself." Rob chuckled.

Mary Beth waved goodbye and followed Peter. John accompanied them, sometimes hopping, and sometimes running. City streets extended five blocks and then Mary Beth entered a cluster of trees. Sounds of battle became muted as they continued.

THE NEXT DAY
SATURDAY AUGUST 22

Peter found Chattanooga streets almost deserted as he headed into the city about dawn. Shelling had stopped about twenty-four hours ago, but he needed information to decide if the bank should evacuate. The dirt roads had potholes, and the church had lost its steeple. The hardware store sustained damage to the front, but most buildings remained intact. He headed far enough toward the river to see the Union cannons still in place. Along the riverbank, numerous gaping craters gave testimony to the shelling, but the pier remained undamaged. Coming back to the Haskell's, he noted many citizens stood in line to buy tickets at the train station.

He believed the Union readied to take the city, but he would wait to see what Mary Beth had learned at the hospital.

An Hour Later

Out of breath and tired, Mary Beth entered the Haskell's dining room where Jane waited for her. The cook had laid out sassafras tea and fresh rolls, and the aroma of fresh baking made Mary Beth's stomach growl. How odd to compare the sparkling china and silverware with the rustic hospital she left moments before.

Jane pulled out a chair. "You look weary. Sit down and let me fix you tea."

"Thank you." Mary Beth placed a hand on her base of her neck and inhaled to calm herself. She accepted the tea and took a sip.

"What did you find?" Jane asked.

Mary Beth had hurried back. What she found worried her. "I offered them the medicines and the basket I packed them in, which they accepted. They are evacuating as fast as they can."

Jane's complexion lost its color. "Oh, dear. Does that mean a battle?"

"You would think they would need a hospital if fighting were imminent." Mary Beth swallowed the congestion in her throat. "Maybe they want to move the wounded men out of the way. I cannot say."

"Wait." Jane looked toward the front door. "I see your husband coming."

"Good." Mary Beth pushed aside the biscuit, not able to swallow anything more.

Jane left the room and returned with a sweaty Peter.

"Peter?" Mary Beth rose from the table and went to him. "What did you find?"

He handed her a slip of paper. "Someone shoved this at me. Read it to me."

Mary Beth opened the paper and read aloud.

Dear Sir,

Our newspaper would like to continue publishing as long as possible. Since many are evacuating, may we set up our press in your vault where we would be safe from cannon fire?

Sincerely,
Rebel Staff

Peter laughed. "The newspaper staff thinks the city is evacuating. At least someone has a use for the vault we built."

"That's not funny, Peter. I love our bank," Mary Beth said. He put his arm around her.

"Come and have some tea." Jane waved toward the chairs. "Everything appears less stressful if you have eaten."

Peter sat down and drank some tea. "Very good, Jane. Thank you. What did you find, Mary Beth?"

She told him what she learned.

"When I made the evacuation plans, I thought we would pack and leave the city right away." Peter reached for a biscuit. "We may have a few days."

"That's what I understood," Mary Beth said. "What do you propose?"

"We must decide what records we must have and make plans to secure them."

"And of course, the gold. If we aren't leaving, where do we store the gold?"

"Good question." Peter spread his arms. "We have a vault for safety. But, if we move gold out of there, we must be reasonably sure we can protect it."

"At this point, we have a huge responsibility for that money." She locked her eyes with Peter's. "We have no idea where the battle will take place, so how can we guard it?"

"I think we should pray before we decide." Peter took her hand.

Chapter Thirty-Four

Mary Beth walked into her office and shut the door against her husband and bank employees talking in the office behind her. Peter had assigned her to handle the banking history. So many records filled her office. They included accounts for individuals and businesses that owed them money. How could she leave anything that contained private information? If only she could burn what they could not take out. Yet this was an emergency, and she had to save enough for the bank to function. Nothing more.

She must pray.

Dear Father, we have protected this material carefully for many years. Please guide us as we evacuate. Keep this from falling into the wrong hands.

Once she opened her eyes, she realized the latest ledgers would be essential and would decrease what they kept in their possession. Now she must find a crate.

She left the office and tiptoed through Peter's office where Mr. Riddle, Mr. Grant, and Peter whispered together about the evacuation. She took a right down the stairs and then another right again to the basement. The room across from the vault contained a simple table and chairs where employees ate meals along with crates and filing cabinets of old files. She lit an oil lamp on the table and glanced around for an item to use for storage. Bennet's leather satchel sat against the wall. Riddle must have forgotten to return that to the widow, but the size would work for a number of ledgers. Maybe she could use it and return it later.

When she picked it up and looked inside, she saw several letters Bennet wrote to his wife but never mailed. The men who cleaned the sheriff's house must have left these. Surely Mrs. Bennet would want them. Curious, she opened a letter and read. The word bank leaped out at her, and she couldn't put the missive down.

A Few Minutes Later

Peter took a deep breath as Riddle and Grant left his office. They had hammered out a creative solution, and he prayed their plan would work. At moments like this, he longed to chat with his late father, but Father had never managed a bank during war. Seeking God was much better, but that meant walking by faith.

However, he determined to be prepared for the invasion. He reached into the cabinet behind him and pulled out his rifle and counted his ammunition.

"Peter!" Mary Beth rushed in, breathless.

Her expression worried him. "What's wrong?"

"I found a satchel Bennet left in the house he bought. I was going to use it to store the recent ledgers, but I found letters to his wife. He came to Chattanooga to find a spy at a financial institution." Surely, he wouldn't object to her reading them, but she held them out to him.

"Let me see." He grabbed the papers and read.

She leaned toward him and lowered her voice. "I believe Evans was the spy."

Peter took a deep breath. He was not sure.

SUNDAY MORNING
AUGUST 30

Mary Beth let her gaze wander around the sanctuary as she entered with her husband. The sparse congregation was already singing without organ music. Sunlight streaming through the stained-glass windows always made her worshipful. She needed worship and praise today with Chattanooga on the brink of war. This morning she saw more Confederates than last Sunday, but the Union had fired on them and remained across the river.

Peter nodded toward the left.

She saw his family and allowed him to guide her to the pew where Mrs. Chandler sat.

Peter stepped aside and Mary Beth lifted her skirt so she could ease past Mrs. Chandler and sit by Ruth. Mary Beth scooted toward Ruth making space for Peter between herself and her mother-in-law. She was thankful Peter took her cue and sat beside her.

"Mother keeps asking what is going on at the bank," Ruth whispered.

Mary Beth met Ruth's gaze. "She must ask Peter."

Ruth snickered, and Peter leaned over to give his sister a warning scowl.

Mary Beth focused her attention on the service—she needed God's wisdom and comfort. In the middle of the chorus, Peter's body relaxed and eased toward hers. His eyes were closed, and he was obviously not praying. She nudged him, and he jerked back into a sitting position.

What made her husband so sleepy?

Haskell Guest Room
That Evening

Again, Peter eased himself out of bed once he was certain his wife was sleeping. After putting on dark clothing, he slipped out of the house and hurried to the bank to meet Riddle and Grant in the bank foyer. He hoped he did not have to continue this many more nights, but he must secure bank records. Last night, he had been up all night hiding the gold.

Once there, he unlocked the door and crept into the darkened room. Although he could not see them, he knew the other men were there. "Grant? Riddle?"

"I am here," Grant said.

"I am here," Riddle said. "We have sorted through what we think we can burn tonight."

"Very good," Peter said. "We must move silently as we transport the crates."

"Your wife had a brilliant idea," Grant said. "No one will guess we are burning these at your ruined home."

"Yes. And I want her ignorant of what we are doing in case she is questioned later." Peter would do almost anything to keep his wife safe.

Hopefully, they could finish before dawn so Mary Beth would never know.

SEPTEMBER 8

The morning light roused Peter when the maid drew open the curtains, but he did not want to rise. He had spent eight nights burning records most of the night and pretending he was fine during the day. How much sleep had he missed? At least last night, he'd managed a full eight hours since he and his men completed the burning process. Someday he would pay them for their time—that is, if he ever had money to do that.

Mary Beth shook him. "Honey, you need to wake. Mrs. Haskell planned a special breakfast today. Besides, we promised to sweep out the vault for the newspaper, remember?"

He groaned and rolled over. This morning he should hop out of bed like he was rested, but every muscle in his shoulders ached. Banking never made him so sore. "What did you say about breakfast?"

"Mr. Weston smuggled us bacon last night when he brought your mother to visit. Remember?"

How could Peter forget? When he saw Weston with his arm around his mother, Peter's stomach knotted. Did this mean he would soon have a stepfather? With one motion, he sat up on the side of the bed. "I am out of bed."

"Yes, but Peter, I am already dressed. Hurry up."

Peter could not imagine a reason to hurry.

LATER THAT MORNING
C&R BANK FOYER

The sound of marching brought Mary Beth to the bank window. "Peter? Peter! The soldiers are going somewhere."

"What?" His voice came from the basement.

She turned to see him coming toward her with brooms.

Peter handed her a broom. "I will start in Grant's office, and you can work here."

Mary Beth nodded toward the windows. "Where are they going?"

Peter shrugged and turned toward the offices. "They did not send me their memos."

"I did not realize we had so many soldiers in the city." A wagon with ammunition came into view. "Look at that and tell me what you think."

Peter walked up behind her, resting his body against hers, and kissed her neck. "It appears they are leaving town, but I have guessed wrong before."

Mary Beth tried to ignore the tremor in her stomach. Her heart told her this was a historic event and maybe a bloody one. "What are we going to do?"

Peter, who remained behind her, squeezed her arm. "You and I are ready to leave the city. If either army fires one shot, we go."

"Correct." She steeled herself. She knew they had prayed before preparing for every contingency. Right now, she could sweep while she watched and listened.

An hour passed, and silence enveloped the city. Mary Beth had collected a pile of dirt, dust, hair, and paper scraps while taking note of the activity outside the bank.

However, suddenly she heard marching again, and she ran to the window. "Peter, the Union army is moving in."

Peter came into the foyer. "This floor looks great."

"See." She pointed.

He hurried to the window and threw an arm around her shoulder. "Yes. The Union is taking the city. Let's go upstairs to the office to watch."

Sending prayers heavenward, Mary Beth went upstairs. At the window, she allowed Peter to fold her in his arms.

A sudden banging caught their attention.

"I think someone's at the bank door," Peter said, releasing her. "I shall see who it is."

Mary Beth worried what that might mean. Would the Union arrest citizens? Would they be forced to leave town? She took a deep breath to control her voice. "Why not go together?"

He smiled. "I like that."

The two of them made their way down the steps, through the foyer, and straight ahead to the door. Three armed soldiers dressed in dark blue stood there. The middle one had sandy blond hair and brown eyes.

Mary Beth gasped. "Evans!"

The soldier spoke up, "You knew me as Evans, but I am Lieutenant Daniels of the Union Army Secret Service Bureau. I am taking possession of this bank for the Federal Government."

"Not Dixon?" Mary Beth asked.

"No. I used that alias in Atlanta," he said. "You must have investigated further."

"Yes." Mary Beth was so tired.

"May we go home?" Peter asked.

Lieutenant Daniels nodded. "Where can we find you?"

"We are staying with the Haskell family," Peter said.

They had lost the bank.

Chapter Thirty-Five

Union soldiers filled dusty Chattanooga streets as Peter and his wife strode to the Haskell home. Soldiers were chopping down trees, removing fences, swiping livestock, and taking food items from homes as they marched. Peter had nothing to fear. The Federals had already taken all he had—his job, his business, his vault, his key. His home remained damaged and uninhabited. At the moment, half his furniture sat in the rental house, and half sat in the burned house. Without a job, what did a man do?

He was tired.

They entered the sitting room where Mrs. Haskell rose to greet them. "We were worried about you. Would you like some tea? It always lifts the mood."

Mr. Haskell rose from a red brocade love seat and motioned for them to sit there together.

Mary Beth sat down, and Peter perched beside her.

"The Union took over the bank," Mary Beth said. "Perhaps they will request we manage it. They have no reason not to trust us, and you cannot assign a bank to anyone."

Peter rubbed his neck. "I am sure the Union has many bank managers. They do not need us."

He grimaced at his own words. All those nights burning records had worn him down. He should send a message to his mother and then rest. "I would like to lie down."

LATE THAT EVENING

Mary Beth sat down on a chair beside the bed to remove her stockings as she prepared to retire. She still could not believe the bank belonged to the government. Banking had formed the center of their life. Now they had nothing. At least the Haskell's had offered them a comfortable place to stay. Peter had fallen on the bed fully dressed, and he stared off into space. "What are you thinking?"

"I have been praying." He ran his hand over his mouth. "I am a banker. I have a degree, and I am good at what I do. We shall buy the bank from the government."

"What a good idea." Mary Beth clapped. "How can we make that happen?"

Peter rose and paced. "I am thinking about that."

"Before we do that, we need to clear up this cloud hanging over us. People need to know we had nothing to do with those murders."

"No. You let me worry about our reputation." Peter glared at her. "You are alive, and I want you to stay that way."

Mary Beth did not want to wait for Peter to act.

THE NEXT MORNING

Right after breakfast, Mary Beth left with Peter for the sheriff's house to collect rent. She was thankful Peter remembered he still had a source of income. She could not believe how the city had changed. Union soldiers had set up tents all over, even in the Haskell's yard. She and Peter had to step around their tents to avoid damaging them. The soldiers had chopped down all the trees and were building breastworks fortifying the city.

Once they reached the sheriff's house, she stopped. "I should speak with Ida while I am here."

"I shall come for you when I finish." Peter nodded. "Do not leave here without me."

Mary Beth had been praying all morning, and she prayed again for both of them. Walking to the right, she went around the house to the basement entrance and knocked.

Ida opened the door—her face was covered in bruises. Her abdomen was protruding now, making the pregnancy obvious.

"Ida, you look terrible." Mary Beth touched her cheek.

"Actually, I am much better. I am learning what makes him angry so I can avoid getting hurt."

"I need to go through your husband's things."

Ida scrunched her face. "He might kill you."

"The Confederates have left the city. So, you should be safe."

"No," Ida shook her head. "He told me he had a different commission and would not leave right away."

"He cannot walk through town in a gray uniform anymore." Mary Beth nodded toward the soldiers camped in her yard.

"Now he's dressing in regular clothes so he can come and go."

"I shall be fast, please." Mary Beth was ready to get on her knees.

Ida opened the door wider. "Very well. I shall keep watch. At least, I warned you."

Mary Beth hurried around the apartment and looked at everything. Any papers or orders he might have received would give her information about his role, but she particularly wanted to see what medications he might have. In the closet, she found a couple suits and long sleeve shirts, and Ida's clothing.

She left the closet and went to drawers in the highboy. She pawed through socks, underwear, suspenders, handkerchiefs, and loose change. Finally, she found what she was looking for—a medicine bottle. She twisted it open. The smell was licorice without the red berries. With this information and the pictures that identified Stanford, she was almost certain he poisoned the grocer.

Ida ran in. "Quick, I see him coming. Hide under the bed."

Mary Beth slid underneath and listened.

"I saw that banker walking toward the house," Stanford said. "Did you ask him to come?"

"No." Ida said. "I have not talked to Mr. Chandler."

"Stay away from his wife." Stanford growled. "I have to deliver a report, so do not expect me until late tonight."

"Very well." Ida's voice sounded frightened.

The door slammed and Mary Beth came out, sweating.

Ida rushed into the bedroom. "He just left. You had better leave soon."

Mary Beth peeked out the window. "He is heading south, so I should be safe. Besides, Peter is asking the soldiers upstairs for rent, so I have an escort."

Mary Beth hoped Ida was safe staying here.

Energy flowed through Peter as he left the sheriff's house. This was his first time to receive paper money printed by the Union. The soldiers gave him seven dollars for rent. Since the Union proclaimed it money, legal tender, he could purchase wood and building supplies to fix their house. At least he could work while he made plans to buy the bank. His next stop would be the dockyards where he would get what he needed.

He went around the back of the house, and Mary Beth came out of the basement apartment. She wore a scowl, and he wondered what Stanford had been doing.

"Ida lives in fear, and I wish I could help her." She shrugged.

"Her husband evacuated with the army, right?"

She shook her head. "No. He has another commission and wears everyday clothing."

"That sounds like a spy to me."

"I agree." She grabbed his arm. They had left the sheriff's yard and were heading into town. "Did you forget? We are not going to the bank. To get back to the Haskell's house, we turn here."

He nodded in the direction of the Tennessee River. "I want some lumber for repairs. Now that I have rent money, I can get started on our house."

Suddenly Peter heard a shot and then another from behind him. His heart raced as he pulled his wife down to the dirt road. "Someone was firing at us."

Military darted toward them with guns drawn. Peter stood slowly and helped his wife up.

"I'm Lieutenant Shook, and I need your firearm."

"I have none." He swallowed hard as soldiers checked his pockets. His heart was still thumping hard.

"The shots must have been fired toward you." Shook grimaced. "Do you have any enemies?"

"Not that I am aware of." Peter was reviewing his friends and acquaintances, and he could think of no one except McDonald and Stanford. Did he dare say that? He had no proof.

"I advise you to stay in your home. Better yet, leave town." He stalked away.

Soldiers returned to their duties building fortifications and setting up sandbags. As they neared the river, another soldier approached. "You cannot go any further."

Peter had feared the military might refuse him entry. These people from the north did not know him. "Where can I buy lumber to repair my home?"

"You will need a pass from the general. All available wood is being used for breastworks."

Peter ground his teeth. "Very well. I shall obtain a pass and return."

He had lost the bank, but a band of soldiers would not defeat him.

Chapter Thirty-Six

Peter fingered the note in his pocket as he walked past the picket fence and up to the porch of his house where Mr. Riddle awaited him. Several soldiers had pitched tents in his front yard. Two of them built a small fire and had a kettle over it. His secretary sat on the porch and approached as he got closer to his house. "Riddle. I got your note. What can I do for you?"

Riddle grinned. "Two of our customers have given payments to me, so I felt like I should pass them along to you. I didn't feel comfortable taking this to the Haskell's home, so I asked you to meet me here."

"Thank you, sir." Peter accepted the gold Riddle offered him, and then he gazed into the older man's face. This man had worked for his father, but he was not just an employee. He was a trusted friend. "We are still banking—in exile."

The two men laughed together.

"I need a job, sir."

"And I need an employee." Peter inhaled as he organized his thoughts. The Union took the bank building, but not his customers and their money. He had no plans to lose Riddle or Grant. After all, he had rent money in his pocket to buy wood. "Let's make this our headquarters.

The bedrooms are empty because we moved furniture into the rental house. When we aren't banking, we can repair the burned areas."

"I assume you are including Mr. Grant? He is experiencing the same situation."

"Yes. I want him back." Peter rubbed his forehead as he thought. "In fact, if either of you have cash you would like to contribute to buying back the bank, I welcome that."

Riddle chuckled. "I shall communicate that to him."

THE SAME DAY

Anna had never gone this long without hearing from her son, and she worried. Maud reported the Union army had encamped all over the city. She would never venture out by herself until calm returned. Despite her unbearable headache, Anna heard a scuffle at the front door. She adjusted the damp cloth on her head to sit up. "Ruth, dear. Please see who is at the door."

Ruth, with John trailing her, headed out of the sitting room.

Anna hoped it brought good news. She was not going to venture out until Weston arrived, and he had not come.

Ruth appeared carrying notes. "Mama, one of these was penned yesterday, right after the soldiers came into the city."

"Read them." Anna could hardly breathe, and she would not be able to decipher a word.

"The first is from Peter, and he said soldiers came and took possession of the bank. He and Mary Beth are fine."

Her mother gasped. "What? That's terrible. How unfair. I shall have Weston look into the situation. He knows everyone."

"The next one was written this morning from Mary Beth. She says Peter wants to buy the bank from the Union and wants your help."

Anna sat up. Peter needed her, and she always rose to the occasion. "Bring me writing materials. I shall reply right away. Of course, I will see he has what he needs."

THE NEXT MORNING
HASKELL SITTING ROOM

Peter rose when Lieutenant Daniels entered the room in dress uniform with gun and sword. Peter never thought he would see the man he knew as Evans again, and certainly not in here. However, he would take advantage of the opportunity to see if the military was open to selling him the bank. "Good morning, sir."

"Good morning. We entered the bank, and we found printing materials in the vault. That surprised us, and I thought I would ask where you put the records and gold."

Peter chose to be honest without telling him the hiding place. "I evacuated the bank since the money does not belong to me. I want my clients to trust me completely."

"And the printing supplies?"

"I allowed the newspaper to use the vault for a few days before they left the city. I had nothing in there, so I saw no reason the room could not be used."

"That sounds generous. I worked for you almost a year, sir. I have the greatest respect for you."

"I appreciate that." Peter took a deep breath before he brought up the subject on his mind. "I have noticed the Union has taken advantage of Mr. Haskell's law degree, and I commend them since he is an honest man. I would like to know whether the Union would be interested in selling the bank to me. I would cooperate fully in dispensing the payroll."

"Possibly." Daniels raised his eyebrows. "I shall add my recommendation. You do not favor the Confederacy?"

"I was trying not to stir up trouble, but I cannot sanction a government that allows slavery even though I believe in states' rights."

"I feel sure you will have to sign a pledge that you support the Union, and we do use legal tender. Congress authorized printed money. Union money is green and black."

Peter's heart rate sped up. He did not expect to have Daniel's support. "I would willingly do that."

"I will bring this situation to the general's staff." Daniels turned to leave.

Peter whispered a prayer for that to happen soon. "I stand ready at any moment to bring my case."

"Of course. You remember I know you well."

"One more item." Peter stood, wondering how much Rosecrans would be involved. He might turn over such details to those under him. "I would like to report someone shot at me and my wife this morning while we were downtown."

Daniels frowned. "That is serious. Do you suspect anyone?"

Peter related his concerns about Stanford.

"Confederate soldiers have left the city, though."

"Yes. However, Stanford's wife says he has a new commission, and my wife saw him yesterday in plain clothes. They live in the sheriff's old house, which the bank purchased."

"I shall pass along this news."

"May I ask what your assignment was in Chattanooga?"

"That is confidential, but I will tell you. My superiors sent me here to find a spy with liberal financial resources."

"What was your conclusion?"

Daniels laughed. "I was your only spy."

Peter looked around and realized his wife had left the room.

"I saw her leave too," Daniels said. "Based on my observations of you, I believe I can trust you both.

AT THE SAME TIME

Mary Beth hurried out of the sitting room while Daniels was talking to Peter and went in search of Jane. News Daniels brought energized her, and she had to talk. She ran toward Jane's room and had to force herself to wait for her friend to answer.

"What?" Jane opened the door holding her finger in a book. "What are you worried about?"

"Evans used to work for us, but he was assigned to find a spy."

"You are not making sense." Jane turned down the corner of a page and closed the book. She stepped back and motioned Mary Beth to a chair by the bed while she eased onto the ruffled bedcovers. "Come in and explain."

Mary Beth recounted the bank's recent upheavals. "A man plotted to get our bank. He was trying to either kill our reputation or make our bank crash. Now I know the person is probably a spy based on what Lieutenant Daniels just told Peter."

"I know you." Jane raised a brow. "You have someone in mind. Who?"

"I believe Weston is the man. He is a financier who makes loans, and he's obsessed with building a larger empire. He also has an uncanny ability to get tea or coffee or whatever in short supply. I could use your help to clear our reputation."

"Me? I know nothing about banking." Jane placed a hand on the base of her neck. "Have you noticed soldiers line our streets?"

"Peter and I visited the sheriff's house yesterday in complete safety, and we can purchase food during the day."

"Great." Jane rolled her eyes. "So what do you recommend?"

"I would like to look around Weston's office for documents, papers, letters, and notes. He has always offered us delicacies like coffee or sugar. What if we visited and requested something special for Peter's mother?

"Weston would see through that because Peter's mother would ask for what she wanted."

Mary Beth nodded. "You are right; however, her birthday is nearing. We could ask if he could obtain a special brand of tea or coffee for her."

"You told me the Union holds the bank, which means clearing your name will have no effect."

"Peter will buy it back." Mary Beth sounded confident, but she prayed he succeeded.

Chapter Thirty-Seven

Early Afternoon That Day

A nap had restored Anna, and she woke ready to assist her son. She had no intention of entrusting any more of her own cash to Peter because she didn't want to lose it all. Weston, however, could do whatever Peter needed. He could connect Peter with money and the right people. Plus, her timing was great. If she arrived close to dinner, Weston would expect her to dine with him, and then see her home. She bathed, washed her face, and donned a light blue dress which enhanced her best features before leaving. As she walked down the narrow lane, she wished for the carriage they once owned before the war.

Weston had a palatial residence on Lookout Mountain, but he also had a home just north of the city right on the river. He told Anna he'd stay in town this week and she walked about thirty minutes before she arrived at the large white house, which faced the Tennessee River. Anna had to walk past the open library windows. She could hear voices.

"Imbecile! What were you thinking? Discharging a gun …"

A muffled reply.

"Such stupidity. I have spent hours concealing your mistakes."

Anna knew Weston was speaking, but she had no idea who he spoke to. This represented part of him she had never seen and did not like.

She paused a few feet from the window to listen. However, she heard no more, and she continued around the house to the porch bordered by large white columns and knocked on the front door.

After a brief delay, Weston opened the door, "Anna, what a pleasure. Come in and relax. I do hope you stay for dinner."

Anna wondered which man was Weston. The man who spoke roughly or the man who stood before her now. She might not mention the bank to him either. "I have been so uneasy since the Union took the city, but at least I heard from Peter."

Weston smiled and escorted her inside. "Tell me the problem. I shall see if I can put things right."

Mr. Weston's Home
The Next Morning

Mary Beth exchanged glances with Jane as they entered the Weston sitting room. "How elegant."

Jane pointed to the fabric of the sofa. "I think this is silk."

"Yes." Mary Beth eased onto the sofa beside her friend while fingering the cloth. Weston had done the room in shades of champagne which was set off by mahogany paneling. A lavish oriental rug combined the wood tones with a touch of red.

"Are you sure this was wise?" Jane had a deep line between her eyes.

Mary Beth did not want to admit she was terrified. Weston would be a challenge to unravel, but she had to prove he was their man. "I have prayed, and I refuse to give up."

"Good afternoon." Weston walked into the room spreading his arms wide. "What a privilege to entertain such lovely ladies. I hope Mr. Haskell and Mr. Chandler are both well?"

Jane glanced wide-eyed at Mary Beth.

"They are well, thanks." Mary Beth tried to match his relaxed tone and hide her anxiety. "All of us survived the Union occupation. We are not quite sure how much freedom we have yet though."

"We are under martial law." Weston sat in an overstuffed wing chair across from the sofa. "I am sure General Bragg wants Chattanooga back, and you can be sure Rosecrans has plans to take the mountains around the city. There will be a battle. The question is where it will take place."

Mary Beth shuddered.

"There's good news. Your medications are useful to both sides, and everyone needs a banker." He nodded at Jane. "Your father's law degree will make him valuable too."

"I suppose everyone will want to keep us alive. Isn't that good news, Jane?"

"Hmm?" Jane opened her mouth and closed it again. "Oh, yes."

"But I can see the talk of war makes you uncomfortable," Weston said. "How I miss having a lady around the house. What can I do for you?"

"Mrs. Chandler's birthday is coming up, and we wonder if you know how we could obtain a gift for her?" Mary Beth believed she sounded too on edge, but he had been talking about war. "Maybe some nice fabric?"

"Coffee?" Jane blinked. "I thought she liked coffee."

"She does." Mary Beth touched her arm. "And I know I mentioned that to you, but I have had time to think more."

"I recently gave her coffee," Weston said.

Mary Beth willed herself to relax. "Jane and I discussed what she might want, and coffee came up. We have been staying with the Haskell family."

"That's right. Your house is still damaged. I commend your thoughtfulness." He tucked a cushion behind his back. "You must know how fond I am of your mother-in-law. She loves to mother you."

Mary Beth had a lot of affection for Peter's mother, even though she tried to manage their lives too much sometimes. "She sews very well, and we have not been able to find textiles ever since the war started."

"I recall she bought some in Savannah." Jane frowned.

"Yes. That was a year ago." Mary Beth smiled at her friend. Jane had not caught onto her ploy. "Anna bought some for Ruth. She will not buy for herself when her daughter is in need."

Weston stood. "You choose what kind of fabric and what color. I shall be thrilled to oblige. And anytime you want to drop by and chat, I would love to get to know you better. After all, I may be getting married to Anna soon."

An idea came to Mary Beth, and she chose without mulling it over. "Do you mind if we wander around your house? I might find something just the right color."

Jane caressed the sofa. "This color and cloth would be perfect."

"Please look around." Weston smiled. "You may find something you like better."

Mary Beth could be wrong. Weston didn't seem secretive.

Mary Beth kept a lively pace while leaving Weston's home. While she believed she succeeded in her initial encounter with him, she had no desire to stay longer. The evil he represented made her angry, and she longed for the safety of the Haskell home. Jane, who strode along beside her, was falling behind and breathing hard. Besides oppressive humidity made the morning feel warmer than it was. "Did you see anything that made you suspicious?"

"Not at all." Jane sighed. "I cannot imagine why you are so sure."

"I have a feeling he wants our bank."

"Why? From the looks of his home, he is not needy."

"I agree, but I know I am right." Mary Beth could not explain her hunch. The return journey took them past more and more soldiers. She had to walk with more care when they arrived at the border of the town. Soldiers had erected tents everywhere.

"These soldiers make me edgy. Can we hurry home?"

"Of course." Mary Beth sped up and steered her friend away from town.

"Mary Beth?"

She turned to see Dr. Smith coming alongside. "Hello, doctor. Weston just told us we are under martial law."

"Yes. However, the services you and your husband offer are essential. Right now, you should be busy preparing medications for the upcoming battles. If I can assist you, please let me know. The authorities have been respectful and will listen to our concerns."

Mary Beth suppressed thoughts of war and considered the preparations she had on hand. "I could use Ruth's help."

"Very good." He waved as he turned into the city. "I shall see she arrives safely at the Haskell home where you are working."

Mary Beth wished she had asked about the bank.

ONE WEEK LATER

Peter had arrived at his home headquarters earlier than usual this morning. Grant had set up an appointment with a potential client, and Peter wanted to ensure he was prepared. The exiled bank looked good. He had purchased from sutlers who came to sell goods to the military. He and his staff had repaired the roof, and the kitchen section of the house neared completion. With odd scraps and bricks Peter had set up a rustic office in one bedroom. He even had obtained a small supply of clean paper. Records Mary Beth rescued from the bank building remained in Bennet's old portfolio, which Peter carried with him. Once the war ended, he would make sure his staff reimbursed the family for its use.

Grant knocked at the open door and stepped inside. "Riddle has seen a man moving around in the wooded area behind us. He acts as if he does not want to be seen."

Peter had been concerned people would be getting curious about their repairs to the house. Their banking activities must remain under wraps. The Union would likely object and maybe arrest him, and the spy who targeted his bank could continue his torment. "Mary Beth and I should move back in. Our presence here would prevent snooping, especially with my wife preparing medications in the kitchen."

"It won't explain Riddle and me," Grant said.

"I can claim you as domestics." Peter rose and handed him the broom. "Clean off the front and back porch. Perhaps that will allay suspicion for today."

Peter whispered a prayer for the safety of the bank.

Chapter Thirty-Eight

The Next Day

Mary Beth hurried down Main Street toward the grocer while marveling at the increased numbers of military walking the streets. Crowds thronged the train depot too, and she wondered how many injured soldiers would arrive. Today she was out to purchase herbs since her garden was damaged by those who put out the fire. Besides, she wanted to see how Mrs. Nelson fared after her husband's passing.

A bell over the door rang as she entered the store, something Mrs. Nelson must have installed. The shelves appeared better stocked than Mary Beth expected, and several other customers milled about. Molly came toward her. "Good morning. How is your mother?"

"She still cries a lot, especially at night." Molly did not meet her eye. "How can I help you?"

"I have a list of dried herbs." Mary Beth pulled a list from her pocket.

"I shall have to ask Mama about a few of these." Molly left for the back room.

Mary Beth looked over the various baskets while dodging other shoppers. Finally, Mrs. Nelson came out with her youngest daughter clinging to her skirt. After reaching into her apron pocket Mrs. Nelson pulled out a cloth sack, which she pressed into Mary Beth's hand. "Good to see ya, ma'am. I am giving you my quarterly payment even though the bank is not open right now. I hope your husband is well."

Mary Beth whispered a prayer of thanksgiving as slipped the bag into her purse. "Thank you. Peter has been cleaning up the damage to our house. We would like to move back in."

"I do hope you can. It's possible I can assist you with that project if I know what you need. You are such a nice couple." Mrs. Nelson wiped a tear.

"Mrs. Nelson, my husband and I both appreciate you." Mary Beth touched her arm as she swallowed a lump in her throat. The war and the problems it caused made you thankful for friends. "We are honored to have you as a customer."

"Molly is sortin' through those herbs you need. I'll be a sendin' her out to your place when she is done."

"We are staying with the Haskell family right now." Mary Beth did not want her sending herbs to the empty house.

"Yes'm. We will get it there."

"Thank you." She offered Mrs. Nelson the brightest smile she could muster and allowed her gaze drop to Mrs. Nelson's youngest child.

The daughter stared at Mary Beth with widened eyes. "But why did you kill my daddy?"

The store grew quiet, and Mary Beth felt overheated. How do you tell a child you did not hurt her father?

"No. You mustna' say things that. Your papa done drunk himself to death, child. Tis no fault of Mrs. Chandler."

Mary Beth must clear their name.

SEPT 19
JUST AFTER DAWN

Mary Beth, accompanied by Ruth and John, entered the Haskell basement to pack up medical supplies. John would assist with lifting the crates when they were full, but now he carried paper and pencil. Today she and Peter would move back home. She dreaded the process, but she would enjoy being back in her own house. Yesterday Peter had borrowed crates from the grocer and bought several bundles of straw from farmers. "Ruth, take all the dried herbs and pack them in this crate. I will use the straw to protect our jars."

"What about the cooking utensils?" Ruth picked up the mortar and pestle.

"We have large baskets for those items, but I think they are in my room."

"I can find them when I finish here."

Mary Beth was so thankful for Ruth. "Thanks."

John plopped down at the table they used to grind herbs and sketched.

Mary Beth pulled several jars off the shelves against the wall to put in crates.

A series of blasts erupted in the distance.

She jerked, banging the shelf behind her. An avalanche of empty jars cascaded onto the brick floor. Ridiculous. She glared at the mess of broken glass. The detonation was far enough away, the explosions posed no danger. Perhaps her reaction came from being tense for too long.

John stopped sketching and fetched the broom. He swept and dumped the shattered glass into the trash bin.

"Great job, John." She marveled how the Lord provided. While he worked, she peeked at his drawing—a man climbing out a window. What had he seen?

Peter came in. "Dr. Smith reports a major battle going on just over the river in Chickamauga. They are going to need medications."

She sighed, thinking of all the suffering. "I am going to need more jars. I accidently broke a number of them this morning."

Ruth paused with her hands full of dried herbs. "Why not ask Weston to find some? He brought some stunning beige silk for mother."

"Good idea." That might give Mary Beth a chance to interact with him again. Or, even better, maybe she could go through his papers and documents to uncover his guilt.

Two Days Later

Peter's stomach churned as he waited in the sitting room of the house he had planned to rent from Mr. Haskell's client. Sweat ran down his back as he glared at the mismatched furniture and light green walls. What irony. The Union general living here now had the keys to C&R Bank and would allow Peter to plead for the right to purchase his own bank.

A noise in the back of the house made Peter's heart beat faster.

A heavy-set man with a graying beard, and dark wavy hair entered from the stairwell in the hallway. "Good afternoon, I am Major General Thomas. How can I assist you?"

Peter cleared his throat. "I am Peter Chandler, former owner of C&R Bank. I have a degree in banking and finance."

The man sat down on the sofa across from him and laughed. "You are the man who surrendered an empty bank building."

"I did." Peter sat up straighter. "The money belongs to my clients, so I evacuated the bank before you occupied the city. When someone gives me their money, I consider that trust sacred."

"What devotion." He puffed out his chest. "Daniels recommended you highly, but I am hard to convince. Tell me why you should own the bank."

"First of all, I am highly qualified to handle the money. I graduated with highest honors from Dartmouth. I have remained on the gold standard since I believe the Confederate paper is just that. Worthless. My investments earn five to six percent interest per annum."

The General whistled.

"You are going to need a banker who knows how to work with the paymaster, and I will cooperate fully. I have an excellent reputation, and I know key men in banking all over the south."

"Are you invested in the railroad?"

"I am. I still hold northern investments even though I have not received dividends since the war began. At present I have a large warehouse full of cotton the Union may purchase right away."

"Daniels reported there were some accusations against some of your employees."

Peter paused, knowing he must watch his words. "I would vouch for any of my employees without hesitation."

"How much will you give us?"

Peter pushed a document toward him, hoping that number was enough.

Thomas read the entire document, turned it over, and held it up to the light, seemingly looking for a watermark. "Have the papers drawn up. As long as there are no pending criminal charges hanging over employees, I shall sign them."

Peter sprang to his feet. "Thank you, sir!"

Mary Beth carried yet another basket packed with medication. Ruth who strode beside her had piles of sheets for bandages, and John lugged jars of soup for the wounded soldiers. They headed to their church, which the Union had possessed after tearing out the pews to make a hospital. As she drew near, she tried to ignore the pile of bloodied limbs the surgeons left.

An orderly met her inside. "Oh, good. We need more medicine."

Dr. Smith followed behind him. "Particularly quinine. I fear infection is spreading through the wounded."

"We also brought soup for the patients and sheets for bandages." Mary Beth transferred medication from her basket to the nurse's desk.

The head nurse entered. "I cannot thank you enough for this soup. We have not seen this many injuries in any single battle. The military said sixteen thousand men were wounded in two days."

Mary Beth groaned. "That's horrible. Is that just the Union?"

Dr. Smith nodded. "I understand the numbers are about the same for the Confederacy."

"I had best keep prepping medications, but I must have more glass jars." The thought of that many men wounded made her stomach uncomfortable. "I shall do all I can."

Ruth gave the sheets to an orderly. "Mr. Weston promised us more, and we are going there now to see if they have arrived."

"Is it safe?" Mary Beth could imagine her husband worrying about her walking so far.

"Yes." Smith nodded. "Tell them your mission. I think the soldiers will cooperate."

She wanted jars, but more than that, she wanted evidence. Maybe today she would get that.

Chapter Thirty-Nine

THE SAME DAY

Peter was reorganizing his makeshift desk to find more room for his work when a scratching sound caught his attention. He looked up and burst into laughter at Riddle, who stood at the door of his office. "You have leaves in your hair and a few twigs."

Riddle's face turned bright red as he brushed the array from his hair. "I have been hiding in the bushes, like you asked. And I have the evidence you need."

The flush on his friend's face was amusing, but he refused to comment. "I appreciate your willingness to humiliate yourself. Tell me what you know."

"I overheard Stanford and McDonald discussing the bank. McDonald killed Bennet, and Stanford killed the grocer in hopes of spoiling our reputation. They indicate Weston's distaste with many of their choices. Right now they are on their way to meet Weston at his house."

Peter glanced at the time. "Mary Beth is supposed to go to Weston's today to pick up glass jars. She hoped to go through the man's desk for clues, and she will snoop. Considering what you know, we'd best send her help."

Grant walked in. "Anna was supposed to confront Weston today as well. She has been poking into his files and found things that look suspicious."

"Oh, dear." Peter could not lose his wife and mother. He grabbed his pistol. "Pray for me."

Mary Beth sat on the gray silk sofa fuming. She had waited for Weston for more than thirty minutes now, and she would rather be grinding up herbs for medication. Ruth wandered around the room examining each piece of furniture, oohing over the exquisite decor. John had drifted off, which was typical. He usually stayed in the vicinity but never sat still.

Mary Beth leapt up. She had to act. Now. If she could locate the place Weston did business, maybe she could solve the murders. "I am going to search."

"I will go with you." Ruth pointed to a door. "How about that way?"

Mary Beth walked straight ahead into the dining room and saw a kitchen to her left. To her right, however, a hallway led to a library. Bookcases lined two walls from the floor to ceiling. This might be the place. A filing cabinet was built into the wall on either side of a huge executive desk. A floor length window behind the desk had burgundy drapes pulled back with burgundy tasseled rope. She looked around and listened for Weston's return. When she heard and saw nothing, she opened the first drawer. Weston kept a file on each company he dealt with and maintained records on how much he invested, listing each dividend he received. She flipped through company names, looking for anything on Chattanooga.

"I love books." Ruth pulled one off the shelf. "Such pretty leather covers."

"Look through those and see if you discover any papers." Weston might hide documents there rather than his files.

Ruth giggled. "I shall enjoy this."

Mary Beth walked around the house and gazed outdoors before she continued. When she saw no one approaching, she returned to the office and the huge desk. The front drawer had pens and ink. On the left, she opened a deep drawer that extended the depth of the desk. Empty envelopes and blank paper filled half the drawer. Once she took those out, the drawer did not look deep enough, and she suspected a false bottom. She tapped the empty drawer until she found a catch. When she sprang it, a brown book lay inside, filled with small writing.

She sat down at the desk and started reading. This was a diary, of sorts, but she could not tell what year it started. The writer told a story about a beautiful young dancer who lived in Europe. Weston once said he missed having a lady in the house. Perhaps this was his lady, but the material had nothing to do with spies. Where else should she look?

A sudden noise caught her attention.

"What are you doing?" Weston stood in the open door. "His eyes narrowed, and his forehead wrinkled with deep creases.

Her face blazed as she glanced around at the mess she'd made. Envelopes and paper covered the top of his desk. Ruth had tossed leather books on the floor after shaking them out. An escape option would not come to mind. She must think fast. "I came for my jars, but you weren't here. I figured I would find them somewhere in your home or at least records of where you bought them. This is important. Patients could die."

McDonald and Stanford entered behind Weston. Stanford raised his pistol and fired, shattering the window behind her. Mary Beth slid to the floor under the desk, quivering. Now she was in real danger, and she probed her mind for a scheme to save herself and the two children.

Maybe she could bargain with her life and have Ruth and John go free.

"You idiot! At least you have horrendous aim. I should have never hired you," Weston said. "I'm tired of hiding your mistakes."

More gunfire erupted. Some from inside, but at least one shot came in from outdoors. Mary Beth prayed and stayed under the desk. With shots coming both directions, she might put herself in danger if she tried to ease out. Her heart pounded as she thought about Ruth and John. Had they left the room? What could she do to protect them? If Ruth or John could stay alive and tell their story, Peter could buy the bank. But if those two young friends died, she would not be able to live with herself.

"Mrs. Chandler? Miss Chandler? John?"

That was Evans. Daniels. She wanted to peek out, but she shook all over. "Is it safe?"

"Yes, ma'am."

She inched out. Weston, McDonald, and Stanford lay on the floor, bleeding. It took a moment for her to realize they were dead. The room spun, but then she saw Ruth in the hallway, crying while embracing John. Mary Beth wandered out into the hallway. Mrs. Chandler lay on the floor, dead.

Mary Beth embraced both Ruth and John. She could not believe what she saw, but looking again did not make it any more real.

"I apologize." Daniels pressed his lips together. "She got caught in the crossfire. I think she must have come to see Weston."

Chapter Forty

Once again Peter occupied a chair in the dreary green sitting room with hodge-podge furnishings. This time Mary Beth, her eyes bloodshot with crying, sat opposite him on the somewhat-more-plush bluish green sofa. Teary-eyed, Ruth huddled beside her, and John wandered around the room. Daniels, who wore his blue dress uniform, held a sheaf of papers he continued to rustle. Riddle occupied a straight chair beside Peter. He kept his eyes on the floor.

"I feel sure Thomas will not be much longer." Daniels tapped the papers he held. "He wanted all of you here, despite your grief."

Ruth sobbed on Mary Beth's shoulder.

"I am sorry." He shook his head. "It's military protocol."

At last heavy footsteps came from outside, and Major General Thomas entered with several other officers. He turned to the men with him. "I have a matter here to clear up. Come by in an hour or so to finish our business."

Daniels stood at attention.

"At ease. I apologize for keeping you waiting." He went to the rustic table that now sat off to the side of the room. "I need to hear what happened to clear the bank employees of any guilt."

Daniels handed him the papers. "Let me start, sir."

Thomas nodded. "Please."

"Let me introduce the people here. We have Peter Chandler and his wife, Mary Beth. They owned C&R Bank. Peter's sister, Ruth, is beside Mary Beth. John is Ruth's friend. He seldom speaks, but he is a witness to these events. We have several of his sketches. Mr. Riddle serves as Peter's secretary. He has evidence which he overheard about the men involved in the shooting."

"Welcome." Thomas nodded to each. "We are here to establish the bank's reputation."

Daniels continued. "The Union brought me into the South because they suspected a double agent who was involved in high level finances. I was given a wife and kids to substantiate my story, and I worked for a time at an Atlanta bank. In the short time I spent there, I cleared the employees there, but I advised my superior officers that the double agent resided in or around Chattanooga. Since we were going to take the city, finding this man was vital."

"About a year ago, I lost an employee and started searching for a replacement," Peter said.

"I was still at the Atlanta bank at the time and heard about the offer. We put together a recommendation letter from the bank I used to obtain the job. When we received a letter from C&R Bank, an employee in Atlanta was supposed to verify my identity. It appeared he failed, which later brought Mr. Chandler there asking about me."

"I could tell they were divided on the handling of Mr. Charles Daniels, but I did not know why." Peter laughed.

"We hired Mr. Evans." Mary Beth said, sniffling. "And we grew fond of him. Evans did excellent work and proved trustworthy."

"That was the name I took," Daniels explained.

"I discovered the Confederacy hired Bennet to find the spy, and he suspected our bank too," Mary Beth said. "Bennet picked a fight with our bank manager."

"Wait." Peter raised a hand. "We had a burglary first. Who did that?"

"Bad man." John pulled a sketch from his pocket and gave it to Peter.

"John, is this Lieutenant McDonald?"

He nodded.

Peter handed the sketch to Thomas. "We are not sure how John knew this. Here he depicts confederate Lieutenant McDonald climbing out the basement window of the bank, which we know the burglar did. After that robbery, I bricked up the window and completed the vault to protect our gold."

Thomas glanced around the room. "Lieutenant McDonald is where?"

"Shot today." Daniels said. "He is dead."

Thomas cleared his throat. "Please continue."

"It appears Bennet had a hot temper, and he physically attacked the bank manager," Daniels continued.

"Is the bank manager here?" Thomas asked.

"No." Daniels said. "He was not involved in the event today. Mr. Riddle."

Riddle cleared his throat. "Peter and I have been repairing Mr. Chandler's house after a fire."

Peter raised a hand. "We believe Stanford set our house on fire as part of his attack on the bank. I am not sure I can prove that."

"I can." Mary Beth raised her hand. "I gave Stanford's wife some medication in a fancy lavender jar. After the fire, I found part of that jar, burned and broken, but I am sure it was the same."

Riddle spoke up. "As we repaired the house, we noted men in the woods who appeared to be watching. Since we wanted to ensure the building remained secure, I volunteered to act as security by hiding in bushes and mounds of leaves. Today I heard McDonald take credit for shooting Bennet, and then he had the grocer place the blame on the bank manager. Sergeant Stanford then poisoned the grocer, and he acted in such a way to throw blame on Mary Beth Chandler. In particular, he suggested to the youngest child that Mary Beth mixed the poison to kill her father."

Mary Beth groaned. "I wondered why she seemed so certain."

"My interaction with bank employees was the reason I met Mr. Weston. Weston was wealthy, and he was always looking for ways to expand his financial empire. We know he passed and received messages from both Union and Confederate, which made me wary of him. I believe he masterminded a robbery involving Mr. Field who was bringing dividends to C&R Bank. I located the money and returned it to the bank."

"You are the one who put the gold in the filing cabinet?" Mary Beth's eyes widened.

"I am." Daniels looked at his stack of papers. "And I experimented with taking gold and receipts to see if any of your employees might be involved with Weston."

"We found that in your desk," Peter said.

"I wanted Henderson to arrest you." Mary Beth hugged Ruth closer and rubbed her arm.

"We come to today." Daniels took a deep breath. "I believe he was courting Mrs. Anna Chandler as another means to ingratiate himself with bank owners."

"Where is she?" Thomas looked around.

"Murdered in the cross-fire." Daniels said.

Ruth cried harder. Mary Beth hugged her closer.

"She was beginning to suspect Weston," Peter said. "She told me several things he said recently did not fit together. I knew she wanted to talk to him, but I had no idea she would show up like she did."

"We have been closing in for some days," Daniels said. "Including false messages and overlapping times to rattle him. He was particularly clever, so I had to involve a network of men to confound him. I had several pose as Confederate spies from Jefferson Davis as well."

Mary Beth spoke up, "I put together herbal medications for the military hospitals, and I had asked him for a supply of jars. I really needed them too, since I broke a good many moving back home. I went there today to get them, but Weston was not there."

"Riddle overheard McDonald and Stanford bragging about what they had done. He heard they were meeting with Weston," Peter said. "So, I asked Daniels to go for Weston and asked him to watch out for my wife and mother."

"We had already surrounded his house and watched Mary Beth Chandler enter with John and Ruth. Weston showed up, and McDonald and Stanford followed right behind him. When we heard gunfire, we moved in to protect the family," Daniels said. "Mrs. Anna Chandler showed up after the shooting began. I regret her death more than I can say."

"Does anyone have a question?" Thomas asked.

"Someone shot at Peter and me when we were moving in here. Does anyone know who that was?" Mary Beth asked.

"Mother overheard Weston scolding someone about shooting in town. I believe it was Stanford. I am also thankful he couldn't shoot, or we might both be dead," Peter said.

Mary Beth spoke up, "The grocer's wife confided she became concerned after the robbery because a new merchant approached her husband. I don't think it's related."

"Anyone else?" Thomas asked.

The room was silent except for sniffling.

"We accepted a few quarterly payments after you entered town," Peter said. "I thought I had better tell you in case you heard that elsewhere."

"Mr. and Mrs. Chandler, you and your employees possess incredible stamina and courage to live through this. I cannot believe you stayed on the gold standard. If you had not, I could not consider allowing you to continue. You are unstoppable. Please accept my commendation. I will officially return the bank to your possession." Thomas signed a paper he then handed to Daniels.

Daniels handed documents to Peter, Mary Beth, and Riddle. "We need a signature on this oath of loyalty to the Union."

"And that concludes my business." Thomas stood.

"But the money? I was going to buy the bank from you," Peter said.

"Read the document Daniels has. We will accept a dollar in gold, and then we will return the keys." He left the room.

Peter laughed, tears rolling down his face.

Chapter Forty-One

November 1863
Office of C&R Bank

A cool breeze came in from the open window, rustling the stack of papers Peter had to sign. In an attempt to keep them from blowing away, he placed a small stone bust of Lincoln on top of them.

He looked around his office and smiled. How he enjoyed the open window that faced the Chattanooga streets. The bookshelf across from him belonged to his father, but he had included a full-size American flag to stand beside it. Behind him hung a huge portrait of his father, and a small oval painting of his wife graced his desk. Every day, he thanked God he could own the bank the government once occupied. He loved his job. He loved his city. He loved his wife.

"Peter?"

He looked up to see Mary Beth in his open door.

Wind from outside rustled the curls around her face. "We have a problem in the vault, and I know you will want it fixed before the paymaster arrives tomorrow."

After what he had been through, he was confident nothing could arise that God could not guide him through. "What sort of problem?"

"I shall show you." She waved for him to come downstairs.

He was so close to completing the document he had been reading he did not want to stop, but his wife seldom asked for him unless it was necessary. After scooting back his chair, he put down the paper and accompanied her downstairs.

She stood at the door of the vault. "You must go in to see it."

He walked in and found a bassinet against the back wall. "What does this mean?"

A smile blazed across her face. "Dr. Smith says we will need one in a few months, maybe as early as May. Do you have any ideas where it should go?"

"Not inside my vault."

He pulled his wife into his arms. "Praise God. The wait was worth it."

"I agree." She pulled away and gazed into his eyes. "I learned a few things these past few months."

"Tell me."

"Perseverance sums it up." She took a deep breath. "While we were trying to solve the mystery surrounding the bank, I spoke with Reverend McCallie. He said life presents tough moments, but you have to pursue God and then reflect his glory."

"Perseverance." Peter nodded. "We were doing the right things seeking the Lord, but we needed to let others see the glory of God in our lives."

"That's right. I was grumpy with you at times, and that was wrong. Reflecting God's love, reflecting gold is work, but I'm going to try hard to stay there because I'm confident God will take care of us."

"That sums it up for me too." Laughter bubbled up from Peter's soul. "Will it be a boy or a girl?"

"We'll be busy reflecting God's love and glory until we find out."

Author Note

Reverend T. H. McCallie and his wife, the former Ellen Jarnagin, lived on the spot that is now First-Centenary United Methodist Church. He served as pastor of First Presbyterian Church and as a civic leader as Chattanooga grew. Ellen was an active person, always keeping her home open to visiting pastors or anyone needy. She often cared for wounded soldiers during the war. The couple had sixteen children, and eight lived to become adults. Today a major street bears the McCallie name as does a boy's school, which two of their sons founded.

Dr. Milo Smith earned his medical degree from Philadelphia Medical School and moved to Chattanooga in 1838 with his sister. On several occasions, he served as mayor. He loved Chattanooga, and residents demonstrated their fondness for him by naming their offspring after him. During the war years, he lived on Cameron Hill with his wife, Caroline. He worked for the Confederate military in the city while caring for Chattanooga citizens as well. A brilliant man, he had many interests and helped found First Presbyterian Church. Dr. Smith was known for his generosity and never requested payment for his services.

Glossary

Bill—paper used in place of gold. Confederate bills were not legal tender, which means such bills could not be used for certain transactions.

Broken bank note—paper currency issued by a bank that went out of business.

Dollar—Our founding fathers chose the dollar for United States Currency. Colonists never had enough currency and tended to use foreign coins that came when they traded. They preferred the Spanish silver dollar which had a consistent amount of silver. They often cut the coin into eight pieces called 'bits.' Two bits equaled a quarter.

Invest—extending a loan with interest to support or expand a business.

Gold standard—using only gold or silver as payment for debts.

Legal tender—paper money used to buy and sell in place of precious metals such as gold.

Specie—gold or silver used for exchange.

Sutlers—tradesmen who come into an area during a war. They sell goods to the military.

Tender—to pay for goods or services.

About the Author

Cynthia loves younger women and enjoys using new technology to encourage them. She grew up in Chattanooga, TN, where she attended the Erlanger School of Nursing. After she married Ray Simmons, she homeschooled their five children through high school, including her youngest son, who has severe disabilities.

Unafraid of tough topics, Cynthia writes The Big Question column for Leading Hearts Magazine. In addition, she and her husband host apologetics' discussions with college students over tea.

An avid reader and writer, she served as past president of the Christian Authors Guild, teaches writing workshops, and directs the Atlanta Christian Writers Conference.

Cynthia adores history and longs to peruse every archive she comes across while traveling. When speaking and teaching, she includes lively vignettes from history and laughs about how she loves women from the past.

She hosts and produces "Heart of the Matter Radio" and does Cynthia Chats and #momlife encouragement videos.

Cynthia loves to help her readers and enjoys messages, so visit her website and give your thoughts. www.clsimmons. com